JUST TO BE WITH YOU

The Sullivans

Bella Andre

JUST TO BE WITH YOU

~ The Sullivans ~

Ian & Tatiana

Ian Sullivan, the powerful and wealthy CEO of Sullivan Investments, has never failed at anything in his life...apart from love and marriage. Certain that he'll never take the plunge again, the last thing he expects is for a beautiful actress to turn his perfectly organized world completely upside down.

Tatiana Landon, one of the hottest talents in Hollywood, has been waiting for true love her whole life. When she meets Ian, she's certain she's finally found it...along with a passion that sizzles hotter than anything in her wildest dreams. All she needs to do now is find a way to convince him to take the risk of loving again.

Ian soon realizes that Tatiana is just as focused on winning his heart as he is on locking it away. But when unexpected circumstances thrust them into a world where real-life rules don't apply, will Ian finally recognize Tatiana as his one true love?

A note from Bella:

When I first met Tatiana Landon a year and a half ago while writing Smith Sullivan and Valentina Landon's love story in *Come A Little Bit Closer*, I immediately liked her. She was intelligent, full of love for her family, passionate about her acting career...and it was clear that one day she was going to make some guy very, very lucky.

Of course, I had to pair her with a Sullivan! What other man would do? And as I began to write about the Seattle Sullivans, I quickly realized that Ian Sullivan was the perfect match for her...and she for him. As the eldest of the five siblings in the Seattle branch of the family, Ian most definitely needed to have his world knocked off its axis by a beautiful, honest, and irresistible woman with whom he couldn't help but fall in love. I hope you love Tatiana and Ian's story!

If this is your first time reading about the Sullivans, you can easily read each book as a stand-alone—and there is a Sullivan family tree available on my website (http://bellaandre.com/wp-content/uploads/2014/02/SullivanFamilyTree.pdf) so you can see how the books connect together.

Happy reading,
Bella Andre

CHAPTER ONE

Rain fell steadily outside the floor-to-ceiling windows of the Sullivan Investments skyscraper, just as it had for the past several days. Coffee shops seemed to outnumber all other retail outlets in the city two to one. And Ian Sullivan's sister, Mia, had already texted him a half-dozen times to remind him that he'd better not show up late to dinner at their parents' house tonight because of a last-minute meeting.

And yet, despite all that, it was good to be back in Seattle.

Surprisingly good.

Ian had worked out of the London office for the past several years, and his European investments were thriving as a result. But now that Sullivan Investments was on the verge of making a massive investment in eAirBox, an innovative cloud-based digital storage company based in Seattle, it had made sense to finally head back home. Plus, two of his siblings would be getting married and starting families soon, and Ian had already missed too many pivotal moments in his siblings' lives by being an ocean away.

In any case, Ian was glad that he'd been able to keep it all in the family with the deal he'd made today with Jake McCann on his very successful chain of McCann's Irish pubs. Jake was not only a genius at coming up with artisanal brews, he was also married to Sophie, one of Ian's cousins from San Francisco. Though he knew he was breaking one of the tried and true rules of doing business, in Ian's experience, working with family had always been not only enjoyable, but also extremely profitable.

"I'm glad we were able to make this deal work, Ian," Jake said through the video conference feed set up in one of Ian's smaller conference rooms on the 15th floor.

Jake's T-shirt put his tattoos on full display, and though he was an incredibly intelligent guy with great business sense, it wasn't much of a stretch to look at him and guess that he'd come from a pretty rough upbringing. Ian would never have imagined that his soft-spoken librarian cousin and Jake would work as a couple, especially considering the story that Jake had gotten Sophie pregnant during a one-night stand. But they'd turned out to be one hell of a good team, and Ian was happy for both of them.

"I've got a lot of respect for what you've done with your pubs, Jake. Everyone here is glad we can be a part of your expansion." When Ian's head legal counsel excused himself from the meeting to take an urgent call, he took the meeting in a personal direction. "How are Sophie and the twins doing? Smith and Jackie must be getting big."

"Hold on a sec and I'll show you." Jake got up from the chair in his home office and returned a short while later with a kid squirming under each arm. "Kids, say hi to your Uncle Ian."

Jake and Sophie's twins were ridiculously cute as they waved and grinned at him. Jackie had crumbs all over her hands and face, and Smith's dark hair was standing on end as if he'd just woken up from a heavy-duty nap.

Ian didn't have a clue how Jake managed to run his business so well and have time to take care of his wife and kids, too. Marriage was the only thing that Ian had ever failed at, so badly that he'd come out of it one hundred percent certain that a wife would never—and *should* never—be in his future again. Which meant kids were out of the picture, too. Fortunately, there were plenty of Sullivan babies to spoil rotten.

Ian had just said his own hellos to the twins when they wriggled out of Jake's grip and made a break for it. Ian heard Sophie's laughter as she scooped them up just before she came in range of the camera's lens.

"Hey, cuz." Sophie seemed utterly unperturbed by the fact that her kids were not just squirming like crazy now, but were also trying to pull each other's hair. "I'd love to catch up more, but since it looks like I'm going to have to break up a baby brawl in a minute, I wanted to let you know that I'm supposed to tell you not to be late to your mom and dad's house for dinner tonight. Or else."

"Mia texted you, too?"

Jake and Sophie just laughed as they split the kids between them and Smith's and Jackie's wails began. "Say hello to everyone for us."

After shutting down the video conference feed, Ian headed for his office down a long open hallway that looked over dozens of cubicles. At fifteen minutes past six on a Friday night, everyone had already left. Though he'd been back at the Seattle headquarters for only a week and a half, Ian had seen for himself that everything in the office was running with perfect efficiency. Organization and order had always been crucial components of his success, along with a laser focus and an unwavering determination.

Only once had he made the mistake of letting himself be spontaneously thrown off course. But in the wake of his messy marriage and even messier divorce, he'd been even more careful to make sure that the women he connected with were willing to play by the rules that would keep them all safe from future messes: no entanglements, no emotions. Just hours of pleasure when they were together, and nothing at all that lingered when they weren't. And if anyone thought giving up love was something to grieve, that's because they didn't know how much relief there was in knowing he would never hurt a woman again by promising her something he would never be able to actually give.

At the threshold of his office, Ian shook all thoughts of love and romance aside before he stepped inside. Love had no place in the worldwide empire he'd built, and he was glad for that fact, especially when he needed every ounce of his focus right now to do whatever it took to finally close the eAirBox deal.

Mentally drafting an email to his board regarding the new counter-offer he was planning to make on Monday morning, Ian was halfway to his desk when he realized he wasn't alone. His large leather chair was turned away from his desk so that the back was facing him...and the most stunning bare legs he'd ever seen were crossed over the arm of it, the woman's shiny red heels tapping out a fast rhythm in the air.

He couldn't immediately place the legs, but the scent was one he'd come across only once before, at his cousin Marcus's wedding in Napa

Valley a handful of months earlier. Equal parts vanilla and spice, the combination was at once innocent and so powerfully sensual that he was overwhelmed with the need to breathe her in just one more time, and then one more time again.

Tatiana Landon.

If she were anyone else, Ian would immediately have alerted her to his presence. But he needed to take a few moments to steel himself against the powerful way the beautiful actress affected him. And at the end of a long, hard week, he found it took him more than a few seconds not only to solidify his walls, but also to make absolutely sure that they would remain impenetrable.

Finally, he cleared his throat. But her feet didn't stop tapping out the beat and she didn't turn the chair around. Her evocative scent grew stronger when he moved closer, and he gritted his teeth against the potent impact it had on him as he reached for the top of his chair to turn her to face him.

He'd only just begun to spin the chair when she let out a little shriek and jumped halfway out before falling back into it. One hand was pressed over her mouth, the other over her chest, her legs tucked beneath her on the big leather seat as she stared up at him with big green eyes.

Before he could stop himself, Ian was drinking in the gorgeous expanse of skin on display from the way the skirt of her dress rode up her thighs. Her long hair was loose around her shoulders and her skin was flushed from the fright he'd given her.

Was there another woman on the planet this beautiful?

By the time she pulled out her earbuds and slid her legs out from beneath her, she was laughing. "You scared me."

If he'd thought she was beautiful before, watching her laugh, so free, so easy, showed him he'd had no idea what real beauty was until now. He'd been the one to startle her, but just looking at her had *his* heart beating too fast.

"How long have you been waiting in my office?"

"A little while. Your assistant wanted to let you know that I was here, but I asked her not to interrupt your meeting. Of course, that was before I knew that you have absolutely nothing worth snooping through in your office." She paused to look more closely at him. "You look pleased, so I'm hoping that means your meeting was a good one."

"It was," he said, even as he worked to bank his surprise that she could read him so easily, or so accurately. "Jake and I had a lot of final details to iron out before the contract of our new agreement can be drawn up, so our meeting went longer than we planned."

"Are you talking about Sophie's Jake? You're investing in McCann's Pubs?"

"I've been interested in his company for a while and the timing was finally right." Wait a minute—he didn't need to give her any explanations about why he hadn't been in his office to greet her. Especially since she hadn't let him know she was coming in the first place. "Why are you here?"

Her lips curved up at the corners, just the slightest bit. Almost as if she thought his total lack of manners was...cute. "It's nice to see you again, Ian."

Damn it, she was right—he was being a jerk. But only because she threw him off in a way no one else ever had.

"You, too." But he knew that wasn't good enough when his cousin Smith would be getting married to Tatiana's sister, Valentina, soon. With any other member of his extended family, Ian would have been friendly, regardless of the circumstances under which he was seeing them. He shouldn't be treating Tatiana any differently. "You look lovely."

She flushed slightly, looking down at her dress and smoothing a hand over a lock of hair. In that moment, it struck him that she seemed a little uncertain. As if she wasn't actually sure he meant it. As if she wasn't one of the most in-demand and sought-after movie stars in the world who could have any man she wanted falling at her feet.

When he'd met Tatiana at his cousin's wedding, Ian had been surprised by the air of innocence she had about her. And just as he had then, he reminded himself that anyone who had come of age in Hollywood couldn't possibly be innocent. It was simply part of her skill as an actress that she was able to make even a cynic like him believe in innocence that wasn't there.

"Thank you," she said softly, as if his compliment had meant something more to her than just a polite greeting. Her eyes were shining when she smiled up at him. "I'm excited about being in Seattle to work on my next film. Which is actually why I'm here. I'd like to ask you for your help with something."

Ian ran his company—and his life—using a combination of calculations, well-thought-out strategy, and what he felt in his gut.

Right now, his gut was telling him to prepare for trouble.

Instinctively sensing he should put space between himself and Tatiana, he gestured for her to have a seat on his couch while he moved to the chair behind his desk. But it was yet another miscalculation where she was concerned, because now he could not only smell her perfume, he could also feel her warmth on the leather where she'd been sitting.

"Is there an issue with financing for your new movie?" Over the past few years he'd worked with Smith to help finance several films, and it was one of the areas where Ian and his executive staff had agreed to increase their focus in the coming year. But investing in a film that was having issues wasn't part of his plan, and even as he asked Tatiana the question, Ian was already working out how to make this clear to her in a way that wouldn't upset her.

"No, everything is going great on the back end with the production. That's not what I need your help with."

Ian should have been relieved that she hadn't come to ask him for money. But instead of relief, his tension only grew. Because if she didn't want his money, what could she possibly want?

Trouble, he thought again as she came to her feet, a whirl of irrepressible passion and energy.

"Each role I play is different, and I love learning about new careers, new worlds. I'm not a method actor by any means—I can't imagine putting my real life on hold so that I can stay completely in character while filming—but it *is* really important to me that I fully understand the character I'm playing, inside and out." She stopped and smiled at him, clearly reading his mind as she said, "I know you're probably sitting there wondering why I'm telling you all this."

He would have had to forcibly repress the urge to grin at her breathless monologue were it not for the fact that his gut was still churning with a sense of impending danger. "I am."

"The character I'm playing next becomes a billionaire overnight when she inherits a huge company and ends up having to run a multinational corporation much like yours. I'd like to shadow you, Ian, for the next couple of weeks as research for my role."

She wanted to shadow him?

Of all the things he thought she might want from him, he'd never have come up with this in a million years. But that didn't mean he didn't immediately know what his answer had to be.

No.

Of course, because she was nearly family, he'd temper his refusal with kindness. Not only would he and Tatiana be seeing each other at family events for the next sixty years, but if his sister Mia found out he'd done something to hurt Tatiana's feelings, she'd forever crucify him for being an unhelpful jerk.

"First off," he said, "I'm not a billionaire."

It was a goal that had driven him for many years until he was so close to making it a reality that he could practically taste it, and every additional hour he needed to work to reach that goal was well worth it. It was one of the reasons the eAirBox deal was so important to him, not just because it would be a brilliant move for Sullivan Investments, but also because it would push him straight into billionaire territory. For Ian, the zeros on his bank statements weren't just a barometer of success and professional victory, they also meant security. And though he'd already set up a trust funds for everyone in his family, it was important to him to know with absolute certainty that they'd all be taken care of in the future, no matter what.

"No, not yet," she said with a nod, "but I've studied your holdings and I'm guessing your next big investment will get you there."

Yet again, he was surprised. But this time, it was the intelligence in her gaze that caught him as she spoke about researching his financial holdings. Stranger, though, was the very offhand way in which she talked about his near billion-dollar net worth, as if she didn't particularly care how rich he was.

Ian knew very few people to whom his wealth didn't matter, and most of them shared his surname. Sure, Tatiana had done well with her acting career, but they both knew he could buy and sell her a hundred times over. Considering she was a woman who clearly liked pretty things, like the red shoes she was wearing and the gems sparkling at her ears, his wealth *had* to matter to her, didn't it? Especially, the cynical part of his brain added, if she thought there was a chance he might ever spend some of it on her.

"In any case," she continued, "from what I've already learned about you while doing some preliminary research, you're the perfect CEO for me to shadow for my role. You're focused. You're driven. You obviously know how to pinpoint ideas that will be successful and profitable. And on top of that, you give back to the community. You won't even notice I'm here while I'm shadowing you. I'd like to take notes for myself, of course, but I'll sign an ironclad nondisclosure agreement, and I promise that not one word of what I hear and see in your office will ever leak. Monday morning, I'll show up wherever you tell me to, at whatever time you tell me to be ready."

Just that fast, visions of Tatiana doing whatever he told her to do assaulted him. Only, they weren't in his office in those visions...they were in his bedroom, and she was naked and flushed with need, and he was touching all those soft curves she wore so beautifully.

Damn it, this was exactly the road he couldn't let himself walk and was the perfect reminder of why he couldn't possibly let her shadow him. Because while he was normally known for his self-control, from the first time they'd met, nothing about his reaction to Tatiana had been anywhere close to *normal.*

"I've just returned to my Seattle headquarters from London, as I'm sure you already know from your research," he said with a lift of one brow, "and it's a particularly busy time for the company. In addition to my usual workload, I've got several important events to manage and business trips coming up, as well."

Tatiana listened to his excuses without looking away from him. The brightness of her smile had dimmed a bit, but her determination still shone brightly as she said, "I know I haven't given you any warning, so maybe if I wait until your schedule eases a bit—"

"My schedule never eases."

When her expression softened with concern, Ian was reminded of the way his mother and his sister looked when they were worried about him.

"I'm sure there are other CEOs in Seattle who could work with you." And no doubt every last one of them would jump at the chance to spend a couple of weeks with her. But even as he reached for his phone so that he could give her their numbers, he hated the idea of Tatiana sharing an office with any of them. What if one of them tried something with her?

"I know there are plenty of other CEOs in Seattle I could call. But you're special, Ian. And I'd very much like to shadow you for this role."

Half a dozen further reasons why he couldn't say yes lay on the tip of his tongue, but he was well aware that only one was really true: He didn't trust himself with Tatiana for an hour, let alone a week. Already, from nothing more than this one short conversation, the sparks and the heat between them were stronger than he could ever remember with another woman.

The less time they spent together, the better it would be for both of them. Tatiana was a young, talented beauty with eyes full of wonder and dreams and the certainty of endless possibilities. Whereas Ian knew from first-hand experience just how impossible some things really were. He'd already crushed the wonder and dreams and endless possibilities in his ex-wife. He'd never forgive himself if he did the same to Tatiana.

So though he wished he could spare her feelings, he knew it wouldn't be wise to sugar-coat his answer and give her hope that he'd change his mind. "No."

Surprise didn't flicker in her eyes. But disappointment was there, and it twisted in his gut despite the fact that he was doing the right thing. Because if he ever made the mistake of touching her—if he ever let himself have her even for an hour—he couldn't imagine a world in which he'd ever be able to let her go again. Especially not to find pleasure with another man.

He'd learned at Marcus and Nicola's wedding that Tatiana dreamed of long white dresses and lacy veils, and had been picturing her own wedding since she was a little girl playing in the backyard in her mother's wedding dress. Ian could never again be a part of that dream for any woman, regardless of how much he wanted her.

But even as he moved to take a step away from her, she was closing the distance between them in her sexy red heels. Her skin was flushed and soft looking as she stopped barely a breath from him to ask, "Why?"

He understood, suddenly, why she'd been such a success. It wasn't just that she was a great actor. She also didn't seem to know fear, didn't hesitate or hold things back where other people would instinctively have done all of the above in the face of his firm *no.*

"I heard all of the reasons you've just given me," she continued in the same forthright and open manner with which she'd spoken to him in Marcus's Napa Valley vineyard months ago, "but none of those are the real reason you're saying no, are they?"

For a moment—one split second of temporary madness—he was tempted to show her exactly why. To drag her into his arms and steal a kiss that she'd never forget. To show her the force, the power, that the intense attraction between them had.

And the damage it could do.

Self-control asserted itself just in time for him to curl his hands into fists in his pockets instead of in her silky hair, and he was carefully weighing his words, measuring his response, when his office door flew open.

"Aha! I knew I'd find you here, still working. Ford is waiting in the car downstairs to drag you to Mom and Dad's house right aw—" His sister, Mia, suddenly realized he wasn't alone. "Tatiana, I didn't know you were in Seattle already. It's so great to see you again!"

As the two women hugged hello, Mia shot Ian a look over Tatiana's shoulder—one that had him gritting his teeth even harder than he had been before his sister arrived, all because he could read Mia's mind.

Ian and Tatiana sitting in a tree
K-I-S-S-I-N-G

When they were children, everything could be boiled down to such simple sentiments. But life wasn't that simple anymore, and hadn't been for a very long time. Heck, Mia ought to understand that after how difficult things had been between her and Ford Vincent. The rock star was now her utterly devoted fiancé, but during the previous five years, their relationship had been a radically different story.

As the oldest in their family, Ian had done his best to watch over Mia since the day his parents had brought her home from the hospital—a tiny, innocent bundle wrapped in soft blankets. He'd made sure to take care of her when she skinned her knee, when she fell from the bars in the playground, when she took a tumble on the ski slopes, when she'd needed help staying up all night to study for a test. She'd always been there for him, too, making him laugh with her silly antics, even once he was in college and things had begun to fall apart for them as a family...and there hadn't been time for much laughter anymore.

Later, when they were both adults, his sister had tried to be there for him again when he'd been going through his divorce. But instead of letting her, he'd left the country. In the years since, he still hadn't shared the finer details of his divorce with anyone, including his sister, but that didn't mean she was clueless. She knew he wasn't interested in love, romance, or marriage again, even if she didn't know exactly why.

Mia let go of Tatiana to move into the circle of his arms, and as he pressed a kiss to the top of her head, he knew for sure that he'd made the right decision to come back to Seattle. He'd missed his sister a great deal during his years in London.

"I'm glad you're back, big brother," she said as she hugged him tighter. Of course, the second she let go of him, she went straight back to poking around in his private business. "It looked like I interrupted a pretty serious discussion between the two of you." She didn't even try to be subtle as she asked them, "Did I?"

"I was in the neighborhood," Tatiana said with an easy smile. "So I decided to drop in and see if I could catch Ian before he headed out for the night. I'll be playing a heroine who inherits a big company, and I figured watching your brother in action for a little while might provide some helpful research."

He was amazed at how smoothly she'd told the truth, while also deftly saving him from having to admit to his sister that he was a jerk who had flat-out refused to help her.

"Interesting," Mia said in a tone that told Ian *precisely* how interesting she found the whole situation. Far too much for his peace of mind, which was already teetering on the edge of sanity simply from being this close to Tatiana. "Did you learn anything yet that you'll be able to use for your role?"

Tatiana's eyes held his for a brief but heated moment before she turned to smile again at his sister. "Only that CEOs are busy. So busy that their sisters have to come and make sure they leave the office at a reasonable hour on a Friday night."

Mia shot him another pointed look. "You did invite her to dinner at Mom and Dad's tonight, didn't you?"

"I'm afraid I didn't exactly let him get that far," Tatiana said, saving him from his sister's wrath yet again. "Besides, I should really spend tonight going over the new changes the screenwriter made."

"Come to dinner with us, Tatiana." Even to Ian's own ears, his request came out sounding like gravel was coating his vocal cords, so he tried again. "Our parents would really love to have you there."

"We would *all* love it," Mia corrected, her disapproval over the way he was handling himself around Tatiana coming through louder and clearer with every passing second. "And I refuse to take no for an answer, so the changes to your script will just have to wait a few more hours."

With that, his force-of-nature sister linked her arm with Tatiana's. As they headed toward the elevator, Mia called over her shoulder, "Hurry up, Ian, otherwise people are going to realize their rock-star hero is sitting outside in the car waiting for us and then we'll be really late to Mom and Dad's."

In London, Ian had been in charge of not only one hundred percent of his business, but of his personal life, as well. He'd barely been back in Seattle for a week, and already his family was meddling. But only, he reminded himself as he grabbed the bouquet of flowers he'd bought for his mother, because they loved him.

Which meant he'd better brace himself for a whole lot more meddling tonight at dinner.

Especially if he wasn't able to hide his reaction to Tatiana any better than he had so far...

CHAPTER TWO

Ian's office had looked just the way Tatiana thought it would. Perfectly ordered, with everything exactly where it should be and, most of all, everyone working hard to please him.

She smiled at that thought, knowing just how easy it was to feel that way. Heck, she didn't know him very well beyond their one meeting at Marcus and Nicola's wedding in Napa and what she'd heard about him through her sister and the other Sullivans...and yet she already found herself wanting to do something, anything, that would put a spark of approval into his dark eyes. Eyes that seemed to be full of so many mysteries—and so much barely banked heat—that every time she looked into them she couldn't help but be completely and utterly drawn in.

Again, she smiled, but this time, entirely different kinds of sparks were the reason. The kind that had made her feel warm and flushed and tingly all over every time she'd thought about Ian Sullivan during the past few months.

She'd wanted to know if her memories of the instant connection she'd felt between them in the vineyard had been real. After only fifteen minutes with Ian in his office, she knew the answer.

Yes, the sparks were real...and getting hotter by the second.

Especially after he'd said his terse *No* to her request, and she'd moved closer to ask him why. Maybe, she acknowledged, it was a little bad of her to get such a kick out of provoking him. But how could she resist the way his eyes lit with heat and emotion that he couldn't seem to contain around her? Her appearance had clearly shaken up his otherwise neatly ordered life. Even her red heels and sparkly earrings had seemed to grate on him, as if bright colors were expressly not permitted in the Sullivan Investments headquarters.

During the first couple of hours she'd been waiting in his office, she'd pulled up her script on her phone and read through it another two times. After having gone over it more than a hundred times already, she'd hoped to finally find the clue to her character's soul that she'd been looking for. Alas, the glorious *aha* moment she so badly needed remained elusive. Frustration at spinning her wheels had her closing her script in momentary defeat and turning on one of Nicola's pop songs in her headphones that never failed to lift her spirits.

She hadn't planned on Ian finding her listening to music, but perhaps it had been the perfect way to greet him, she thought as he opened the back passenger door of Ford's Tesla for her. Sexy as sin in his dark suit, he somehow managed to look rough and rugged even beneath perfectly tailored wool. Plus, he smelled amazing, like a pine forest in the cool of night. But what had sent her heart racing even faster was when he'd put his arms around his sister and held her tight, pressing a kiss to the top of Mia's head, his expression one of pure love. Now, as he slid into the backseat beside her, she realized he was carefully holding the bouquet of flowers that had seemed so out of place in his office, obviously intended for his mother.

"Look who I was lucky enough to find in Ian's office," Mia said to her fiancé as she got into the front passenger seat beside Ford and gave him a kiss on the lips.

"Tatiana," Ford said as he turned to greet her, "it's great to see you again so soon. Have you started filming your new movie already?"

"Not quite yet. I've got a couple of weeks until we begin, so I'm still in character-research mode." But since she didn't want to admit that she'd just run into the first role she couldn't figure out, darn it—and her brain wasn't exactly working at top speed anyway with Ian sitting so close—she asked Ford and Mia, "How are things going for the two of you?"

She relaxed in the supple leather backseat while Ford and Mia quickly filled her in on what they'd both been up to since she'd last seen them. Throughout, however, Ian sat stiffly beside her. She wouldn't be surprised if he was still irritated by her request to shadow him, but something told her she wasn't the only reason for his unease.

Tatiana had personally been witness to the horribly awkward moment when Ian had first met Ford. The rock star had been secretly making out with Mia in a storage room at Marcus and Nicola's wedding. Tatiana would never forget the fury she'd seen on Ian's face when he'd thought Ford was taking advantage of Mia. Things had continued to be strained when they'd all been seated at the same table during dinner and toasts, and just as she had on that day, Tatiana wanted to try to help smooth things over with everyone. The problem was, she didn't yet know Ian well enough to do whatever would have helped to set him at ease.

In order for Tatiana to do her job well in front of the cameras, she not only needed to look deep into other people's personalities, she also had to look inward at her own. As a result, she knew herself to be both curious and impulsive. Which meant that, in the months since meeting Ian at the wedding, she simply hadn't had the self-control to keep her curiosity about him at bay. A few quick online searches had been enough for her to learn that his marriage to Chelsea Adrienne, a flawlessly beautiful blonde even by Hollywood standards, had ended several years ago. Since then, he'd been photographed with a series of equally stunning women at various events, all of them tall and dark-haired and willowy, with cool expressions.

While stopped in downtown traffic, the light of a street lamp enabled Tatiana to study their combined reflections in her window. Ian was dark and brooding and possessed such masculine beauty that it was no wonder stunning women flocked to his side. And as for her...well, *tall and dark, willowy and cool* were pretty much the exact opposite of her green eyes, reddish-blond hair, and lush curves.

Fortunately, as an actor, her slightly off-center looks had helped set her apart from the thousands of other women vying for parts. On a personal level, however, she honestly didn't have enough experience with men to know if *off-center* could ever have a chance of competing with *stunning.*

When they arrived at the Sullivans' house, Ian got out, then held the back passenger door open for her again. Regardless of how badly he might want to keep a distance between them, he had been raised to be a gentleman.

She'd walked the red carpet in front of hundreds of cameras many, many times. But her nerves had never been quite this high, and though the rain had finally stopped falling on their drive, she stumbled in her heels on the wet bricks of the driveway. Ian caught her against him before she could go down, and the strength and the heat of his body against hers, along with the potent fragrance from the bouquet she'd just accidentally crushed between them, actually had her gasping aloud.

They'd done nothing more than shake hands at the wedding. And though he'd been easily affectionate with his sister, Ian had been careful not to touch Tatiana in his office, not even to shake her hand.

But now, as she stood for a few perfect seconds in the circle of his arms on his parents' driveway on the cool, damp Seattle evening, Tatiana felt more warmth, and more arousal, from one accidental touch and the intensity of his gaze, than she ever had with another man.

Is this the real reason you don't want me to shadow you? she silently asked him.

When his eyes darkened even further—and his grip tightened on her waist as if he wanted to draw her closer right before he abruptly released her—she was almost positive he'd just given her his answer.

* * *

The next few minutes were full of happy greetings and laughter that helped settle Tatiana down from the emotional and physical whirl that Ian's arms around her had set off. Claudia and Max Sullivan were, just as he had predicted, thrilled to see her. She felt so welcomed by them that she could almost pretend she was a Sullivan herself.

The bouquet of flowers, thankfully, wasn't too badly off for her falling into it. And when Ian gave them to his mother, then folded her into a hug that had Claudia's eyes tearing up from pure happiness at having her eldest back home, Tatiana's eyes threatened to well up, too. After hugging his father, even the old family dog who looked to be losing his sight got a friendly pat from Ian and his toy rope thrown across the room for an impromptu game of fetch.

Yes, Ian was clearly a tough-minded businessman who was more than a little cynical about love and romance. But at the same time, he obviously had a very soft spot for his family, just as she did. And ever since her sister, Valentina, had become engaged to Smith, the Sullivans had felt like her family, too.

A few minutes later, though it was clear that Claudia and Max wanted her to relax with a glass of wine while they finished dinner preparations, Tatiana said, "Please, I'd really like to help in some way." Claudia had pans on every burner on her stove and dough for homemade pasta sitting on the counter, so Tatiana tucked her hair up into a quick ponytail, washed her hands, and said, "When

Valentina and I were kids, we used to have bake-offs all the time. One day I surprised her with pasta I made myself, which is my way of saying I promise I won't screw up your hard work if you'll let me help roll out the spaghetti."

"The first time I met Mary Sullivan—although she was Mary Ferrer at the time and such a famous model I was more than a little bit nervous around her—she made us all fresh pasta that tasted like it came straight from Italy." Claudia smiled, thinking back. "Max's brother Jack was still trying to convince Mary to officially date him at the time, but it was clear to me that Mary and Jack were already head over heels in love with each other. Ian was a toddler way back then and you won't be surprised to hear that he fell in love with Mary that night, too, when she read him his favorite book. Ever since, the two of them have had an extra close relationship." Claudia laughed at herself, as she added, "All of which is *my* very long-winded way of saying that I've had a heck of a time eating store-bought pasta ever since, and I'd love your help."

"Hey Mom, Dad," a deep male voice called from the back door, "I picked up the cream you asked for."

Dylan Sullivan was the youngest male in the family, and Tatiana had often thought that he was also the biggest charmer of the bunch. Where Ian was the serious and responsible eldest sibling, Dylan had a carefree ease about him that was instantly appealing. It didn't hurt that the boat-builder and sailor was also an extremely good-looking man.

It wasn't until Dylan came around the counter to put the cream in the refrigerator that he saw Tatiana. "Why didn't someone tell me the prettiest girl in the world was going to be here?" He swept her up into his arms, and she laughed as he spun her around in the small space.

But a few seconds later, when her body started to heat again, it wasn't because she was in Dylan's arms. She didn't need to see or hear Ian to know that he must have walked into the kitchen. Though he was still halfway across the room, she was intensely aware of every breath she took, the brush of her eyelashes over her cheekbones, the swift beat of her heart.

Dylan put her back down on her feet, and when she glanced over at Ian, she saw that his eyes had darkened again. Was it because his brother had been touching her? Was it because she'd laughed with Dylan?

Or was it simply because sparks flew like crazy whenever she and Ian were in the same room?

With carefully steady hands, she continued rolling out pasta. Sliding onto a kitchen stool across from her as he uncapped a beer, Dylan said, "I already thought you were the perfect woman, but if it turns out you can cook, I just might have to propose to you right now."

"You'll have to fight me for her," Adam said as he suddenly appeared in the kitchen and pulled her toward him in an easy and affectionate manner to give her a kiss on the cheek.

"Adam, Dylan," Ian said, "Dad needs our help moving the cord of firewood into the shed before dinner."

"Duty calls," Adam said with a grin. He gave her another kiss on the top of her head before removing his hand from around her waist. "But don't worry, I'll be back to flirt some more with you soon."

Claudia was laughing even as she shook her head at their antics. "How will you ever manage to choose between my sons?"

When Tatiana was on set in front of the cameras, she was a master at controlling her expressions so that they suited the character she had been hired to play. But she'd always promised herself that in real life she would never act, would never hide what she really felt from the people she cared about. She'd seen too many actors whose entire lives were lived as though they were always onstage in front of cameras. For Tatiana, make-believe was so much fun because she lived in a fantasy world only part of the time.

So instead of forcing a joking response to roll off her tongue, when the kitchen door had closed behind the men, Tatiana lifted her gaze to meet Claudia's. "They're all great, and I love spending time with your family. But—" Was it crazy for her to even think of speaking about her budding feelings to Ian's mother? Especially when she was still working out, moment to moment, exactly how far those feelings reached?

"You've already chosen, haven't you?" Claudia's eyes held hers. "Ian."

Tatiana blew out the breath she'd been holding as she nodded. She hadn't spoken to anyone about her crush on Ian yet, not even her sister. Especially not her sister, who would likely freak out about Tatiana possibly setting herself up to get hurt.

"I know it might sound crazy." And crazier still that Ian's mother was the person she suddenly found herself spilling everything to. But the truth that Tatiana hadn't been able to shake for months was that it had felt like love at first sight when she'd met Ian at the wedding. "We hardly know each other."

"Feelings don't work on a timetable," Claudia said gently. "Sometimes it takes five years for a couple to figure things out, like it did with Mia and Ford. Sometimes it takes fifteen or twenty years, like it did for Rafe and Brooke. And sometimes, it only takes a few seconds to fall at first glance...and to feel deep inside your heart that you've found something special that will last forever."

Ian had never flirted with her. He had never touched or kissed her with careless affection. And yet, from the first moment she'd spoken to him, she'd felt as if she belonged to him. Now, as she spoke with his mother, she had to wonder, was what she was feeling more than just a crush? Was it something that could turn into the kind of forever that Mia and Ford and Rafe and Brooke had? And even if it was, would it make any difference to Ian, when she could still remember every word they'd said to each other at Marcus's wedding?

* * *

"It was such a beautiful wedding, wasn't it?" were her first dreamy words to him after the ceremony. She'd been so overwhelmed by the love all around her, not just between the bride and groom, but among all of the Sullivans who had found their true loves. They were so free with their smiles for one another, their gentle touches, their kisses. Falling in love with Smith had made Valentina more relaxed and happy than Tatiana had ever known her sister could be.

But Ian had only said, "Marcus and Nicola are both good people."

She'd realized with no small amount of shock that he hadn't been as overwhelmed by all the love at the wedding as she had. Trying to understand how that could possibly be, she'd said, "I take it you're not a big fan of love?"

It had been his turn to look surprised by her pointed question, maybe even intrigued despite himself, as he said, "I have no doubt that the two of them are in love."

Tatiana wasn't usually the kind of person who deliberately got in a stranger's face and asked him deeply personal questions within the first five minutes of meeting him. But Ian Sullivan had drawn her in a way no man ever had, so she'd gone another step further and asked, "So if it's not love that bothers you, it must be marriage?"

Again, he hadn't directly answered her question. Instead, he'd turned it around on her. "How old were you the first time you dressed up in a wedding gown?"

She hadn't hesitated to tell him her fun memories about how she used to put on her mother's wedding dress when she was four or five and pretend her dog was the handsome prince she was marrying.

When she was done, he'd simply asked, "How often do you think those fairy tales come true?"

Oh, how she'd wanted the fairy tale to come true right then and there—for Ian to turn out to be the man she'd been waiting for her whole life. Looking back, she was sure every one of those desires and dreams were in her voice and on her face as she softly told him, "I hope that they come true all the time."

He'd looked stunned, and they'd simply stared at one another. His eyes had grown darker and more intense throughout their conversation, and she'd been struck by how attracted she was to him. Shockingly so, with every inch of her skin feeling overheated, her breath coming faster, even her breasts feeling fuller as they pressed against the bodice of her dress. She'd wanted so badly to reach out to touch him, had been so tempted to go to her tippy-toes and press a kiss to his mouth that would surprise him even more than her questions had.

But she simply hadn't had the first clue how to do any of those seductive, enticing things. Sure, she knew how to play sexy for the screen, but in real life? The truth was that she'd never met a man about whom she felt strongly enough to want to be sexy with him...not until Ian.

So though she'd been standing there in front of him with her heart racing and her skin flushing, rather than doing anything seductive or enticing, she'd finally settled for an awkward smile and a semi-apology for quizzing him about love and marriage in the middle of the vineyard.

* * *

Tonight, as she'd watched him be so incredibly sweet with his sister and mother, Tatiana couldn't help but wonder at Ian's insistence that love was no more than a fairy tale. Tatiana had always trusted more in what people did than what they said.

And what Ian *did* was love the heck out of his family, who loved him right back—a love just as strong, just as true.

"Does he know how you feel?" Claudia asked, drawing her back from her vivid memories of that first, strangely intimate conversation with him.

Tatiana was about to say no, but then she remembered the way he'd reacted to her when he'd been holding her in his arms on the driveway. As if he'd felt their sudden connection just as strongly, just as deeply, as she had.

"Maybe." She had to laugh at herself and amend her response. "Probably. Because as you can see, I'm not exactly going out of my way to hide it. Not even from his mother." Since she was already being utterly reckless by talking about her feelings for Ian with his mom, Tatiana figured she might as well ask, "Got any tips for me about how to woo your eldest son?"

Claudia's laughter was just as warm as the arms that enfolded Tatiana into a hug. "He'd be a fool not to fall for you, sweetie. And the one thing I know for sure is that I haven't raised any fools."

"No, you most certainly haven't," Tatiana agreed, "but even so..." She paused, trying to think of a tactful way to put it. "Ian's already made it pretty clear to me how he feels about romance."

Claudia simply nodded as she turned back to the stove. "Tell me, for most people who want to act for a living, once they realize just how difficult it is to get any parts at all, let alone good ones, how long does it take them to give up their dreams?"

"Usually, it's a matter of months. Although there are some who stick it out for a couple of years before they throw in the towel."

"Did you ever consider giving up, Tatiana?"

"No." It had never even been a possibility. "Acting is such an integral part of who I am, I've never even thought about doing anything else. I love it that much."

"And you've always been determined to make it work?"

Tatiana thought about how hard she'd been working to get at the heart of her new character, and the fact that she wouldn't let up until she did. "Yes, I've always been determined."

"Well, people always say that if you follow your heart, you'll never regret it, which I agree with. But what I learned when Ian's father and I were trying to make things work between the two of us way back when, was just how much determination it can sometimes take to stay on your heart's path. I also learned that love is worth the struggle. Always."

It was, Tatiana thought as she slipped the pasta into the boiling water on the stove, both an encouragement and a warning from a mother who clearly knew her eldest son very, very well. Well enough not to shy away from words like *struggle* and *determination.*

Before either of them could say anything more, Max walked into the kitchen, handed Tatiana the glass of wine she hadn't yet had a chance to drink, and asked if she could go tell the boys to finish stacking the wood and wash up, because dinner would be ready in a few minutes.

* * *

As soon as they were alone in the kitchen, Claudia stepped away from the stove and put her arms around her husband. "You know how much I've worried about Ian. Not just since his divorce, but even before that."

"We all have."

"Suddenly, I don't feel like I need to worry quite so much anymore."

Max brushed his wife's hair away from her face, after all their years together still the most beautiful one he'd ever set eyes on. "Because he's back here in Seattle with all of us again?"

She smiled up at the man she'd loved with every single breath from the first moment he'd held her in his arms, just the way he was now. "Because something tells me that he's going to fall in love. For real this time. And that it's going to change everything for him, in the best possible ways."

"Ian? In love? Did he say something to you?" But Claudia knew it wouldn't take him long to figure it out, and a moment later, he said, "Tatiana?"

Ian and Tatiana had been seated together at Marcus and Nicola's wedding, and though Claudia had been seated at the next table, she'd noted the way Tatiana's gaze had continually returned to her son's handsome face. And it had seemed to Claudia that his normally steely self-control had been hanging by a thinner thread than usual around the pretty actress. Tonight when they'd come inside the house, Claudia had seen all of the same signs, on both their parts. Only this time, her son hadn't seemed quite as good at pushing away his obvious attraction.

"Tatiana," Claudia confirmed for her husband, her brain already a half-dozen hopeful steps ahead to another wedding and babies and, most of all, the happiness Ian had always deserved, but had never quite been able to find.

It suddenly occurred to her that if she could have picked out a woman for her son herself, she couldn't have chosen better. Tatiana would never need Ian's power or influence to help her achieve success. She would never need his money. All she would ever ask him for was a love that matched her own for him. Granted, that was the one thing Ian didn't seem to think he had to give. But Claudia was confident that in time, he'd realize the truth of what was in his heart, that there was not only enough love for her and his father and siblings...but endless love for a woman who would finally make his life truly whole.

"She's very pretty and obviously talented," Max said in a considering voice, "but do you really think she's strong enough for Ian?"

Claudia looked toward the door through which Tatiana had just exited. "Something tells me she's going to end up surprising everyone with just how strong and determined she is. Ian, most of all."

Max's arms tightened around his wife. "I hope you're right."

"When," she said with a saucy little grin, "have I ever been wrong?"

Knowing better after several decades of marriage than to answer that one, he simply covered her mouth with his. When the sound of the pasta boiling over forced her out of his arms, both of them knew without a word being said that as soon as dinner was over and the kids all went home, they would be right there in each other's arms again.

CHAPTER THREE

Ian already had his jacket off, his shirtsleeves rolled up and at least two dozen fire logs moved into the wood shed by the time his brothers tore themselves away from drooling all over Tatiana to come outside to help. They'd pulled in Ford, as well, and soon the four of them were making a serious dent in the wood his parents had had delivered.

He hadn't had a chance to see Adam or Dylan since he'd been back. They'd both called a couple of times to ask if he was free to grab a beer with them, but he'd been in meetings each time. He'd been looking forward to finally getting to sit down with his brothers tonight in their parents' house, but when he'd seen Dylan with his hands on Tatiana—and then Adam a couple of minutes later—he'd immediately seen red.

Ian had always been a possessive man, but where Tatiana was concerned he didn't have one damned thing to be possessive about.

She wasn't his.

She would *never* be his.

Hell, if one of his brothers wanted to date her, he should be happy for them both.

His jaw popped hard, and the pain of it had him belatedly realizing that he was clenching his teeth hard enough to break a molar. Damn it, he needed to get his infatuation with Tatiana under control, and fast.

Ian had always been able to calculate sums quickly in his head and could figure out the worth of a risky investment with nearly perfect clarity every single time. But so far, he hadn't been able to figure out how to stop thinking about a pretty girl.

Out on the driveway when she'd stumbled into his arms, the attraction between them had flared up so fast and so hot that he'd been a heartbeat from dragging her into the woods at the side of his parents' property so that he could turn that intense attraction into something even hotter. But though this only reinforced his decision not to let her shadow him, knowing he was doing the right thing by keeping his hands off her didn't do one damned thing to diminish his desperate need for her.

"Heads up!"

Ian dropped the logs in his arms onto the top of the pile and spun around just in time to catch the football before it slammed into his head. He hadn't played in years, but his muscles and his hands still held enough memory to throw a perfect spiral back to Dylan without so much as blinking. They sent the ball sailing back and forth several satisfying times before Adam suddenly decided to steal the ball from Dylan. He quickly lobbed it back to Ian before Dylan got his revenge by sending his Adam flying on the wet grass.

For a few minutes, as he played football with his brothers on the back lawn, Ian felt like a kid again. Back then there'd been no worries holding any of them back, no concern whatsoever about what the future held, no responsibilities beyond remembering to kick their shoes off outside so they didn't track mud on the kitchen floor...and hoping there would be enough light left after dinner to pick up their game where they'd left it.

He'd started with those games in the backyard with his brothers and ended up the top high school quarterback in the Pacific Northwest. But though he'd done even better in college, instead of gunning for a contract with the NFL, he'd traded in his football jersey for a three-piece suit and a career in investing. Still, after all these years, he'd never forgotten the rush of throwing for a touchdown. Every time he closed another big deal, he felt that same rush. Running Sullivan Investments might be a hell of a lot different than the pro football career he'd once dreamed of, but the challenge of bringing his best game and the thrill of the win were the same.

Speaking of challenges, Ian was well aware that he hadn't yet dished any retribution to Ford Vincent for the way he'd screwed around with Mia's heart for five years. Sure, from everything Mia had told him, it sounded like Ford had gone out of his way to atone for his sins, but just because Ian's sister had completely forgiven the guy didn't mean Ian was all the way there himself. Mia hadn't let Ian tear Ford apart at the wedding, or after, but if he acted quickly enough, she wouldn't be able to stop him tonight.

With the center of Ford's chest a perfect target for the football, Ian got ready to let it rip. But a few seconds later, on a curse, he dropped the ball back to his side.

"Mia would be very proud of you for not giving in to the urge. And don't worry," Tatiana said as she moved closer and took the football out of his hands, just in case he changed his mind and decided to nail Ford after all, "it will be our secret that you were even thinking of doing it."

Just then, as his sister came out into the yard and put her arms around Ford's waist, Ian couldn't decide what was harder right then: not letting himself turn to drink in Tatiana's beauty, or keeping his gaze on Ford and Mia while they kissed as if they were alone rather than surrounded by family.

In the end, however, Ian knew it wasn't really a choice. Not only was he slowly starting to accept that Ford really *was* treating his sister the way she deserved to be treated, but the woman beside him drew him like no one else ever had. And even if he should have been focusing on protecting his sister and reconnecting with his brothers, Ian hadn't yet figured out a way to stop himself from losing the thread of anything but Tatiana whenever she was near.

"It was nice of you to help my mother out in the kitchen."

Tatiana's answering smile had Ian feeling as though the football had just nailed him in the chest, right in the spot where he'd been so certain nothing would ever be able to touch him again.

"I love your parents. They're so easy to be with, and to talk to. I can't imagine how any of you kept anything from your mother when you were kids."

"It wasn't easy," he agreed. And yet, just as he'd kept the finer details of his marriage and divorce from his sister, he hadn't talked to either his mother or his father about the situation, either. They all loved him, just as much as he loved them, and he knew how badly they all wanted him to fall in love again, to marry again, and hopefully to have kids this time around. There was no one he wanted to disappoint less than his family. So since he couldn't give them what they most wanted, he believed it was better to keep his own counsel on the reasons his marriage had gone so wrong and why he wouldn't make the mistake of going that route again.

"I think I may have just shared my biggest secret with your mom, actually." Tatiana ran a hand over her skirt in what he was starting to realize was a slightly nervous gesture. "And what's really amazing is that I was only in the kitchen with her for a few minutes."

As Tatiana stood beside him in his parents' backyard, so beautiful that she took his breath away, Ian wanted to know all of her secrets. What did she secretly dream of? What did she secretly desire? And were her secret cravings as sensual, as desperate, and as endlessly hungry as his were becoming?

But he couldn't ask her any of that. He could only say, "If you're worried that she'll give away your secret—"

Tatiana shook her head before he could finish reassuring her. "No, I'm not worried about that. Although I'm sure she'll tell your dad, which is totally fine. In any case, what I really came outside to say was that dinner's ready. I'll go tell everyone else."

He didn't want to relinquish Tatiana to the attentions of his brothers again. But since he didn't have anything to give to her, and he was pretty sure his brothers both did, Ian let her walk away from him...and toward them.

* * *

Tatiana found herself seated between Adam and Dylan at the dining room table, with both of them living up to their reputations as master flirts. She couldn't remember another dinner where she'd laughed so much. Were it not for Ian choosing the seat farthest from her, and remaining almost completely silent during the meal, it would have been the perfect evening.

She was glad she'd stepped into the backyard in time to see Ian playing football with his brothers. She wasn't at all surprised by his athletic ability. No, she thought with a little shiver of desire, she was absolutely certain that he did *everything* with both innate grace and strength. It was the joy she'd seen on his face as he played with his brothers that had her needing to put a hand on the French doors to steady herself.

All at once, she'd been able to see it so clearly—the expensive tailored suit gone and in its place, a football jersey streaked with mud and grass stains. She'd wanted to kick off her heels and dash out onto the grass to get in on their game, if only to be a part of Ian's joy for a few precious moments. She still didn't have the first clue how she was going to get him to change his mind about letting her shadow him, but she was hopeful that a brilliant idea would come to her soon. It certainly helped, in any case, to know that she had his mother's seal of approval.

She also loved watching how sweet Mia and Ford were with each other. Every touch, every look they gave each other was laced with love. At the same time, it was clear to Tatiana that while they were a perfect team now, they had both remained unique individuals. Mia was full of her usual spark and sassiness, and Ford was still a brilliant and bold rock star, through and through. Tatiana was encouraged, yet again, that when people were meant to be together, even if they sometimes had a rough road to travel, things worked out in the end the way they were supposed to.

After they'd cleared the dinner plates and moved into the living room to dig into the delicious chocolate truffles that Rafe's fiancée Brooke had made, Ian's father walked in carrying a large bottle of champagne.

Standing by the fire where the family dog was snoring contentedly, Max said, "It's been a heck of a great year for us Sullivans. First, with Rafe and Brooke getting engaged, and then, Mia and Ford finding each other again." Max gave a warm smile to the man who would become his son-in-law and Mia blew her father a kiss. He popped the champagne cork and poured the fizzing liquid into the glasses Claudia had brought out, waiting until each of them was holding a full glass before raising his. "Tonight, I'd like to make a toast to Ian. We all missed you while you were living in London, and we're very glad you're back home."

Ian hadn't said much all evening, but even so, it was easy to see just how much he enjoyed being with his family. Now, as he smiled at his mother and father and said, "It's good to be back," Tatiana's heart just about stopped in her chest.

Ian Sullivan had the most beautiful smile she'd ever seen.

Why, she thought as she stared at him in helpless wonder, *didn't he smile more?*

The realization that his happiness already mattered so much to her had her hands shaking slightly as she reached out to clink her glass against the others'.

Though Tatiana had become accustomed to often being the center of attention over the years as her roles got bigger and her fame grew, she was glad for a big group to temporarily disappear into while she worked to regain her equilibrium.

Of course, that was right when Max said, "I'd also like to raise a toast to Tatiana for joining our family tonight."

All eyes turned to her, and she wondered if she was as much an open book as she felt. Claudia, and likely Max, already knew how she felt about Ian. But could Mia, Dylan, and Adam see how breathless being around their brother made her?

"You're always welcome here, Tatiana, and Claudia and I both hope you'll consider ours to be your second home whenever you're in Seattle."

"Thank you, Max. Thank you, Claudia." Her words thickened with gratitude for their welcome. "I've had such a wonderful time tonight. It really does feel like being home."

"Don't forget, I've also got plenty of space at my place if you need it," Dylan offered in his charmingly wicked way.

"Thanks for the offer," she said, grinning right back. "Hopefully the owner of the condo I'm renting won't suddenly up and decide to kick me out, but if she does, I'll keep you in mind."

"At least let me take you out for a sail tomorrow."

She wasn't all that great on moving things like boats and planes and trains, but during her years of traveling around the world for work, she'd learned how to tamp down her natural inclination toward motion sickness. "I'd love to go sailing with you, Dylan, but I've got to head to Los Angeles tomorrow morning for the weekend."

"What about Monday then?"

"She's busy Monday."

Everyone turned to Ian in surprise—partly because he'd interrupted their conversation from out of the blue, but mostly because of his tone. One that could quite easily be described as possessive.

Extremely possessive.

Dylan asked, "You are?" at the exact moment she thought, *I am?*

Though they were surrounded by his family in the cozy living room, when Ian looked at her it felt to Tatiana as if they were the only two people in the world. "My first meeting on Monday is at seven a.m. The details will all be on the schedule my assistant will email you."

Dylan looked back and forth between the two of them with raised eyebrows before settling his questioning gaze on Tatiana. "Why are you going to be hanging out with Ian on Monday?"

"The character I'm playing in my next film inherits a really big company, and even though everyone is certain she'll fail, she's determined not to. Ian is so nice that he's agreed to let me shadow him for a couple of weeks so that I can learn what it's like to actually be a CEO." She knew her smile was likely too big, too happy, too giddy. Borderline goofy, even. But maybe if she didn't worry about holding back her own smiles, it would help Ian realize he didn't have to hold in his, either.

Dylan raised an eyebrow in his brother's direction. "That is mighty *nice* of you, Ian, to let Tatiana spend two weeks with you."

Mia smacked her brother on the arm. "I think shadowing Ian in the office is an absolutely *fabulous* idea, Tatiana. Although, I swear that place feels like walking into the CIA sometimes. After you're done with your stint at Sullivan Investments, you'll have to fill us in on all his little secrets."

"Oh no, I would never do that," Tatiana said with utter seriousness. "Whatever happens in his office will stay in his office." She hadn't yet signed an NDA, but even without one, she would never break his confidence, business or otherwise, with anyone. Not even with his family.

Fortunately, Ian clearly had no intention of letting the conversation grow any more awkward, because he drained his glass, then rose and said, "Speaking of the office, I'm sorry to have to eat and run, but I've got a great deal of work to take care of tonight."

Like a finely oiled machine, all of the Sullivan children insisted their parents continue relaxing by the fire while they took their dishes into the kitchen. And even though she worked with rich, famous people all the time, Tatiana got a kick out of watching one of the world's biggest rock stars wash dirty dishes, then hand them to a near-billionaire CEO so that he could dry them. Less than thirty minutes later, the six of them were done cleaning up the kitchen and dining room and had said their good-byes.

As they drove away, Tatiana spoke to Ian in a soft voice that only he could hear in the backseat with her. "Thank you for changing your mind about me shadowing you. I'm really excited about Monday."

She couldn't see his expression in the darkness of Ford's car, but she could feel the heat of his gaze as he turned to look at her. Instead of saying anything in response, he spoke to Ford. "I'd appreciate it if you'd pull over here to drop me off."

Mia turned all the way around in her seat as her fiancé pulled over to the side of the downtown Seattle street. "We're a good dozen blocks from your building, Ian."

Regardless, a moment later, he was out on the curb. "Thanks for the ride. Good night."

"Gotta love my brother," Mia said with a shrug as Ford pulled back into traffic. "He's one of the best men I've ever known, but he's not always easy to understand. Good luck shadowing him next week, Tatiana. I know you won't be able to tell us what you learn, but I hope it turns out to be everything you need it to be."

Feeling like Ian had left holding her heart in his hands, Tatiana said, "I hope so, too."

CHAPTER FOUR

On Monday morning at six forty-five, Ian found Tatiana standing outside the locked front doors of his office building. He'd been certain that as a famous actress, she would not only be late to his early meeting, but she'd also use her tardiness as a way to make a grand entrance.

Yet again, he'd been wrong about her.

"You didn't need to be here for another fifteen minutes."

She slipped the sunglasses she was wearing onto the top of her head as she turned toward him with a smile that wasn't the least bit dimmed from yet another of his rather unwelcoming greetings. And though he'd assured himself he was prepared to see her today, just one look at her incredible beauty nearly took him to his knees on the pavement.

"Time is money on film sets. I assumed it would be the same for you. Plus," she added with another grin that was a thousand times too adorable for his peace of mind, "I've found that being punctual means people will usually forgive me for everything else."

"Everything else?"

"I'm messy. *Really* messy." She said it without the slightest bit of regret or guilt. "Every time I think about cleaning up or organizing, there's always something else I'd rather do."

Order was an integral part of Ian's life. Messes drove him crazy.

No wonder Tatiana made him feel like he was losing it, one beautiful smile at a time.

If he'd been able to think straight, he would have gotten her inside the building before anyone noticed who she was, but because he couldn't get his synapses to fire properly around her, several people stopped to do double takes. He quickly punched in the security code, but by the time the door opened, strangers were already lining up on the sidewalk to ask her for autographs and pictures.

Tatiana was gracious and friendly and didn't seem the least bit disturbed by any of the attention, even from the guy who stood a little too close and didn't ask for permission before putting his arm around her for the photo. Though he was related to several famous people, and his sister was now engaged to a rock star, Ian had never been able to understand how any of them could accept the constant lack of privacy. At his first opportunity, he got her inside.

She was wearing a black coat that covered her from shoulder to ankle, and her hair was pulled up off her neck. Clearly, she'd intended to make herself as unexceptional as possible to passers-by, but she obviously didn't realize that she'd have as much chance of that as she would trying to get the sun to stop rising every morning. Even weeks of rainy days couldn't make you forget what it was like to feel the heat of it on your skin, or keep you from remembering the bright reflection of it on the open waters all around Seattle.

"Does it ever work?"

She stepped into the elevator beside him. "Does what ever work?"

"Your disguise."

She slipped out of her big coat and put her sunglasses in one of its pockets. "Very rarely," she admitted. "Which is why, usually, I don't even bother to try. But I didn't want there to be any problems on my first day shadowing you, so I figured I'd at least give it a shot. Sorry about all that outside. I hope I didn't make us late for your meeting."

Without her coat on, he could see that she'd also tried to dress for the office in such a way that she wouldn't draw attention to herself in any of his meetings. Only, despite the blue blazer and slacks that were similar to what the other women in his office often wore, Ian was certain that no one would ever make the mistake of overlooking her. Not when she was an endlessly intriguing puzzle of innocence and pure sensuality, from the slight wave in the red-blond hair that was threatening to spill out of its pins, down to the tips of the heels she wore as if she'd been born walking on four-inch spikes.

Ruthlessly forcing away his attraction to her the same way he had all weekend long when she'd crept into his thoughts again and again, he said, "We're not going to be late, but if we had been, it would have been my fault, not yours. I should have known to get you off the sidewalk as soon as possible."

"It was fine," she said, as unconcerned with the potential ramifications of her fame now as she'd been outside. "I walked here from my condo, actually. It was really nice to see what downtown Seattle looks like before it wakes up for the day."

She'd walked here? Alone? "Shouldn't you have a bodyguard with you?"

She made a dismissive sound. "No."

"Does Valentina know you're walking around by yourself downtown? And that you're letting strange guys put their hands on you for pictures?"

Her beautiful green eyes flashed beneath raised eyebrows. "I'm sure you taught Mia to watch out for herself. My sister taught me the same things. I'm rather attached to my freedom, but I'm not stupid about it, Ian. I'm careful, I promise. Plus," she added with a grin, "I've taken some karate lessons, so if that guy had done anything weird, I would have knocked him flat with a punch to the solar plexus."

How many times was she going to surprise him? he asked himself as they got off the elevator, then headed for his office.

Of course, his lust-filled brain instantly twisted the question up as he wondered, would he be surprised by the softness of her skin beneath his fingertips? Would the taste of her lips against his tongue be as sweet as he imagined? And what would she sound like as she came apart beneath him? Whimpers? Gasps? Or would she be too breathless for either?

Business, damn it. He needed to keep his mind on business. "Do you have any questions about the schedule my assistant sent you?"

As she pulled a folder out of her bag, her scent played effortless havoc with his quickly diminishing self-control. "Just one." Holding up the three pages that detailed the next twelve hours of his life, she asked, "When do you get a moment to take a breath?"

"Breathing is usually scheduled for just after lunch," he replied, before he could think better of teasing her.

Her eyes widened for a moment before she began laughing. "I'll make sure to pencil it in."

Her scent and her nearness were destroying his restraint moment by moment. *Boundaries.* He needed to make sure the boundaries between them were clear—not just to Tatiana, but in his own head, as well.

But before he could lay down any ground rules, she said, "Like I said on Friday, not only do I not want to get in your way this week, but the best way for me to learn is to see you do whatever it is you would naturally do throughout the week. I truly intend to fade into the background, so please don't give me another thought."

She went to sit down on the couch, but he stopped her with one incredulous word: "How?" He made a sound of obvious disbelief. "You can't even get away with a disguise outside. So how do you think you could ever fade into the background in my office?"

"Blending into the wallpaper is one of the first things you learn in acting class. And I'll have you know," she said with a confident smile, "that I can play a mean wallpaper."

"I don't care how good you are at acting like wallpaper, you're a *star.*" A stunningly beautiful one, no less. "Hell, we both just saw the way people reacted to you outside."

"You're right that your colleagues will probably react at first because they've seen me in a movie or two, but it won't take them long to realize that I'm just a person. And that I'm no different from anyone else."

But couldn't she see? She *was* different. So different that he'd been off his game from the first moment he'd met her.

His assistant knocked on the open door. "Good morning, Ian. Ms. Landon, it's lovely to see you again."

"Please, call me Tatiana, Bethany. And, actually, if it's all right with you and Ian, I was hoping at some point this week that you and I could sit down together so that I can ask you some questions for my research?"

"Absolutely, Tatiana."

Ian's assistant had met plenty of famous and wealthy people over the years she'd been working with him, many of them from his own family. But he could see from the huge smile on Bethany's face that she was especially excited about getting to spend some time this week with his beautiful, sparkling shadow.

"Mr. Thomas has just arrived and is waiting in reception, Ian. Would you like me to bring him in?"

"No, I'll go greet him myself." Before he did, he turned to Tatiana and explained, "Flynn Thomas is the founder of one of the most innovative cloud-based digital storage companies in the world. They're not the biggest, but they're the best, and poised for huge potential growth. I've been working to do a deal with him for nearly two years, and we're nearly there."

He held the door open for her, and when she headed down the hall in front of him, he was cursed with a view of Tatiana's perfect hips covered in navy wool.

Wallpaper. Was she completely nuts?

"Flynn, thank you for taking the time to meet with me this morning. I'd like to introduce you to Tatiana Landon. Tatiana is doing some research for a role in an upcoming movie and has asked to sit in on my meetings today, if you don't have an objection to her doing so. She's signed a nondisclosure agreement, of course."

In his late twenties, Flynn was a hell of a lot more self-possessed than most young tech entrepreneurs. In fact, it was precisely because he was nobody's fool that he hadn't yet taken an offer from anyone and still held the reins on a company that was increasing in worth by leaps and bounds.

"It's very nice to meet you, Tatiana," Flynn said, and as they shook hands, Ian could have sworn he held on to Tatiana's just a little too long. "You were brilliant in *Gravity*."

Tatiana flushed at his compliment. "Thank you. I hear you're brilliant, too."

What the hell? Were the two of them flirting?

Rationally, Ian knew it shouldn't matter one bit who Tatiana flirted with, and yet he couldn't quite bank his irritation as they made their way into the conference room where

Bethany had set out an array of breakfast food and drinks.

Flynn didn't normally care for small talk, so Ian didn't offer any. But today, the other man was full of questions for Tatiana, particularly regarding some of the more technical aspects of moviemaking. She graciously answered his questions, and Ian's irritation notched up another level at the certainty that this hugely important meeting was about to be completely derailed. But when Flynn pulled out a chair for her at the conference table, she simply smiled and said, "I'm going to grab a seat over there, thanks." Taking a chair in the far corner of the room, she opened her notepad and began to write down some notes.

Flynn's eyes remained on her for a few moments. He was clearly entranced, but when she didn't so much as look up from her notebook and seemed as if she was totally in her own world, he finally turned his focus to the sheet of paper Ian had put on the table in front of him.

"This is my new offer."

Flynn whistled low and long. "You got the board to agree to these terms?"

Ian nodded. He'd spent the entire weekend doing just that, as a matter of fact. "They're as enthusiastic as I am about working with you and your company."

Flynn looked down again at the enormous figures on the page, running one hand through his hair as if he couldn't quite take it in. But even though nearly anyone else on the planet would have jumped at what Ian was offering, Flynn was not only one of the most independent-minded individuals Ian had ever met, but he'd also been jerked around by a couple of other investment firms the previous year. It had made him increasingly cautious about the idea of partnering with anyone.

Ian sat back in his chair to make sure Flynn knew the pressure was off, even though the full truth was that Ian would do pretty much anything to make sure this deal didn't fall through. He knew it was crazy to feel this way after all these years of success and the huge sum of money in his bank account, but Ian had never been able to completely bury his fear over not having enough money during those years in college when his family had been in dire straits. An enormous deal like this one would go a long way to buffering that sense of security that he'd been chasing ever since.

Finally, Flynn said, "I like you, Ian. Your track record is great, and the numbers you're talking now aren't bad, either. But how do I know you're not just in it now for the hard sell, and then when we do the deal, you'll pass me off to someone lower down the chain?"

"I'm committed to you and your company, Flynn. And you're right, I am a straight-up guy, so I'm going to give you my word that if you agree to partner with Sullivan Investments, I will personally continue to work with you." It would be a hell of a lot of extra work on top of a schedule that was already packed, but Ian frankly relished the challenge and the opportunity to work with someone as innovative as Flynn Thomas.

The other man took his measure in silence. Ian didn't have any problem with that. On the contrary, he appreciated working with someone who thought first and acted only after weighing all of the pros and cons of the situation.

"I'll be out of town until next Tuesday," Flynn said. "Let's meet again then, at which point I'll give you my final decision."

"Sounds good." Especially since between now and next Tuesday, Ian planned to find a good half-dozen more ways to sweeten the deal so that Flynn wouldn't be able to say no. "If you've got a few more minutes, any chance you can take me through that new technology you mentioned yesterday?"

Flynn's face lit at the chance to switch from business to technology, and though he had finally seemed to completely forget Tatiana's presence as he pulled out his tablet and started talking Ian through his newest innovation, Ian hadn't.

Not for one single second.

CHAPTER FIVE

"I thought *I* worked hard," Tatiana said five hours later when they were in the back of his town car on the way to a lunch meeting, "but I'm starting to feel like being on a movie set is closer to hanging out at the spa compared to what you do every day." She didn't need to refer to the schedule Ian's assistant had given her, because she'd memorized it. "I assumed all you did was play with money and keep your eye on changing market conditions, but so far today you've already had meetings about a major tech acquisition, expanding your office further into Asia, a huge fundraising event that you've been spearheading, and now we're heading to lunch to discuss chemistry with a professor from the University of Washington."

It was the first chance she'd had to talk privately with Ian since his first meeting of the day, and though she'd done nothing more than sit in on his meetings to take notes, she felt worn out simply from observing his pace, his intensity, his drive. Slipping off her heels for a few precious moments, she unbuttoned her blue blazer, loosened her hair from its twist, and slid her feet beneath her on the leather seat.

She felt good about how well she'd blended in this morning. Even Ian had seemed to forget all about her. Not that she had stopped reacting to him, however. All morning in his presence she'd felt overly warm, as though her body was constantly on alert for something.

No, not just *something*. For a look. For a touch. And, in her most hopeful moments, for a kiss. One stolen in a deserted hallway as he pressed her up against the wall, his muscles hard against hers, his lips hot as they devoured hers.

Heat swamped her again as she fumbled for the button that would lower the window. Finally, it let in the cool, damp air. She lifted her hair off her neck and let it blow over her.

"How," she asked him as the heat of his gaze on her kept her warm despite the cold rushing through the window, "do you do it?"

"How do I do what, exactly?"

Tatiana wanted to know so many things about him that, honestly, even she wasn't sure which question she was asking in that moment. She wanted to know how he made her feel so much, so quickly, and with so little effort. She wanted to know what had put the darkness into his eyes, and the hard edges around his mouth where smile lines should be. She wanted to know how he could sit at a dining table with a family who wanted nothing more than to love him, but still hold himself just far enough away from them so that they couldn't get all the way past his walls.

But since she also wanted to understand the businessman she'd observed during the past five hours, she asked, "How do you run at this pace, hour after hour, day after day, without getting even the slightest bit winded?"

"It's my job."

She held in an irritated sigh. She'd known he was going to be a tough nut to crack, hadn't she? Heck, his mother had all but held up flashing neon signs of the words *struggle* and *determination* while they were making dinner.

"Yes, but it's a job you no longer need to work at half as hard as you do, especially when you've already had more success than most people could ever dream of. Take Flynn Thomas and his company. I know you're excited about the chance to work with him and he's clearly brilliant at what he does, but I'm sure you could get him to take the deal without offering to give up so much of your own time and energy. And yet, you didn't hesitate to give him your word that you wouldn't hand him or his company off to anyone else."

"The same thing could be said of you and acting—that you no longer need to work at it half as hard as you do when you've already had so much success. But that isn't stopping you from taking on new roles, is it?"

Tatiana understood this was Ian's way of trying to deflect her question away from himself. All morning she'd watched as he talked with employees and colleagues, and while he remembered the details of all their lives, he made absolutely certain that the personal conversations he had with people never circled back around to him. And she'd also noticed how careful all of those people were to stay perfectly within the boundaries he set for them.

When, she wondered, was the last time anyone had thrown caution to the wind and tried to smash through those boundaries?

It was tempting to try to do just that in the back of his town car while they were stuck in lunchtime traffic. But it was still too soon. Way too soon. Hurling herself like a wrecking ball at his stiff and starched-up boundaries within the first five hours of shadowing him wouldn't do either of them any good.

Patience. Somehow, she needed to find a little of it.

So, instead of pressuring him to answer her question just yet, she answered his. "I keep taking new roles because I love what I do." And her love for what she did for a living, at least, really was that simple. "Being an actor was always my dream. I love to make people happy, to know that I've helped them forget about their lives for a little while. Make believe, and disappearing into characters while in front of the camera, is just as much fun for me now as it was when I was a little girl wearing a tiger costume in my first commercial for a zoo. Because even when the outfit got hot and scratchy and all I could think about was yanking it off and throwing the stuffed head as far as I could, I already had enough passion and desire for acting to say my lines another dozen times until the director was satisfied. And what I remember most of all about that day is that when I was done, I felt like I'd achieved something really great. Not just filming a zoo commercial, but that I'd faced the challenge down...and won."

It was precisely what she was hoping to do again with this new role. Just as soon as she figured out her character's motivations, which would hopefully happen any day now. Especially considering the studio had tens of millions of dollars riding on her new film.

"Now that I think about it," she said, "I don't really need you to tell me *how* you do what you do. I think I can understand that well enough from my personal experience with my career. What I'd rather understand is *why*."

Though he'd rather flippantly responded to her first question by saying it was his job, she didn't think he'd do the same thing now. Already, she'd learned that while he wasn't the easiest person to do business with, he was fair.

And he respected a well-thought-out question just as much as he did a well-researched answer.

"I was twenty-one when I started Sullivan Investments."

Over and over throughout the years, people had remarked to her about how much she'd accomplished at her age. Still, she was a little stunned to think that he'd begun his rapid climb to the top when he was two years younger than she was now.

"So this was always what you wanted, the same way I wanted to act?"

"No," he said in a low voice, "not always."

When he didn't say anything more for a few long moments, she nearly reminded him that she'd signed an NDA and wouldn't ever repeat what he told her now to anyone. Only, she suddenly realized, this wasn't business anymore. It was no longer research.

It was personal.

"What did you want, Ian?" She gestured out the still-open window at the tall, shiny skyscrapers. "Before all of this?"

He was looking directly at her, but his eyes were slightly unfocused, as though he was looking through her into the past. "I wanted to play football."

She'd seen him throw the ball, knew just how well it fit into his hands. "I've only shadowed you for a few hours, but one thing I already know for certain is that when you want something, you get it. So it wasn't that you weren't good enough, was it?"

His eyes cleared as he refocused his gaze on her. "I was good. But things changed and football didn't make sense anymore."

"Why?"

"How many times are you going to say that word to me?"

She didn't hesitate before answering him with the truth. "Lots and lots of times."

Irritation warred with amusement on his face, and she thought she saw the corner of his mouth twitch as he said, "If I answer this *why*, will you do us both a favor and not say it again during the rest of this ride, at the very least?" As soon as she nodded, he said, "I went into the investment business in college so that I could pitch in during a rough time my dad was having with his job. Once I started working, I quickly found out that I was good at it."

"*Good* is a bit of an understatement considering one of your colleagues said..." She opened her notebook and pointed to her notes. "*It's as if he has investing ESP.*"

His grin came and went so fast, she might have thought she'd imagined it if she hadn't been able to feel the power of it still radiating straight into the center of her chest.

Right where it was starting to feel as though her heart was beating only for him.

"I like what I do, Tatiana. I like the money, the security, and the peace of mind that comes with being good at it, too."

"But it isn't just about your own financial security, is it?" She thought back to the meeting they'd just left with the head of the Seattle Family Foundation. Ian was to be the master of ceremonies at a big fundraising event on Friday night, and he'd given just as much focus, just as much passion, during the meeting with the charitable organization as he had in any of the others that were all about corporate revenue and profits.

"You never forget what it's like to wonder if you'll lose everything." Again, his eyes clouded as if he was back in the past. "Even once you've got more than you need. If we can teach mothers and fathers, and their kids, the kinds of skills that will mean they'll land on their feet, it might not solve all their problems, but hopefully it will at least give them something to aim for when times are tough."

"So you don't just want to give them hope, or temporary solutions, but the possibility of a good future." She liked it—liked it a lot. "I didn't want to interrupt during your meeting, especially since the event is less than a week away, but the biggest issues seemed to revolve around visibility for the organization. I know this might sound kind of dumb, but something simple like me being photographed at the event on Friday night in some designer dress might help a little bit to raise awareness about what you're working toward." She felt a little embarrassed as she told him, "It seems like whenever I attend anything in a pretty dress, the pictures are all over the Internet and magazines for the next few days. And if it would help a good cause..."

"It doesn't sound even the least bit dumb, Tatiana, and it would definitely help raise visibility for the foundation."

"So it's a date?"

His eyes darkened for a moment before he nodded. "It's a date. I'll let them know you'll be attending and, if it's okay with you, they can alert the press in advance."

"Sounds great," she said, her heart cartwheeling in her chest.

Okay, so it wasn't a *real* date, but at least she'd be spending Friday night with Ian. And it hadn't been nearly as difficult as she'd thought to get him to open up to her a little bit, had it?

"Thank you for answering my questions, Ian." Belatedly remembering she was supposed to be asking because of her research on CEOs, and not just because she wanted to know every little thing about him, she said, "I think it's going to help a lot with my role."

"You know, if you hadn't been such a good little tiger all those years ago, you would have made a good journalist."

Warmth shot through her at his compliment. "Actually, I played a journalist a couple of years ago."

"The twist at the end of that film was pretty surprising."

"You saw it?"

"Your movies are very popular, you know."

"Yes, but I also now know firsthand just how busy your work schedule is."

"Even I take a couple of hours off here and there, Tatiana."

Something about the way Ian said it, with the innate Sullivan lady-killing charm that his other brothers let fly much more freely than he normally did, immediately made her think of him taking time off for *sex.*

Her next breath caught in her throat as desire hit her with far stronger force than it ever had before. Ian was, clearly, a very physical man despite the hours he put in at the office. She assumed he worked out based on how fit he was, but something told her that hitting the gym wasn't the only way he liked to get his blood pumping.

It was moments like this when she felt every inch the virgin no one would ever believe she was given the handful of sexy roles she'd played so far. A more experienced woman would know how to amp up the sensuality in the car with nothing more than a few alluring words.

But, for the first time in a very long time, Tatiana was suddenly completely tongue-tied.

CHAPTER SIX

Every eye in the restaurant turned to them as they walked inside and Ian silently cursed himself for not having thought to change the reservation to a more private location. Because, while Tatiana barely seemed to be aware of all the stares and excited whispers, Ian knew it had to grate on her. Hell, it grated on him like crazy, and he wasn't even the famous one. She'd told him she could take care of herself, but even if she knew some martial arts, she was small enough—and trusting enough—that Ian knew he could have her beneath him and helpless within seconds if he wanted to.

The thought shouldn't have been so arousing, damn it, but fifteen minutes alone in his town car with Tatiana after five hours of breathing in her seductive scent in conference rooms had made it difficult for him to string a straight thought together, let alone put the brakes on his attraction to her.

"Ian, my boy, what a pleasure it is to see you."

Ian shook George's hand, glad that the man's grip was just as hearty as ever. "Professor, it's been too long."

Ian had been looking forward to this meeting since they'd arranged it a couple of weeks ago. George Collingsworth had not only been his favorite professor at the University of Washington, he was also an expert on fuel chemistry and synthesis. When the opportunity had arisen for Sullivan Investments to become a major partner in a company that specialized in new fuel-replacement technologies, he'd asked George if he could meet to give him some advice.

His old professor looked just as he always had, his shock of white hair in complete disarray, the pieces of his suit put together in a seemingly random and color-blind way. There was one big difference today, however: His normally preoccupied expression had been replaced by a huge smile.

Tatiana had that effect on everyone, from young tech geniuses to professors who were usually lost in the wilds of their brilliant minds. Even, Ian had to admit, normally laser-focused businessmen like himself.

He was just about to introduce them when George declared, "You've brought your beautiful wife with you!" Clearly, Ian thought, they'd just come across the one person on the planet who had no idea who she was, which was further brought home when George said, "Tell me your name, my dear."

"Tatiana."

"I'm George, and I must say it is positively wonderful to meet you. What a beauty you are, and with such intelligence in your eyes. Truly, you remind me of my own late wife. It's been fifteen years since she passed away, and I still miss her every single day."

Her face had lit up the moment she set eyes on George. But now empathy moved across her features. "I'm so sorry for your loss."

"That's very sweet of you." George's eyes twinkled as he looked back at Ian. "You're a very lucky man, Ian."

From the moment he'd found Tatiana in his office on Friday, Ian's world had shifted farther and farther off its axis due to his inability to stop wanting her. Now, George's honest mistake threatened to shove it all the way off.

Of course, the way Tatiana turned to him with her own grin and twinkling eyes didn't help one damn bit. Especially considering that he had to not only struggle to drag his gaze from hers...but also to keep from pulling her against him for a kiss that wouldn't do a damn thing to disprove George's incorrect assumption.

"We aren't—" A breeze from the open door of the restaurant blew the vanilla scent of

Tatiana's hair to him, temporarily making him lose his train of thought.

In the end, she was the one who finally clarified things. "I'm really flattered that you think I could be Ian's wife, George, but I'm just a friend."

His old professor frowned, looking between them. "I know chemistry when I see it, and not just in the lab. If the two of you aren't a couple, it's a damned shame." He looked between them again before seeming to make up his mind. He muttered something Ian couldn't quite make out, but that sounded a heck of a lot like *Just a matter of time.*

Ian had never been a man pulled forward by fate, luck, or coincidence. He'd always made his own choices, forged his own deliberate path. But even as he silently denied that what his professor had just stated could ever be true, he suddenly couldn't stop wondering if he really was as in control of his life—or his heart—as he wanted to think he was.

George pulled out a chair for Tatiana and after they were all seated and had placed their orders, he said, "Tell me about yourself, my dear."

"I don't want to take up too much of your time with Ian. I know he's really been looking forward to speaking with you."

"My wife wasn't one to draw attention to herself, either, but just like you, she was too beautiful to hide in the shadows." He gestured to the glass of wine the waiter had just poured. "Now drink up and start talking."

Tatiana laughed, clearly delighted. "Okay, but I really am going to make it quick so that the two of you can get down to business." She took a sip of the excellent dry white wine and made a small sound of pleasure that reverberated all the way through Ian's system. "I'm an actress and Ian is helping me do some research for a new role I've taken on."

"I once had dreams of the stage," George admitted. "And I would have been perfect for the role of Gilbert and Sullivan's Captain Corcoran...if only I could dance or hold a tune."

Laughing again, Tatiana said, "*HMS Pinafore* is one of my favorites, too." All it took was Tatiana softly humming a tune, and soon both of them were spontaneously singing a funny back-and-forth about monarchs of the sea and rulers of the Queen's Navy and sisters and cousins and aunts.

At the end of their impromptu performance, Tatiana gave George a hug. "Thank you for making my day with a Gilbert and Sullivan sing-along. And now, since I know the two of you have important business to take care of, I'm going to excuse myself for a minute so that you can get started without my further distracting you."

Both Ian and George stood when she left the table, and Ian nearly went after her to make sure she didn't get hassled by an overzealous fan. When he finally made himself sit down, his professor said, "You can't take your eyes off her."

Knowing better than to try to deny the truth, Ian explained, "Tatiana told you she's an actress, but what she didn't mention is that she's also very, very famous. Strangers get really excited about meeting her and often forget to keep normal boundaries. I didn't think about how difficult it might be for her to come here for lunch."

"Well, whether or not she's famous and you're worried about her fans taking advantage of her has nothing whatsoever to do with you not being able to look away."

His old professor's tone didn't brook any argument, so Ian didn't try. And when George pulled out a folder with the information Ian had sent him, he was glad to finally settle down to business. Only, Ian simply couldn't concentrate while Tatiana was gone.

But when she finally returned and took out her notepad, though Ian should have finally been able to concentrate on what George was saying, the truth was that her nearness made it just as difficult for him as her absence had.

* * *

It was eight p.m. when Ian got home for the night. He'd dropped Tatiana off on the way and learned that she was renting a condo in a building just around the block from his. So close that he could practically look out his living-room window and see her.

She'd been barely stifling her yawns by the time they made it to the last of his meetings, but had blamed it on the Mexican food they'd had delivered to the conference room. He'd seen his female cousins eat plenty of times, so he knew not every woman picked at her food the way his ex-wife had, but he was still stunned by how happily—and thoroughly—Tatiana munched down her burrito. Chelsea had only dabbled at modeling, and yet she'd been terrified of ever gaining a pound. Tatiana didn't seem to give it a second thought.

Not, of course, that she should, considering her figure was beyond gorgeous. And as he headed into his bedroom to take off his jacket, then loosen his tie and pull it off, he couldn't help but wonder if she was also stripping out of her clothes.

Damn it, now that he was finally alone, he needed to rein in every last ounce of focus and get the work done that he hadn't been able to concentrate on all day...not stand in his kitchen like an idiot and daydream about what color lingerie Tatiana was wearing beneath her clothes.

Most nights he went from his office building to his home office without a break. Work had always settled him down, even in the midst of his terrible divorce. Settling in behind the desk in his den, he took out the contracts he'd brought home and began reviewing them...but when he realized he'd been rereading the same clause on page three for the past fifteen minutes, he pushed back from his desk.

A workout, that's what he needed. A really, really, really rough one that would obliterate every last thought of Tatiana Landon.

Though he was no slacker in the workout department, Ian pushed himself running sprints on his treadmill twice as hard as he normally did. Even better, by the end he was running so fast that he couldn't think about anything but keeping his legs and lungs working in tandem. By the time he moved on to the rack of weights along the back wall of his home gym, he was finally starting to feel like his old self.

At the very least, two weeks of being shadowed by Tatiana were going to be good for his cardio.

Damn it, there she was again, creeping into his head. Turning on the TV, he figured multi-tasking by doing weights and catching up on the financial news he'd missed that morning would keep her out of his head. Only, instead of international stock market tickers coming up on the screen, he found himself looking straight at Tatiana's beautiful face.

She couldn't have been more than sixteen when the program currently being referenced by the financial analyst had been filmed. They showed her speaking only a few lines of dialogue, but that was all it took for him to see that her humor, and the emotional tug she managed to portray even in the midst of what should have been a silly scene in a high school cafeteria, was the glue that had held the show together.

He should have turned it off. But just as he'd been unable to stick to his *No* when she'd asked to shadow him in the office, he found that he couldn't bring himself to look away from Tatiana on his TV, either.

CHAPTER SEVEN

The following afternoon, Tatiana dropped onto the couch in Ian's office to make the most of the rare, and extremely precious, fifteen-minute window in his schedule. If she had been alone, she would have closed her eyes and taken a speed-nap. Then again, if she hadn't been shadowing Ian, she would have been moving at a reasonable pace all day like everyone else on the planet.

Ian, she had decided, was superhuman. He didn't just deal with his crazy schedule...he thrived on it!

It didn't particularly help that she hadn't gotten anywhere near enough sleep the night before. After he'd dropped her off at her condo, she'd been dying to strip off her clothes and sink into her bathtub. But she'd known that once she got into the hot water, she might never be able to drag her exhausted bones out again, so she'd forced herself to pull out her script and study it one more time.

Surely, she'd hoped, something she'd learned from shadowing Ian all day would be what she needed to get a handle on her upcoming role so that the director wouldn't fire her on the first day of filming. But by the time she'd finally crawled beneath the covers, she was no further along with her script than she'd been before. And, of course, once she was in bed, her brain refused to shut off, taunting her as she tossed and turned with images of how good Ian had looked in his suit, how sweet he was with his old college professor, how kind he was with his employees.

And how utterly, completely untouchable he remained.

Ian stepped into the office just then and went to sit down behind his desk. "You seemed really interested in that last presentation, Tatiana."

She peered at him from beneath lids that felt really, really heavy. Barely holding back yet another yawn, she nodded. "It was great." The truth was, however, that she hadn't taken in a word of it after the opening slide. The presenters' monotones had lulled her straight into dreamland.

"I'm glad you thought so, because I was hoping you could help me make a decision on one of the three approaches they presented."

Her lids lifted a little higher. “Decision?” She licked her suddenly dry lips. “You want my help?”

When he nodded, her brain did a quick scan of the forty-five-minute presentation. Maybe if she tried really hard, she’d remember something the presenters had said. *Anything* they’d said. But after a few seconds of concentrating hard enough to give herself a migraine, she still drew a blank.

A very sleepy blank.

Clearing her throat, she said, “I should probably review the slides and corresponding documents again before offering my opinion.”

“Surely you can just review your notes.”

In only a day and a half, she’d nearly filled up her notebook with her thoughts and impressions of what it took to be a successful CEO of a big company. But while her notebook had been open on her lap this afternoon, all she’d managed was a jagged blue line as her pen skidded across—and off—the page.

“I really just wanted to listen this afternoon.”

“Ah,” he said, nodding again, “that explains why you had your face resting on your hands and your eyes closed. So that you could listen better.”

“Okay,” she finally admitted, “I might have lost the thread of the meeting at some point—” Like the beginning one. “—but I’m sure no one but you noticed.”

"*Lost the thread,*" he echoed, a small smile playing on his lips. "That's an interesting way of talking about falling asleep in a meeting."

"Falling asleep?" She felt her face flush and wished, for the first time, that she was as good an actor in real life as she was in front of the cameras. But unfortunately, her brain was sleepy enough that it continued to let her mouth run amok. "That's crazy."

He shrugged as if he were going to let it go, but just as relief came over her, he sneakily hit her with, "You were snoring."

"I don't snore." Ian had to be joking, right?

The small grin he gave her was so surprisingly intimate that it almost felt as if he'd reached out to caress her skin. "You sounded just like a sleepy little tiger."

The goose bumps she got from the caress of his voice were no match for her chagrin as she dropped her face into her hands. "How embarrassing." She felt horrible that the presenter must have known how bored she'd been, because if Ian had noticed her snoring, surely everyone else in the room had, too. "I feel like I should apologize to—" Ugh, what were their names?

"Bill and Francesca?"

"Right, Bill and Francesca." God, she was so tired her brain felt like it was folding in on itself. "I'd hate for them to think I thought their presentation was boring."

"Didn't you?"

"Can you ask me that again after I've had a good night's sleep? Because by the time you dropped me off last night, it was all I could do just to take off my clothes before falling into bed."

Just that quickly, with one teeny-tiny little mention of stripping off her clothes, the air in the room shifted from teasing to desire.

Again, it occurred to her that if she'd had more experience with men—any experience at all, really—she would have known how to capitalize on a moment like this. Surely, other women must know how to turn a heated moment into an equally heated kiss. Or more. Because, as he stared so hungrily at her mouth that her lips began to tingle from nothing more than the intensity of his gaze, she could have sworn that Ian wanted her just as much as she wanted him.

Unfortunately, it was just as clear that he was *not* going to be the one to make the first move.

In the day and a half that Tatiana had spent shadowing Ian, she'd seen just how well he treated his employees and the companies he worked with. She'd witnessed time and again his focus, his determination, his intense drive to win. She'd seen him soften around his family at the wedding in Napa, especially the little ones. No question about it, Ian Sullivan was a good, strong man with a great family behind him.

Which was why she still didn't understand why he was so careful not to let anyone in too close. Especially her.

He was so careful around her, in fact, that apart from the attraction he didn't always manage to hide, she didn't have any idea what he really thought of her. And now she'd gone and fallen asleep in the middle of one of his meetings.

Way to impress, Tatiana.

"Tatiana, it's okay."

"No," she said with a morose shake of her head, "it's not. I came here to shadow you and stay in the background, not to embarrass you in front of your employees."

He pushed away from his desk, moving toward her instead of away for what felt like the very first time. "I fell asleep in a meeting once."

She couldn't stop her mouth from falling open. "No way."

"Way," he said with a full-fledged grin that was so sudden, and so beautiful, that it snuck up on her and pretty much stole away the last part of her heart that he hadn't already claimed. "And I'm afraid I snore a heck of a lot louder than you do."

She couldn't help but laugh then, not just at the image of the perfect and unflappable Ian Sullivan falling asleep in a meeting, but because he'd obviously told her the story to make her feel better about her own gaffe. Why would he do something like that if he didn't care about her, at least a little bit?

And when his laughter joined with hers, it was the sweetest sound Tatiana had ever heard.

She'd seen him smile several times during each workday, usually when one of his family members called. Clearly, they were all thrilled that he was back home. And though she knew firsthand just how crowded his schedule was, she'd also heard for herself how patient he'd been on the phone with his cousin Gabe's eight-year-old daughter when she'd asked him some questions for a project she was doing about the Sullivan family tree.

Maybe it was the lack of sleep that had her suddenly throwing her inhibitions to the wind, or maybe it was just how good it felt to laugh with him, but she suddenly needed him to know, "You have the most wonderful smile, the most infectious laugh. I could listen to it all day."

For a moment, she could have sworn he was going to close the rest of the distance between them and give in to what had been growing more inevitable with every second they were together. But instead, he abruptly looked away from her and frowned. Taking one step back, and then another and another, until he was nearly at his desk, she thought it looked like he was smelling something that bothered him.

By the time the unmistakable scent of Chanel No. 5 hit Tatiana, she realized Ian's ex-wife was standing in the doorway.

CHAPTER EIGHT

Chelsea Adrienne was even more stunning in person that she'd been in her pictures online...and clearly didn't notice that Tatiana was in the room as she swept toward Ian in a very expensive couture dress.

Bethany was only a couple of steps behind her.

"Ian, I'm sorry, I tried to tell Ms. Adrienne that you were busy—"

"It's all right, Bethany."

His assistant shot Tatiana a worried look before leaving the office and closing the door behind her with a soft click.

"To what do I owe this pleasure, Chelsea?"

Just moments ago he'd been full of so much warmth and humor. Now, both were gone as he regarded his ex-wife the way one did an animal that might strike at any second.

"You closed the deal with Amando's two weeks ago."

"And now you've come to offer your congratulations?" His voice was so carefully modulated that although Tatiana thought it might be sarcasm, she wasn't quite sure.

"You began those negotiations when we were married. In fact, I was the reason you even knew about the Italian shoemaker in the first place when you saw how many pairs I had in my closet." She posed as though she'd reached the end of a runway before telling him, "I want my share of the deal."

Tatiana had watched Ian carefully for the past couple of days, and while it had been impossible not to see the walls he put up around himself, she'd never seen his gaze turn this cold. But there was something else there, too, something worse even than the coolness.

Something that looked to Tatiana like guilt.

Still, when he moved behind his desk, opened a drawer, and pulled out a checkbook, Tatiana nearly gasped in surprise.

"Here." He gave Chelsea the check, then pushed away from his desk. "My next meeting is about to begin. I'll walk you out."

His ex glanced at the check to make sure the figure he'd written on it suited her, then opened her Chanel purse and dropped it in without so much as a thank-you. But though she'd gotten what she'd come for, she didn't follow Ian to the door. Instead, she shifted into yet another predatory pose. "I hear you're the bachelor everyone wants to catch now that you're back in Seattle." She laughed, a floating sound that grated on Tatiana's nerves despite how light and airy it was clearly supposed to be. "Don't worry, I won't tell any of them what being with you is really like."

Tatiana couldn't stand it anymore. She tried never to play off her star power unless she absolutely needed to. But right here, right now in Ian's office as his bitchy ex-wife tried to hurt him, she was extremely glad to be one of the best-known actresses in the world.

Unfortunately, she was wearing a rose-colored cashmere sweater and black slacks rather than the kind of fashion-forward outfit that could compete with what Chelsea was wearing. Fortunately, however, after years of transforming herself on a daily basis in front of the cameras, Tatiana knew better than nearly anyone else how to turn *simple* into *spectacular*.

"Ian," she said in a soft voice, "I'd love an introduction."

Tatiana purposely remained sitting on the couch while Chelsea spun around to face her. Once Tatiana knew she had the other woman's full attention, she made certain her every movement as she rose gracefully was so easy and so confident that it was perfectly clear she wasn't trying to compete with Chelsea on any front—beauty, sensuality, or personality.

Tatiana had quickly learned in Hollywood that only an insecure woman needed to compete. The truly successful, truly confident women always forged their own paths, and didn't give a fig what anyone thought about them or their choices, fashion or otherwise.

"Tatiana," Ian said in a tense voice, "this is Chelsea, my ex-wife." Tatiana could see that he was worried about what was about to go down between the two women in his office, and she wished she could reassure him.

But right now she had to hold focus on avenging him.

Ian might not be hers, but five minutes ago she'd been certain they were at least on their way to becoming friends. And she refused to tolerate anyone speaking to one of her friends the way his ex-wife just had.

Tatiana forced herself to take a couple of steps toward the horrible woman. "Hello," she said, holding out her hand in such a friendly way that there was no way his ex could have refused to shake it. Since there was no better way to let the very competitive woman know she wasn't a threat than by giving her an honest compliment, Tatiana said, "Your dress is beautiful."

"It is, isn't it? It's always such a thrill to wear a one-of-a-kind Christianna original."

Tatiana could have spectacularly one-upped Chelsea by informing her that she had just been asked to become the face of Christianna's couture design house in Europe. But she wasn't here to compete for the crown of Queen Bee. She was here to put the other woman in her place as quickly as possible so that she'd leave Ian alone.

Then again...thinking about Ian's check burning a hole in Chelsea's purse helped Tatiana decide that sometimes it might not only be okay to stoop a little low, but it might be downright necessary.

"I'll be sure to let Christianna know you're pleased with her designs when I see her in Paris in a couple of weeks for my Golden Globes fitting."

Tatiana might have laughed at the jealous fury that leaped into the woman's eyes were she not still so furious about the way Chelsea had marched in and demanded money from Ian.

Money he'd given her without a fight...

"You're so much curvier than you seemed to be in your last film," Chelsea said in a voice so sweet it practically gave Tatiana a sugar rush. "I hope your fitting goes well."

This time, Tatiana couldn't stop her laughter from bubbling up and out. She'd met plenty of competitive actresses in the past ten years, but Ian's ex trumped them all. "Casting directors usually just jump past *curvy* and go straight for the word *fat*." But she'd already easily shrugged off the insult. "I know Kate Moss said nothing tastes better than being thin, but I'm pretty sure she'd change her mind if she ever tasted the chocolate truffles we had for dessert at Ian's parents' house on Friday night."

"You're not fat," Ian growled as he moved between them. Turning his scowl on his ex, he said, "You got what you came for, Chelsea."

"I know," Chelsea said, holding up her hands as if he was the one on the wrong foot, rather than she. "You're ready for me to leave so that you can get back to business. Believe me, I remember what it was like being married to you. Business always came first then, and clearly it still does." His ex gave Tatiana a pitying glance. "I don't know how the two of you met..."

With every word that fell from the woman's blood-red lips, Ian's tension seemed to rise, and the instinct to protect him from anything else his horrible ex-wife had to say had Tatiana reaching for his hand. "We met at a wedding."

The need to protect him quickly turned into something that ran even deeper as she stared down at her hand in his and was rocked by such a strong jolt of sensual—and emotional—awareness that she found herself confessing, "I don't think I've ever seen a man look better in a suit." But it was what she saw on his face when she looked up into his eyes that had her continuing to speak straight from her heart, only for him, their audience completely forgotten. "All it took was one handshake for me to fall for you, Ian." Palm-to-palm, the memories of that first time they'd touched came rushing back.

"Trust me," Ian's ex-wife said, shattering the moment with all the precision of a baseball hurled straight through a plate-glass window, "Ian might be good in bed, but even the best orgasms in the world don't make up for what it's like to live with him. Or should I say, *not* live with him, since I promise you that after he gets over his current infatuation, even you are only going to see him when he needs to screw away his tension from a business deal gone bad."

"It's past time for you to go, Chelsea." This time Ian put his hand on her arm to make sure she didn't linger. Unfortunately, her heavy scent did.

Tatiana would never be able to wear Chanel No. 5 again.

She had wanted to teach his ex-wife a lesson, but she hadn't planned on doing it like that, by finally opening up her heart to Ian so suddenly. And so completely. It was simply that she hadn't had it in her to lie about her feelings for him—not even to his ex-wife.

Interestingly, though, Tatiana was certain that it had also been the best possible way to strike out at the other woman. Because nothing could have infuriated her more than knowing how thoroughly she'd been forgotten by her ex-husband.

Chelsea was his past.

And Tatiana had just made it perfectly clear, in perhaps the most unplanned and non-well-thought-out way possible, that she hoped to be his future.

CHAPTER NINE

Tatiana's mind raced with a half-dozen different ways to approach Ian when he came back into his office. Would it be better to act like nothing had happened? Or should she try to cut the tension from what she'd witnessed with a joke that he wouldn't see coming and wouldn't be able to resist laughing about?

If she were in his place, she finally decided, what she'd really want was an ear, a shoulder, someone to gently talk through the whole situation with. Of course, that meant she'd need to force her own emotions into the background so that she could help him.

So then, if she'd been so sure about the best way to deal with things, why was the first thing out of her mouth when he walked back into his office, "Why did you give her the money?"

Only, she knew exactly why she'd said it, didn't she? Tatiana had never been any good at hiding her feelings. Especially when she felt more for the man standing in front of her than she could ever remember feeling for anyone else.

There was only the barest hitch in Ian's gait as he moved to his desk to pull something up on his computer screen. "I have more money than time to deal with lawyers," he replied in a voice utterly without inflection or emotion. "She knows that and capitalizes on it."

What he'd said about his money-to-time ratio was certainly true, but in Tatiana's mind it didn't come anywhere close to explaining what had happened. She frowned as she thought about the scene between Ian and his ex-wife.

One thing continued to stick with her: the guilt she'd seen in his eyes.

"You think you owe it to her—whatever she asks you for—don't you?"

Ian Sullivan had a masterful poker face, and she'd thought more than once that if he hadn't become a captain of industry he could easily have ruled the high roller tables in Vegas without breaking a sweat. But she could have sworn she saw a crack appear as she continued, "Why? Why would you think you owe her anything? I saw the way she acted. I see the way she *is*. What more than what she's already gotten from you do you think she deserves?"

Every time she said the word *why,* Ian's eyes flashed hotter, darker. He'd always held his inner fire in check, but now she expected it to burst free. Finally.

"I'm late for my next meeting."

Tatiana was momentarily stunned by the way Ian completely ignored her questions. Stunned into utter silence, actually.

She'd never known anyone who could shut down—or shut her out—so quickly. Or so thoroughly. And maybe, Tatiana told herself, that's where she should let the whole thing go. Any rational woman would.

Only, there was more than just what had happened between Ian and his ex-wife to deal with, wasn't there? Specifically, when she'd said, *"All it took was one handshake for me to fall for you, Ian."*

She wasn't ashamed that she'd finally admitted her feelings to him, and she didn't much care that his ex-wife had heard it. But she couldn't imagine sitting through a bunch of meetings with it hanging between them...or worse, with Ian pretending she'd never said it at all—as if what she felt for him didn't matter in the least.

So even though the rational part of her knew the timing was all wrong, that in the wake of dealing with his ex-wife Ian was as closed off as he could possibly be, Tatiana couldn't stop herself from moving closer into his personal space. Personal space that he'd just made perfectly clear he wanted to keep as his alone.

She reached for his arm. "About what I said at the end—"

"Forget it, Tatiana."

Now her eyes were the ones leaping with fire. "I can't forget it. I won't."

"You have to. We both do." As open as he'd been when they'd been laughing together fifteen minutes earlier about her falling asleep in the meeting, he'd now swung all the way to the far side of *closed*. "This next meeting will be even more boring than the one we just came out of, so you might as well skip it. I'll see you tomorrow."

Having dismissed her, he walked out of his office, leaving her standing alone with a difficult decision to make, one that she couldn't believe had become so thorny in such a short time. Should she do what he was obviously hoping she'd do—and what, at the moment, her stung pride was demanding—by picking up her bag and finding another CEO to shadow? Or should she suck it up and continue forward on the path she'd been so determined to walk just a few days ago?

But the truth was, continuing to shadow him wasn't about her pride. And it wasn't completely about researching her role, either.

The real reason she was going to stay in his life was because she recognized, deep inside herself, that there wasn't any decision for her to make. Not when her heart really and truly had made it for her all those months ago in Napa Valley, when Ian had held her hands in his...and she'd looked up into eyes that she'd been waiting to gaze into her entire life.

Yes, she knew that it was crazy to try for Ian's heart. While he was a caring man, he wasn't an easy one like his brothers. On top of that, he had obviously been terribly scarred by his marriage, his heart now imprisoned behind a thick, seemingly impenetrable wall.

And yet, she couldn't help but feel that it would be so much crazier *not* to try—to let him go without knowing she'd risked absolutely everything first. His mother's words from Friday night replayed inside her head: *"What I learned when Ian's father and I were trying to make things work between the two of us, was just how much determination it can sometimes take to stay on your heart's path. I also learned that love is worth the struggle. Always."*

Just then, Tatiana's phone buzzed from the couch. She picked it up and was both surprised and pleased to see a text from Ian's sister.

HAVING DRINKS WITH THE GIRLS AT MY PLACE. PLEASE COME!

Tatiana considered her options. She could go in to Ian's meeting, even though he'd just made it clear he didn't want her there. She could go back to her condo and read over her script another dozen times. Or she could go to Mia's house, have a couple of drinks, and try to forget that any headway she'd made with Ian had just been stripped completely away.

After texting Ian's sister back and noting her address, Tatiana tossed her phone at her open bag, then headed for Mia's.

* * *

"What a fabulous house," Tatiana marveled as Mia put a glass of wine in her hand the second she walked through the front door. "Is that a tower I saw just behind the house?"

"Complete with thirteenth century stones and everything," Mia confirmed. "It's where Ford first tricked me into seeing him again, and then later proposed. It's my favorite place on the property. He's turning the lower level into a recording studio, which means there will be lots of hot musicians always hanging around," she added with a wicked grin. "No complaints here."

Tatiana already knew the story of how, five years after they'd had a week-long affair and then split up, Ford had posed as an anonymous buyer to hire Mia as his Realtor to find him a house in Seattle. He'd believed it was the only way to get her to see him again, and while Mia had been furious with him at first, beneath her anger had been a deep and true love that had never gone away in the years she and Ford had been apart.

"I love watching the two of you together. Ford loves you so much."

"Sometimes," Mia said with a happy glow, "I wake up in the morning and he's right there, and I still can hardly believe we were lucky enough to get a second chance."

Tatiana was so happy for her friend, for all of her friends and family members who had found true love. One day, she hoped, she'd be the one glowing from being loved so well.

Brooke and Colbie walked in just then and there were more hugs among them all. Brooke was getting married to Mia's brother Rafe that summer. They lived full time on a lake a couple of hours away, but were often in Seattle for business meetings and to see family, though they'd had to miss dinner at Max and Claudia's on Friday night. Colbie was Mia's oldest friend from kindergarten, and she had also gotten married recently, Tatiana remembered when she saw the stack of bridal magazines Colbie and Brooke plopped onto the kitchen counter.

"Here's everything we had between the two of us. Although we already ripped out the pictures of all the good dresses," Colbie teased Mia.

"I swear," Mia said as she poured glasses of wine for her friends, "thinking through the logistics of marrying Ford is like planning a covert military operation. He's just so famous, I honestly don't know how we can avoid helicopters and paparazzi. I'm starting to think we should just throw on some bathing suits one afternoon and say our vows by the pool, then eat burgers and hot dogs at a cookout with everyone afterward."

Even though Tatiana knew Mia hadn't been serious, she had to ask, "Why don't you?"

Mia looked thoughtful. "Now that we're talking about it," she said slowly, "maybe that's exactly what we should do. I'll have to see what Ford thinks, but something tells me he'd be just as happy as I would to avoid the circus."

Mia had turned on the heat lamps on the covered porch that looked out over the lake and had laid out blankets on the seats so they'd be comfortable sitting outside. Brooke pulled a big box of chocolates out of her bag and put it on the coffee table next to the plate of crackers and cheese.

"I know how busy your filming and traveling schedule is," Brooke said to Tatiana, "but I hope you'll be able to come to our wedding at the lake this summer."

"Their plans are super romantic and sweet," Mia said around a mouthful of chocolate truffle.

Brooke smiled, possessing the exact same glow that Mia did. "We're going to spend the weekend with everyone at the lake and then have the ceremony and reception out on the beach in front of our house at sunset."

"It sounds amazing." Tatiana hadn't visited their lake house before, but the pictures she'd seen had shown a really cute lakefront cottage with a beautiful view. "And thank you for the invitation. I'd love to come to your wedding." She turned to ask Colbie, whom she'd met only briefly once before, "You just returned from your honeymoon, didn't you? Was it amazing?"

"Beyond amazing." Colbie's deep blush said more than words would have about just how amazing it had been.

They talked honeymoons for a while longer, until Mia suddenly zoomed in on Tatiana and changed the subject. "So, how is shadowing my big brother at the office going?" When Colbie looked confused, Mia explained, "Tatiana is spending the next couple of weeks at the office with Ian to do some research on CEOs for her new movie. She's been working with him a couple of days already."

Clearly surprised by this bit of information, Colbie said, "Wow, how interesting. I can't wait to hear about what it's like to shadow Ian."

"Rafe and I were wondering how it's going, too," Brooke said. "Do tell."

Feeling slightly flustered at the sudden attention, plus the glass of wine on a fairly empty stomach, Tatiana said, "It's going fine." *Ugh*, that didn't sound right. It was just that the day had ended on such a weird note, and she was still reeling from it. "I mean, it's going great." She took a sip from her glass before repeating, "Really great."

Everyone remained quiet, as though they were waiting for her to say something more. Tatiana had promised not to share any information about what happened in Ian's office with anyone. And she would never spill his business secrets. But she had to know, "What's the deal with his ex-wife?"

"Chelsea?" Mia made a face. "Why do you ask?"

"I met her today." Tatiana held up a hand. "But I promised Ian I'd keep everything that goes on in his office private, so that's all I can say. I shouldn't even have brought it up, and I don't mean to gossip, especially about your family—"

"We know that's not why you're asking," Mia said, cutting off her apology. "You're probably just wondering, *How could he have married her?*"

Tatiana had to reluctantly nod. "When I saw them together...well, I just couldn't *see* them together."

"I'm probably not the most objective person in the world when it comes to Chelsea," Mia admitted, "but I swear to you that when he brought her home for the first time, we all tried to like her. We really gave it everything we could, all of us—my brothers, my parents, my cousins. But in the end she never wanted to be any closer to us than we did to her. I think she was used to getting what she wanted...and she wanted my brother all to herself. No family always in the way. No work commitments eating up both his days and nights, when she was dying to have her picture taken for the society pages in the couture dresses he bought for her."

"But family and work," Tatiana said, "that's who Ian is. He loves you guys to pieces and running his business gives him a rush, every day, every part of it."

"He used to be a lot of fun, too, though you might not see it."

"I saw it when he was playing football with your brothers on Friday night." She smiled. "And when he was teasing me about falling asleep in a meeting this afternoon, neither of us could keep from laughing."

"You fell asleep in a meeting?"

"Evidently," she said, embarrassment flooding back, "I was snoring."

"And Ian teased you about it?" Colbie asked, sharing a look with Mia and Brooke that Tatiana couldn't quite read.

"When he realized I felt really bad about it, he made me feel better by telling me he'd once done the exact same thing."

All three women looked surprised, but none more than Ian's sister. "Let me make sure I have this straight. First he laughed with you in his office and then he went out of his way to make you feel better? Amazing." Mia took a large gulp of her drink, then refilled everyone's glasses. "Anyway, back to Chelsea. I think she planned on changing him. Standard female fantasy, so I guess I can't totally blame her for that." Though it was clear to Tatiana that Mia wanted to. "When he didn't magically change to suit her, from what I could see from the outside looking in, she decided to blame him for not being good enough to her. For not treating her the way she believed he should treat her. And for, and this is a direct quote from a hissy fit of hers that I accidentally walked in on, 'stealing the best years of her life.'"

Everything Mia said resonated with what Tatiana had seen and heard in his office that afternoon. And it also helped to explain why he'd looked guilty and written Chelsea that check. Clearly, he felt bad that he hadn't been able to change who he was for the woman he'd married.

"She's a fool for not loving him just the way he is."

"No kidding." Mia muttered. "But, you know," she said with a speculative glance at Tatiana, "I've always believed there was someone out there who *would* love him exactly the way he is."

Just then, Ford walked onto the patio. "Hey, beautiful."

Mia turned to kiss him, and Tatiana barely held in a sigh at how perfect they were together.

"I can see there's some serious girl talk going down here, so I won't stay."

"Is your guitar calling to you from the tower again?"

He grinned, but there was a sensuality behind his smile that Tatiana couldn't miss—as if the two of them shared a sexy secret about his guitar. "You could come play it for me later if you're in the mood." One more hot kiss and he headed off with a wave good-bye.

All four of the women watched him walk away with healthy doses of female appreciation. But even though Tatiana couldn't deny that he was definitely good-looking in his dark jeans and T-shirt, Ford felt more like a brother to her than anything else.

Only Ian had ever made her heat up the way Mia did when Ford kissed her, or light up the way Brooke did when she talked about marrying Rafe, or blush the way Colbie did when telling them about her honeymoon with her new husband.

As the conversation shifted to the best places in town to find good deals on shoes and purses and all the things Tatiana should do and see now that she'd be living in Seattle for a while, she realized just how glad she was that she'd come tonight. Now that Valentina was traveling with Smith so much, and especially while they were gone scouting locations for their new movie, she'd missed their girls' nights. Especially at a time like this when she felt off-kilter and needed an attitude reset.

Okay, she thought now that she'd had some distance from what had happened in Ian's office, *so she'd told him that she was falling for him*. But since it wasn't her nature to hold her emotions in, Tatiana decided she wasn't going to keep feeling weird about it, or be angry with him for the way he'd told her to forget those feelings.

Because Mia was right—there was someone out there who would love Ian just the way he was.

Her.

CHAPTER TEN

On Wednesday morning at 7:59 a.m., Ian stood in his office and looked down at his watch for the dozenth time in the past several minutes.

Where was she?

Uncomfortable with the thought of Tatiana waiting outside the building, Ian had given her a temporary employee badge. She'd been in early again on Tuesday, waiting in his office with a cup of coffee just the way he took it. Today, she knew his first meeting with his executive staff for their weekly review and planning session began at eight, which meant she should have been here fifteen minutes ago.

Maybe, he thought as he finally headed down the hall to the conference room, she'd gotten stuck on a business call of her own. While he hadn't actually seen her do any business beyond shadowing him the past couple of days, an actress of her caliber and popularity had to be overwhelmed with offers and publicity requests from her agent and publicist. He was amazed, actually, that she'd been able to put it all aside to focus on researching her role.

Or, perhaps her taxi was stuck in downtown gridlock.

Or, maybe it was simply that she'd gotten sick of sitting in his meetings and had decided to sleep in rather than beat him to his office for a third day in a row.

He thought about asking Bethany to get in touch with Tatiana, but if she'd decided to blow off shadowing him today, frankly, it should be a relief that she wasn't here. After all, he'd been more distracted than he wanted to admit. So distracted by Tatiana's beauty and sweetness and intelligence, in fact, that what had begun as teasing, then turned into laughter, had been teetering on the brink of becoming so much more.

Ian never thought he'd have something to thank Chelsea for, but if she hadn't barged into his office yesterday, it would have been too damned easy to pull Tatiana against him to finally taste the gorgeous mouth that had been tempting him nearly every waking—and dreaming—moment since he'd met her.

Reminding himself that this was his chance to focus one hundred percent on work again, he stepped into the conference room and began the meeting.

* * *

It wasn't uncommon for these weekly planning meetings to run from breakfast all the way into the lunch hour. Today, in particular, was bound to be a long one as they prepared to move forward the second Flynn Thomas agreed to the new offer.

Every ounce of Ian's attention should have been on the information and plans that his executive staff were presenting. But all he'd been able to think about for the past hour and a half was Tatiana.

Damn it, where was she?

He pushed his chair back. "I'm sorry, I've got to go take care of something. Please continue without me. Bethany, may I speak with you outside for a moment?" The moment they were in the hall, he asked her, "Has Tatiana been in touch yet?"

His assistant frowned. "No, I assumed her plans for the day must have changed, but that she let only you know about it. Would you like me to give her a call to see if I can find out where she is so that you can get back to the meeting?"

He shook his head, knowing he wouldn't be able to focus on a damned thing until he knew that Tatiana was all right. "I'll call her myself."

He wanted to believe it was traffic or work or boredom that had her staying away today, but what if none of those reasons were right? Yesterday afternoon, Tatiana had said, point-blank, that she was falling for him...and in response, he'd not only completely shut her down, he'd also tossed harsh words back at her.

Words he'd regretted the second they were out of his mouth.

Ian cursed as he headed into his office then pulled out his cell phone and scrolled through his contacts list for her number. Even if she was upset with him, he still hoped she would pick up, if only to reassure him that she was fine…or to tell him exactly what she thought of him being such a jerk to her. Then again, he thought as he realized a strange buzzing was coming from the cushions of his couch, he simply couldn't imagine Tatiana snapping at him, even if she was angry.

What he could still see clearly, however, was the fire—and the hurt—that had flashed through her eyes when he'd told her to forget about the two of them ever acting on their attraction.

Moving toward his couch, he hung up on her voice mail and hit the Call Again button. Moments later, when the buzzing started up again, he reached between the cushions and pulled out her phone.

She'd told him she was messy. Now he was starting to get a sense of just how far that messiness extended, if she'd managed to lose her phone in his office during the few minutes they'd actually been able to spend there the day before.

Ian put her phone in his pocket and stopped at his assistant's desk. "I need to head out for a while."

"Is everything okay? Where is Tatiana?"

Clearly, she was now as concerned as he was about the beautiful actress they'd both spent so many hours with in the past couple of days. "That's what I'm going to go find out." Bethany's eyebrows went up in surprise. In the ten years she'd worked for him, he'd never missed a single planning meeting, even that week he'd had a 104-degree fever and could barely walk a straight line. "If she does happen to call or come by while I'm gone, tell her to call her cell phone, would you?" He walked past the full conference room without breaking his stride.

The ride in his town car from the office to her condo should have taken fifteen minutes, tops, but traffic really was bad today. Normally, he answered email on his phone to make up for the lost travel time, but he couldn't stop thinking—and worrying—about Tatiana long enough to type in a coherent reply to so much as one.

She'd fallen asleep during that meeting yesterday, and he suddenly worried that she hadn't come to the office because she wasn't feeling well. If she was sick, would she know that she could call him or his parents or any of his brothers or sister for help?

Telling himself that he would have done the same for any of his siblings who were supposed to meet him over an hour ago, Ian told his driver to keep heading to Tatiana's place, then got out to cover the rest of the distance on foot.

* * *

When Tatiana's doorbell rang for her meeting with a model who was transitioning into acting and the young woman's mother, she put aside her script and got up to answer it. She'd never made so many notes in the margins of a script...or gotten so little out of any of them.

Every line of dialogue she'd played out in her head this morning had sounded wrong, worse now than they had before she'd started to shadow Ian. It would be easiest to blame the screenwriter, but her problems with the part weren't his fault. They were hers, and hers alone.

She knew she was overthinking it, and yet the more she tried to relax and trust that she'd figure out her character before filming began, the tenser she became. By this point, she'd been gripping and crumpling the pages so hard that they looked as if a teething infant had been gnawing on them.

Plus, even though she'd vowed the night before not to keep feeling weird about what she'd said to Ian in his office yesterday afternoon, she couldn't stop thinking about the way he'd shut her out. And how much it had hurt.

On the way to the door, Tatiana picked up a stray hairband from the kitchen counter and, with a big yawn, shoved her hair into a messy ponytail. She'd always been a good sleeper, which had helped her out a great deal over the years when she'd needed to catch catnaps between scenes. But all the things she'd said to Ian—about *falling for him* and *how could he have paid off his ex* and that *she wasn't going to forget her feelings for him*—had played on repeat in her head all night long, along with the way he'd carefully scrubbed his expression clean of emotion by the time he'd left for his meeting.

She didn't much feel like smiling at the moment, but she made sure one was on her lips as she opened her door. "Serena, hello. It's so nice to see you again." She gave the positively gorgeous model a hug. "Hello, you must be Serena's mother. It's lovely to meet you, Genevieve. Please come inside. Sorry, I know it's a little messy, but I thought it would be easiest for all of us if we met here rather than on a set or in an office."

Serena's mother looked positively gleeful as she said, "I'm so thrilled Smith suggested we meet with you to discuss this role. Serena is absolutely beside herself at the chance to prove herself on the big screen, aren't you, sweetie?"

Serena nodded and smiled, but evidently Tatiana wasn't doing as good a job of covering up her gray mood as she thought, because she said, "I hope you weren't in the middle of something. We could come back later if we've interrupted you."

Catching the horrified expression Serena's mother gave her daughter, Tatiana replied, "No, this is perfect."

Smith had asked if she could do him a favor by running through a couple of scenes with Serena and then giving him her opinion about the budding actress. It was a pretty important role in one of his upcoming movies, and because Serena was untried, he wanted to make sure he wasn't going to regret his casting choice.

Tatiana had worked with models before and apart from the occasional exception, they were never all that great. They looked beautiful, of course, but looking pretty and expressing honest emotion weren't always synonymous. She'd met Serena at a couple of industry events this year, and each time, she'd been struck not only by just how pure the model's beauty was, but by how different she seemed. Quiet, and not overly interested in playing the game, the two of them had had a normal, un-Hollywood discussion about a book they'd both recently read.

"Can I get either of you a cup of coffee?"

When both women nodded, she went to fill three mugs. Tatiana had already had one cup too many this morning, but figuring one more couldn't make her feel any more off-kilter than she already did, she topped off her own cup.

"Is this Smith Sullivan's family?"

Serena's mother was holding a picture Tatiana had taken and framed of all the Sullivans and their mates and kids together at Marcus and Nicola's wedding. Telling herself it wasn't fair that she felt as though her privacy was being intruded on when she'd been the one to invite them to her house for this read-through, she made herself smile again. "Yes, I took it when we were at—"

"Marcus and Nico's wedding!" Genevieve exclaimed. "I can hardly believe there are so many famous people in one family. Not just a movie star, but a baseball star and a pop star and Chase Sullivan, who has won all those awards for his photography and Jake McCann with his pubs. Isn't one of them also a billionaire?"

Genevieve didn't seem to realize she'd breathlessly cut Tatiana off, but Serena looked mortified—just like any normal teenage girl would be when her mother freaked out over famous people.

Ignoring the billionaire question, Tatiana said, "Yes, they are certainly an exceptional group." She brought over the coffee and made sure Genevieve had to put down the framed picture to take hers. "Not in the least because they're all so nice."

"And *so* incredibly good-looking, especially this one," Genevieve said, pointing to Ian. "I'm sure your sister knows how lucky she was to snag Smith the way she did."

Tatiana thought about biting her tongue, but if there was anything she'd proved during the past couple of days shadowing Ian, it was just how bad she was at it. "Actually, Smith was the one who did the snagging." Really, she should shut her mouth before she said anything more, but she couldn't stand the thought of this woman thinking that Valentina had done something to trick Smith into falling for her. "They're very much in love, and his fame is the last thing in the world that matters to her."

"Oh, I'm sure," Genevieve said with a knowing nod. "Over the years Serena has worked with so many stars that we're totally over it all, too. Aren't we, sweetie?"

Serena made a sound that could have meant anything, but it was hard to tell if she was agreeing or disagreeing because she was staring down at the couch cushions as if she was trying to disappear into them.

Tatiana immediately felt bad about not letting Genevieve's thoughtless comment roll off her the way she should have. She was just touchy from lack of sleep...and from not being able to stop thinking about Ian. Besides, she knew how hard auditions were, especially when they all knew that Tatiana's opinion of Serena's acting ability would likely weigh quite heavily into Smith's final casting decision.

She smiled at the model. "Do you need anything else before we do the read-through?"

"No, I'm ready to go."

Tatiana reached for the printout of the two scenes Smith had emailed her, and when Serena didn't take one out, too, started to hand her the extra copy she'd made.

"Oh no, Serena doesn't need that. She has it memorized, don't you, sweetie?"

Working hard to push her irritation away at the way Genevieve kept speaking for her daughter, Tatiana said, "Great. So, why don't we—"

Her doorbell rang again and she stopped in the middle of her sentence. She gave the two women sitting on her couch an apologetic smile. "I wasn't expecting anyone, but if you'll just give me a second, I'll find out what they need." Who could be coming to see her now that Serena and her mother were here? More than that, who even had her Seattle address apart from her family and manager?

Through the peephole, the sight of Ian standing outside her front door was the very last thing she'd expected...and the very, very best.

She flung open the door, grinning like a fool. A lovesick one. "Good morning!"

But he didn't say a word or smile back at her. His gaze ran over her from head to toe, as if he needed to make sure she was really standing there in front of him. He was beautiful as always in his suit, but when she looked closer, she realized he wasn't quite as pressed and perfect as always. In fact, from the windblown look of his dark hair and the scuffs on his usually polished shoes, it looked like he'd jogged to her condo from his office. Which was totally crazy, because why would he do something like that? Especially after the way he'd shut her out the previous afternoon.

"Ian, what's wrong?"

"Why weren't you at the office today?"

"I had a meeting this morning, remember? I told you yesterday that Smith called and—" She grimaced. "I didn't tell you, did I?" Her grimace turned into a full-blown groan. "Sorry, he texted me during one of your meetings, and I meant to tell you afterward, but with everything that happened yesterday, I obviously forgot."

It occurred to her, suddenly, that Ian was probably missing a whole host of really important meetings to come and track her down. "You came all this way to find out why I didn't show. Why didn't you just call my cell?" Maybe, just maybe, it was because he cared more about her than he wanted to admit?

He reached into his pocket...and pulled out her phone. "You left it on the couch in my office.

Actually, it was *inside* the couch by the time I found it."

Oh, so that was why he'd blown off work to come to her house—he hadn't been able to reach her by phone. "Thanks." She knew her voice sounded a heck of a lot flatter than it had just a few seconds ago, but it was the best she could do at the moment. "I was wondering where I'd put it."

But when she reached for it and he put it into her hand, he closed his fingers over hers and didn't let go. She looked up at him in surprise, and what she saw in his eyes had her breath catching in her throat.

"I was worried about you, Tatiana." She watched him war with himself for a few seconds before he finally said, "Yesterday, I didn't deal well with the situation in my office. Not with any of it. And especially not with you."

Oh my. He had melted her heart from the very start, even though he'd been working so hard the entire time to keep his distance. But now that he was finally speaking to her straight from his heart, without any walls up, she realized just how much harder—and farther—she'd fallen for him than she'd been aware of.

Tatiana had never been in love before. But as she stood with her hand in Ian's and his dark eyes holding hers with such intensity, she now knew with perfect clarity that she was all the way there.

"Ian," she began, just as Genevieve's voice sounding from the living room behind her reminded her that they weren't alone.

"You're busy," he said as he started to pull his hand back. "I'll let you go."

"Please, stay." She kept his hand in hers, knowing instinctively that once he went back to the office, all of his walls would build back up, and likely be even more impenetrable. Thinking fast, and talking even faster, she said, "Since you're already here, I'm sure Smith would love your opinion on this read-through, too. In fact, I know he'd be thrilled to have a third party here who can look at things totally objectively." Realizing he had no idea what she was talking about, she dropped her voice so it wouldn't carry to the women sitting in her living room. "Serena Britten is a really well-known model who auditioned for a part in one of Smith's new movies. He thinks she's good, but working with models can be..." How could she put it nicely?

"A pain in the ass?"

Tatiana remembered what she'd learned online when she'd looked up Ian all those months ago—that Chelsea had been a model. She paused, before nodding. "Yes, that's why he wanted to get my opinion."

"Only about her acting skills?"

"Mostly that, but also how I think she'll do in the mix in rehearsals and on set. I haven't seen her act yet, but I like her. And it would really help if you'd be willing to watch us run through two short scenes and give your opinion, as well."

His phone rang then, the specific tone that meant it was Bethany calling. Finally pulling his hand from Tatiana's, he answered it. "Yes, she's at home, and she's fine." He listened to something his assistant said, then asked Tatiana, "How short are the scenes you'd like me to watch?"

She knew how seriously he took his work, and what a big deal it already was that he'd skipped out of a meeting at all. But for him to even consider staying a few more minutes?

Well, if that wasn't a declaration to her of his feelings...she didn't know what was.

"Really short. I promise."

"Please tell them to continue the meeting without me," he told Bethany, then slipped his phone back in his pocket.

Unfortunately, in her excitement over having Ian stay a little while longer, Tatiana had forgotten about Genevieve…and how over-the-top her reaction was bound to be when one of the gorgeous, famous, successful Sullivan men in the picture on her mantel came to life.

But there was nothing Tatiana could do or say to warn Ian, because they'd barely walked into the living room when Genevieve jumped up off the coach, yanking Serena up by the wrist.

"Well, *hello*."

"Genevieve, Serena, I'd like you both to meet Ian." Tatiana purposely left off his last name, hoping that Serena's mother wouldn't make the connection, but between staring at the wedding photo and the stalker-like research she likely did on wealthy, famous men, there was no fooling her.

"Serena, can you believe we've been lucky enough to meet two Sullivan men in one week?"

Serena politely offered her hand to Ian. To his credit, he neither goggled at the model's incredible beauty nor blanched at her mother's handshake that went on way too long. It was, Tatiana thought, as if the older woman was silently trying to tell him, *"You can have either me or my daughter, whichever you choose, big boy."*

"Why don't we get started?" Tatiana suggested in an overly enthusiastic voice as she boldly put her arms around both Serena and her mother to direct them away from Ian. "I asked Ian to stay and watch, as well, if that's okay with you, Serena."

"Of course it's okay," Genevieve answered, actually clapping her hands in delight.

Beyond irritated with the woman, Tatiana moved close enough to Serena to make it clear that she was speaking directly to her, rather than to the mother-daughter team.

"Before we start, I want to ask you to forgive me if I'm a little off my game today. I haven't been sleeping that well the past couple of nights, so I might need a few restarts to get it right."

"You're always so good, I thought you always got things perfectly the first time out."

Tatiana laughed out loud at the idea that she was perfect. Hadn't Serena already seen what a mess her home was? And wasn't it also true that she'd gone and fallen head over heels for a man who obviously didn't want her to feel that way about him?

"Clearly, Smith didn't tell you about the time I couldn't stop giggling in the middle of a really sensitive scene in *Gravity*. I don't know if you've seen it—"

"Of course I've seen it." Serena looked shocked that Tatiana could have thought otherwise.

"Well, you know the scene where Jo is secretly watching Graham cuddling with her baby girl?"

"I cried during that scene."

"Good. You were supposed to cry. But I was punchy from a long week of sensitive and hushed scenes, and I swear every single thing Smith did and said was positively hilarious that afternoon." Thinking back on it, she laughed again. God, she'd been such a twerp. But she'd needed the temporary lift to get through the following hours of giving such heavy and strong emotions to the cameras. "I'm sure he would have strangled me were it not for the fact that we already had ninety percent of the movie in the can and he needed me alive to finish the last ten."

When she saw a real smile on the girl's face, Tatiana knew they'd both shaken off her mother's interference, and were finally ready to begin the scene.

CHAPTER ELEVEN

Ian had been wondering what the hell he was doing sitting in Tatiana's living room with a model and her overbearing mother who clearly was hoping he'd take a shine to either herself or her daughter. He should already be back in the meeting he'd so abruptly walked out of—or at least listening in on his phone as he headed back to the office in the town car.

But then Tatiana started laughing...and, suddenly, Ian knew not only why he was still there, but also why he'd had to come find her in the first place.

Something was poking him, so he shifted on the couch and pulled a paperback book out from behind the cushion. Yes, *messy* was definitely one word for Tatiana. But as he looked around him at her home, he was struck more by its charm than its disorder. Though he knew it was only a temporary residence while she filmed her next movie, she'd filled it with lots of pretty, fun things that he could easily guess made her happy. Lots of framed pictures of her with her family along with a little stuffed tiger on the fireplace mantel that might not have made sense if someone didn't know her.

Ian's thoughts skidded to a halt as he realized he was no longer one of those people who saw Tatiana's beautiful face, her gorgeous figure, her incredible acting skills, and thought he saw the whole picture. Yes, all those things were a part of her, but there was so much more to her. Her humor. Her intelligence. Her devotion to family. And, he had to acknowledge, the way she stuck up for someone she cared about when she'd walked into Chelsea's warpath yesterday with the clear intent of avenging him.

"How dare you act like such a little tramp? You've embarrassed our entire family."

Ian snapped to attention as Tatiana transformed right before his eyes into a furious mother. It didn't matter that she was only a handful of years older than Serena—two sentences was all it took for him to understand the brittle, prideful character she was playing.

"I'm—" Serena faltered, fought back tears, before winning her own character's fight for strength. *"I'm not a tramp."* She tilted her chin up and faced down Tatiana. *"I'm in love."*

"Love." Tatiana spat the word. *"You don't know one damned thing about love. You think it's*

all butterflies and rainbows and groping around in the backseat of that boy's car."

"That's not what it's like! That's not what we're doing."

"Oh, I know exactly what you're doing spreading your legs for him, exactly the mistake you're making. How do you think I ended up with you?"

Serena's eyes widened as her skin paled. *"I knew it. I always knew you thought that."* Her breath shook, her eyes filled with tears that she still wouldn't let fall. *"I was a mistake."*

Tatiana put down the paper she'd been reading from and grinned at the model. "That was great."

Serena looked stunned for a few moments, not able to pull out of her character as quickly as Tatiana had. "Thanks." She took a deep breath, blew it out, then finally smiled. "It felt good."

Genevieve jumped up off the couch and gave her daughter a hug. "What did I tell you, sweetie—you're magnificent. Simply born to play this part!"

Ian watched as the girl shrank back from the extravagant praise, clearly embarrassed by her mother's behavior. Tatiana stood and held out a hand to Serena, drawing the model away from her hovering mother.

"Why don't we do the second scene Smith sent over? If you don't mind, I'd like to try it on our feet over by the window for a change of pace."

When Ian listened to them run through it, he realized Tatiana hadn't actually needed to get them up on their feet or off the couch. She'd done it simply to give Serena some much-needed space to breathe.

Empathy. It was yet another beautiful facet to Tatiana that he couldn't ignore.

Plus, for the first time, he was able to just sit back and watch her. He couldn't have done it when they were having dinner at his parents' house on Friday night, and he definitely hadn't been able to do it while they were in his office. But now, as he sat in her living room, he finally let himself drink her in.

With the faint sunlight coming in the window behind her, he could see all the different natural blonds and browns and reds in her hair, along with the way pretty color rose in her skin as she ran through the scene. Just more of her unique qualities that sparkled too brightly for him to ignore or deny any longer.

But she'd asked him to pay attention to Serena's acting, so he forced himself to bring the model into view as well. She was tall, slim yet curvy, with a staggeringly pretty face. One that would probably bring every other man on the planet to his knees, but did nothing whatsoever for Ian. Especially not when she was standing so close to the one woman who *had* brought him to his knees from the moment he'd spoken to her in the Napa Valley vineyard.

As the two women played out the much longer scene, Ian could see why Smith was producing the film. And no question about it, there was something about the way the model played the daughter. Maybe because it wasn't too much of a stretch from the relationship Serena seemed to have with her own mother.

Or maybe it was simply that Tatiana was so good she made everyone she worked with look good, too.

He'd seen most of her movies before he'd ever met her, and he'd always been impressed by the way she disappeared into each role, especially when she rarely played the same one from film to film. But, Lord, to watch her from fifteen feet away like this...to say his mind was blown would be a major understatement.

She was, in a word, brilliant. But more than that, she made the transformation from herself into someone else entirely look so effortless. He could feel her joy at doing what she was meant to do, at being exactly what she was meant to be, just as she'd told him in the back of his town car two days earlier on the way to lunch with his professor.

When they came to the end of the scene, Tatiana stretched, then shook out both arms. "Phew, that's a rough role to jump in and out of."

Serena looked nervous as she stood with her hands twisted in front of her stomach, but Tatiana quickly reached out to her. "You were great. Really great. I'm so glad we got to do this."

Serena smiled, but now that she was done, it was obvious that her nerves were getting the better of her. Tatiana saw it right away, of course, and said, "Chocolate. That's exactly what we need now."

Tatiana hadn't even made it halfway to her kitchen when Genevieve shot up off the couch and intercepted her. "Oh no, we don't eat or drink empty calories like that—do we, sweetie?"

Serena gave Tatiana a regretful smile. "It was nice of you to offer, though."

"Are you going to talk to Smith today?" Serena's mother asked Tatiana.

Ian was impressed by the way Tatiana, for Serena's benefit, held in the irritation she had to feel about the incredibly pushy woman. "I'll need to talk privately with Ian first, but then, yes, I'm planning to give Smith a call."

Genevieve turned her sharp gaze on him. "Wasn't my daughter great, Ian?"

"She was."

"It's amazing how beautiful *and* talented she is, isn't it?"

"Mom," Serena said, finally speaking up, "we should go." She didn't even look at him, obviously too embarrassed to do anything but say a soft thank-you to Tatiana for doing the read-through with her.

Tatiana threw her arms around the model and said something to her that neither Ian nor Serena's mother could hear, and when Serena pulled back, she was smiling again.

Genevieve held out her hand to Ian. "It was positively *lovely* to meet you, Ian. I do hope we'll be seeing you again, and soon."

Ian had learned early on from his own mother that if he didn't have anything nice to say, it was better to keep his mouth shut. "Take care, Genevieve, of both yourself and your daughter." He would have walked over to say a personal good-bye to Serena, but it was far too likely that her mother would see it as a sign of interest, rather than politeness. He remained in the living room while Tatiana walked the two women out.

* * *

Closing the door behind her a few minutes later, Tatiana slumped against it. "Poor thing, I don't know how she deals as well as she does with everything. Tell me, what did you think?"

"You're amazing at what you do."

She smiled, a big smile that told him how much his compliment meant to her. "Thank you. But Serena's the one up for the role, not me. What did you think of her?"

"She was good. Not polished. Not particularly confident, either. But there was something about what she did that was compelling. Very compelling."

"Raw emotion. She's brimming over with it. It's less that she's trying to act the part, more that she *is* the part. Which is precisely what I'm hoping will happen for me with my new role, that I'll understand it well enough to become the freakin' character soon. Unfortunately, thus far it's—"

She cut herself off with a frustrated little growl as she walked into the living room to pick up the coffee mugs. "I never offered you anything to drink. Want a cup?" When he shook his head, she put them in the sink, then turned back to say, "Thank God neither my mom nor Valentina were stage-mother types. To be fair, though, I can see that it would be hard for Genevieve to have a daughter that beautiful without worrying about people taking advantage of her. I suppose you'd want to do anything you could to protect her."

"Protecting her?" He thought about the way Serena's mother had practically offered her daughter up to him, simply because he was rich and came from a powerful family. "I'm not sure that's what she was doing."

"No," Tatiana said with a sigh. "I'm afraid you might be right. She looked at you like you were a particularly delicious piece of candy that she would have been happy for either her or her daughter to enjoy. When I asked you to stay to give your opinion, I didn't think about how uncomfortable that would be for you."

"It wasn't a problem."

"You should have heard her before you got here, going on and on about how gorgeous all you Sullivans are. I'm thinking I should check the picture she was looking at and make sure there isn't any drool I need to wipe off." Tatiana picked up a framed photo from her mantel and studied it carefully before putting it back. "Looks clean and dry, thankfully."

He didn't recall seeing this picture from Marcus and Nicola's wedding, one where everyone was relaxed rather than posing wedding-style for the shot. "Did you get this from the photographer?"

"No, I took it." She smiled at it, then at him. "I really shouldn't be so hard on Genevieve. All of you Sullivans really are quite pretty."

As he looked at the beautiful woman standing before him, Ian finally accepted that she didn't have a clue just how alluring, how tempting she was herself. On the day they'd met in the vineyard, he'd been so certain it was all an act on her part, that there must be something she was trying to gain by acting so, well, normal...despite all the evidence to the contrary.

Now he knew it wasn't an act. Because though Tatiana was a world-class actress, she was one of the few women that he'd never seen put on an act in real life. Instead, amazingly, she let herself be real, be honest, be vulnerable. He could now see why Valentina and Smith were so protective of her.

Ian found that he wanted to do whatever he could to protect her, too.

Especially from a man like himself.

"It must have been difficult for your father when you decided to become an actress."

"I was pretty young when he passed away. I'd only just started to do a few commercials, so he never had to deal with me falling for bad boys."

"It wouldn't matter how young you were, he would still have worried, would still have wanted to protect you."

"I would have liked that, to know that he was there to take care of me if I needed him." Her words were soft, filled with longing for the father she'd lost far too early. "I always think of him, even now, when something really great happens. I want to run to him to tell him everything, want to feel him lift me up one more time and spin me around in circles until we're both dizzy. Valentina says that she's always felt him watching over us, but I didn't get as many years with him as she did, and sometimes he's so fuzzy in my head..."

Ian didn't think before moving to close the distance between them. Tatiana's grief at losing a parent was so much bigger than what he'd gone through with his divorce, and yet, she didn't try to hold it in or to keep it caged inside.

He didn't know how she did it, how she managed to be so open without fear of getting hurt. All he knew was that he had to be there for her, needed to lift his hands to frame her face as he told her, "Valentina is right, Tatiana. Your father sees you. And he's proud of you, so damned proud. Not just because you're such a success, but also because of the truly extraordinary woman you've become."

Her eyes were shining with tears as she lifted them to meet his. "Thank you. Thank you for saying that, and for watching our read-through...and for worrying about me when I didn't show up at your office."

Her skin was soft, so soft. And so warm that he'd never wanted anything more than he wanted to close the rest of the distance between them and kiss her.

Finally kiss her.

Finally learn if her lips tasted as sweet, and were as soft, as he'd imagined them to be.

In that moment, all the reasons he had for keeping his distance, for staying away from her, fell away as he shifted his hands to thread his fingers into her hair so that he could—

Her phone jumped on the kitchen counter, a loud buzz as it clanked against a set of keys that jolted him back into the real world.

He dropped his hands from her and took one step back, and then another and another, away from the greatest temptation he'd ever faced. And when he saw Smith's face light up her cell phone's screen, guilt at what he'd almost done swamped him.

Valentina and Smith trusted him with Tatiana. He should be protecting her, not fantasizing about all the ways he wanted to take her, how many times he could make her scream his name in pleasure before the next sunrise.

"You should get that," he told her.

"Smith can wait. Right now, don't you think it's more important that we talk about what happened yesterday?" She touched her hair, the silky strands his fingers had been tangling in just seconds before. "And what almost happened now?"

"I was an ass yesterday. I'm sorry."

"I'm sorry for the way I behaved, too. Not for what I said to your ex-wife—I can't stand back and watch one of my friends be attacked without needing to get up and fight for them—but that I poked my nose in where it doesn't belong. Especially when I see what Valentina and Smith have, I can only guess at how hard it would be to lose that."

"What your sister and my cousin have together and what I had in my marriage are not the same at all. From what I can see, Valentina gives Smith what he needs and he gives the same right back. My ex-wife and I never were able to do that for each other."

He stopped, realizing he'd just given away *way* too much of himself...and not only that, but he'd let Tatiana get *way* too close. It was hard enough wanting her as he did, but throwing all these emotions into the mix was utter madness.

She'd said he was her friend, and since Ian knew it was the only path forward for them that could make sense—that could work long term—he told her, "You threw Chelsea off her game in a way I haven't seen before. She was threatened by you. It made her angry. But you shouldn't have had to bear the brunt of it."

"Like I said, no one hurts one of my friends and gets away with it. But I want you to know that I didn't believe her, Ian, not a word she said about you."

"Maybe you should." After all, hadn't his ex laid out the truth of what a relationship with him was like? Chelsea had been angry, but she hadn't lied.

But Tatiana dismissed his warning with a shake of her head, obviously choosing instead to believe that it couldn't possibly be true. "How could I believe anything she says when I feel like I already know you better after a handful of days than she did in all the time you were married?"

It was crazy for him to feel that, too, but he did. In fact, he knew Tatiana so well already that he could read her mind and know she was hoping they were about to leap from being friends to lovers.

He'd already gone too deep with her, shared too much of himself, but before he pushed her away again, he had to at least explain to her why he was doing it. "I like you, Tatiana. A great deal. And I'm glad we've become friends. Which is why I can't stand the thought of hurting you. Not in any way."

"Why do you think you'll hurt me, Ian? Why can't we just jump and trust that we'll help each other with the landing?"

"I can't take any chances with you." He wanted to touch her again so badly—wanted to feel her skin against his fingertips, her body pressed close to his again—that he made himself take another step away from her. "Especially not with you."

She stared at him with big green eyes, and he decided to let her take a good long look this time, to let her see what he made sure to hide from everyone else. That she couldn't want him. Shouldn't want him.

Because he didn't have nearly enough to give her.

But instead of flinching or looking away, she said, "I'm not good at holding in what I feel. And I meant what I said yesterday. I did fall for you that first day we met in the vineyard, and I've only fallen further as I've gotten to know you better." She sighed. "I'm not a terribly patient person, so the fact that I'm pretty sure you were just about to kiss me, but didn't, is really bugging me. Not in the least because I've been dying to know if it will be as good as I've dreamed it will be. But now that you're telling me, flat out, you just want to be friends, and—" She sighed again, shaking her head. "I wish I knew what to do. About everything."

He could see how frustrated she was and was equally frustrated that he couldn't reach out to soothe her without risking a friendly embrace turning into so much more. So instead, he did what always helped him when he was confused. He took things apart piece by piece.

"Call Smith back. And then come with me to the office so that you can keep doing your research for your role." Soon, hopefully, they'd figure out how to keep their growing attraction at bay. Now that it was out in the open, at least—and he'd made it perfectly clear to her that they couldn't do anything about it—things had to get easier.

But as he watched her war with herself, a part of him—a really big part that he wasn't proud of—was praying she'd ignore everything he'd just said and kiss him anyway.

Finally, though, she nodded. "There's just one question I need to ask first before we go ahead as if nothing has changed between us, even though we both know it has."

He braced for her question. "Go ahead."

"Do you really think one teeny-tiny little kiss would be that big a deal?"

"With you," he said, as serious as he'd ever been in his life, "I'm certain that no kiss could ever be teeny. Or tiny. Or little."

"A hug then. Now that we've cleared the air from yesterday, I think we should at least be able to give each other a friendly hug."

Even that was a bad idea, Ian knew, but before he could make that clear, her arms were already coming around his neck.

She was so much smaller than he, but they still fit together perfectly, her soft curves against his muscles, taut with the effort it was taking not to lift her up on the kitchen counter and wrap her legs around his waist so that he could devour her.

He could feel her breath warm against his neck, her long eyelashes brushing his skin as she closed her eyes, then opened them again. He could feel her heart beating against his chest, fast and hard, as they stood in the circle of each other's arms for what was one of the most precious, extraordinary moments of his life so far.

Ian never wanted to let her go, didn't know if he'd ever find the strength to do it, but he also knew he needed to shatter the moment before it spun off into another even more heady one.

"My driver is waiting outside. You can call Smith on the way to the office. That is, if you still want to come with me."

When she finally drew back, cool air rushed in where her curves had been warming him. "I do. Of course I do."

Her words were slightly breathless, and knowing why, knowing that he aroused her that much with only a hug, did crazy things to him. Especially when he couldn't help but wonder just how aroused she would become if he kissed every inch of her, then followed up his kisses with caresses.

She reached for her phone with a slightly shaky hand and was already dialing his cousin as they headed out. "Smith, Serena and her mother just left my place."

He was impressed how quickly, and successfully, Tatiana turned her attention to the job Smith had asked her to do. Especially when he knew firsthand just how difficult—impossible, actually—it was to pull off that kind of focus when they were together.

"Serena's a winner," she told Smith. "There's a depth to the emotion inside of her that, when combined with her beauty, is frankly mind-blowing. Ian was watching, too, if you'd like to hear his opinion. Valentina told you I'm shadowing him to research my new role, didn't she? I'll put you on speaker—hold on a sec."

"Tatiana was right on the money," Ian told his cousin once they were all on the call together in the back of his town car. "Serena did a great job—despite her horrible mother doing everything she could to get in the way."

"You owe Ian, Smith," Tatiana said, "since he barely escaped with his life around that woman. However, I still think you should hire Serena. Just figure out a way to keep Genevieve off the set as much as possible."

"Will do," Smith said. "Thanks, both of you, for your help. And Ian, drinks are on me next time I see you."

But Ian knew that if Smith had even the faintest inkling about his feelings for Tatiana, the very last thing in the world he'd be doing was thanking him or buying him drinks.

CHAPTER TWELVE

All Wednesday afternoon after they'd gone back to Ian's office, and then Thursday while they went on an extensive tour of the massive physical warehouse facilities in which he was considering an investment, Tatiana's brain had been spinning as she tried to figure things out, both regarding Ian *and* her new role.

She'd meant it when she said she was no good at holding things in. She had always been passionate about what she was working on, and once she'd tapped the well of inspiration and passion for acting, she'd never even considered turning it off. Her sister had made more than one worried comment over the years about her putting in long hours and so much emotional commitment to her roles. Tatiana wanted to please Valentina, who had always been more of a mother to her than a sister, but even for Val she couldn't change who she was.

All or nothing.

Go big or go home.

And no matter how high, or how risky, the stakes were, give her all and her best.

It shouldn't be much of a surprise to anyone, then, that she had gone and fallen in love with a man who absolutely, positively refused to let himself do the same.

Since the previous Friday when she'd stumbled into his arms, how many times had he deliberately kept his distance, making certain not to touch her with even the barest brush of their fingers or legs against each other? Only yesterday when she'd been talking to him about losing her father had he forgotten to keep that space between them.

The only thing she knew for sure was that she wanted Ian and he wanted her. Yesterday in her kitchen, he hadn't denied their attraction the way other men might have, because he wasn't a man who lied. Ever.

Immediately, she'd discounted playing the seductress. Not only because she wasn't sure she knew how, but also because she respected Ian too much to trick him like that. If and when they finally came together, she wanted it to happen on honest ground, and to know that they were both all the way in.

As for her new role, while she'd learned a heck of a lot already about how to successfully run a company from watching Ian—he was shockingly hands-on, tough but fair, and made sure to surround himself with brilliant, friendly people who always kept their eye on the ball—she was still lost. Seeing the way Serena had dived straight down into her character when they'd done the short read-through of Smith's script the previous day had only highlighted how screwed Tatiana was.

Good thing the director and producer weren't asking her to do a read-through right now, because it would be a total mess.

She didn't realize her private emotions were spilling out of her until Brian, the owner of the warehousing company, turned to her and said, "Is everything okay? You didn't step on something sharp, did you?" He looked around the concrete floor, clearly worried.

Belatedly realizing the little frustrated scream hadn't remained in her head, she forced her lips up into what she hoped looked like a real smile. "No, I'm fine."

When Ian looked concerned as well, she said, "I didn't mean to interrupt. Please, just forget I'm here."

"Actually," Brian said, "I hope you don't mind my asking, but I'm pretty sure my employees would love a chance to get a few autographs, if it would be okay with you."

"Of course I don't mind. I just don't want to get in your way."

Ian's eyes went dark as he looked at her. "You've never been in anyone's way, Tatiana." He nodded over to the group of workers who were sitting in the nearby break room. "We have plenty of time for you to go and make everyone's day."

Brian took her over and she signed autographs and took pictures and just plain had a great time chatting with everyone. It was so nice to get out of her head for a little while that she was shocked when she looked up at the clock on the wall and realized just how long she'd been at it.

"Ian, I'm sorry," she said as she pushed back from the plastic table. "I've thrown off your schedule."

"Like I said before, we're fine." He gestured behind him to a little girl and her mother who were walking toward them from the parking lot. "Besides, I think you've got a couple more people to say hello to before we head out."

Did he have any idea how sweet he was? She wanted so badly to reach out to him and feel again what she'd felt so strongly yesterday when they'd had their arms around each other in her kitchen.

Instead, she walked toward the little girl with big brown eyes and knelt in front of her. "Hi, what's your name?"

"Keely."

"Oooh, I love your name, Keely."

"I was watching you on TV last night. You're famous."

Tatiana laughed. "I guess so. But you're the one with the awesome shoes that light up. Can you make them sparkle again?"

As the little girl danced around, though Tatiana wasn't anywhere close to having kids yet, she couldn't deny the little tug in her heart.

"If it wouldn't be too much to ask," her mother said, "could I take a picture of you together?"

"Absolutely, but only if you take one for me on my phone, too." Tatiana reached into her bag for it, but by the time she came up empty, Ian was already holding his out.

"I'll take it with mine, Tatiana," he said, having clearly guessed that she'd forgotten it somewhere.

Because he *knew* her.

Tatiana and Keely posed for pictures, first with big smiles, and then making silly faces. After hugging both the little girl and her mother, Tatiana waved good-bye to everyone, then headed for Ian's town car.

"We'll need to head to my place rather than my office for my next meeting," Ian explained, "because I need my video conferencing software. Given the way traffic is looking right now, my home office is at least fifteen minutes closer. And," he said, holding up a hand before she could apologize for making them so late, "I would have asked you to leave your fans if I'd wanted to. But you were making them happy—and they were making you happy, too. So I didn't want to ask you to leave."

Seeing Ian's house would be another window into the man she'd fallen head over heels for. And maybe, she thought with renewed hope after what he'd just said to her about liking to see her happy, it would give her new clues into how to get closer to the heart he always made sure to guard so carefully.

The building he lived in was cool and polished, everything classy and top-of-the-line, from the high-tech elevator controls to the crisply pressed uniform on the doorman who called Ian *sir* and her *miss*.

She could tell Ian was preoccupied with what he was missing in the meeting that had started without him, so when he let them inside and offered to get her a drink, she waved him away. "Go dial in. I'll come find you once I've found drinks for both of us."

He looked undecided for a moment, and she had to wonder if it was because he was afraid she was going to find something he'd kept hidden from everyone else. But then, when his cell phone rang again, he said, "My home office is the door just beyond the living room."

She'd joked about snooping in his office the day she'd come to ask if she could shadow him, but she hadn't actually done it. Now, however, she couldn't stop herself from looking all around his penthouse condo with great curiosity.

Last Friday, Ian Sullivan had been an attractive man she'd been hoping to get to know better, and to set off some sparks with. One week later, though he was still impossibly gorgeous, he was so much more to her than just a sexy man who made her tingly all over.

She'd known he was committed to his family, but until she'd seen him interact closely with his sister, his parents, and his brothers at dinner, she hadn't realized just how much they meant to him. *Everything.* There wasn't anything he wouldn't do for them. Plus, his company had great maternity and paternity benefits, and then there was all the time and effort he was putting into the Seattle Family Foundation fundraising event, when she knew firsthand that time was precisely what he didn't have, and it would have been so much easier just to write a check.

Why had he lived in London for so many years when he'd obviously missed his family as much as they'd missed him?

What's more, instead of ruthlessly directing an executive staff from on high, Ian got right in there with them and was hands-on with each part of the massive business he ran. Somehow, he always managed to find the time, and the energy, for everything he did. How did he make it all look so easy?

As for his ex-wife, Tatiana wasn't surprised that he'd been drawn to the other woman's beauty. But, given how horribly Chelsea behaved toward him, why did he obviously blame himself for the marriage not holding together?

Ian was a mystery that she couldn't stop wanting to solve.

Of course, a big part of her hoped that if she did, then maybe she could also figure out how to get him to give their attraction a chance to blossom into something more. But more than that—even if he never let himself fall for her the way she'd already fallen for him—she wanted to see him smile, to hear him laugh...and to know that he was happy.

Truly happy, with or without her.

As Tatiana walked into his living room, she immediately noticed several touches that she guessed had come from the women in his family who loved him. A quilted throw over his couch that looked like it had been made by his cousin Chase's wife, Chloe. A beautifully sculpted bowl displayed on the center of the coffee table that was obviously one of Vicki Bennett's creations. The first-edition leather-bound classics that his librarian cousin Sophie had likely helped him find through her contacts in the book world. And, of course, a big new box of chocolates that Brooke must have given him as a gift to welcome him back to Seattle.

The finely crafted miniature ship on the mantel above his fireplace was so unique she had to take a closer look, and was amazed when she saw Dylan's name scrawled on the base in black ink. She knew he built full-size sailboats, but she hadn't realized he was just as skilled with models. A few prints were hanging on the walls, each of them drawings of historic Seattle houses. Something told her it wouldn't be too far-fetched to assume that they were a few of the homes Ian's brother Adam had brought back to life.

Yes, Ian's penthouse condo had high ceilings and floor-to-ceiling windows. There was the requisite Sub-Zero refrigerator/freezer and marble countertops. If you didn't look any closer, it might seem like the typical CEO domain.

But Tatiana knew that there was nothing impersonal about it. Not at all.

Because he'd surrounded himself with pieces of the people he loved in every corner of his home.

Maybe, she suddenly thought, Ian wasn't nearly the mystery he seemed. Because when family was at the heart of everything a man was, surely he'd soon realize that he wanted the same thing for himself.

Wouldn't he?

CHAPTER THIRTEEN

Ian felt that they had both made a valiant effort to keep things from being awkward as Tatiana continued to shadow him after the scene with his ex-wife. It was a particularly busy couple of days for him at the office, between plans for the big new acquisition, and the fundraiser less than thirty-six hours away. Too busy for them to have time to talk more about almost-kisses, or for her to offer him any more hugs. And he was glad for it.

Or, rather, he should have been glad.

The problem was that even though Tatiana had made more than good on her promise to stay out of the way while she shadowed him, trying to concentrate on work with her nearby hadn't gotten any easier. She was careful to remain quiet and unobtrusive while he held his meetings, and yet the whole time he was on his conference calls and in video meetings, he could sense her intelligent and perceptive eyes on him. He could smell the vanilla of her shampoo. And he could feel the innate sensual heat of her radiating out to him even from across a large conference room.

He had always been a man who was attuned to and aware of beautiful women, and there wasn't a person alive who would question Tatiana's stunning beauty. But even that wasn't an excuse for the way he continually reacted to her presence. At thirty-eight, Ian had more than enough physical self-control to keep from getting a hard-on around a woman just because she had a pretty face and a knockout figure.

Except when it came to Tatiana.

She'd been so fun, so open, so damned beautiful when she'd been hanging out with her fans at the warehouse a short while ago. And when he'd seen her laugh and play with the little girl who had been so in awe of her...well, Ian wasn't made entirely of stone, even if his ex had said more than once that he was.

One day, Tatiana was going to make someone a great wife, and she was going to be a beautiful mother, too. He just hoped like hell that the guy she ended up choosing would be worth it and be good enough for her.

His brothers, and his single cousins out in Maine and New York, were among the only guys on the planet who might be good enough for her. And yet the thought of her with any of them made his gut clench tight, then tighter still.

Again and again, he found his gaze drifting to where she sat on the leather seat in his home office, her head bent over her notebook, her pen moving steadily across the page. He wondered what she thought of where he lived, if she thought his neat and tidy living room was impersonal and cold compared to the well-lived-in mess of hers. Did she think he was a hard-ass? Did she find his intense business focus boring?

And did she have even the faintest clue that it was taking absolutely every ounce of self-control he possessed not to lift her into his arms, carry her to his bed just down the hall from his home office, and take her?

Damn it, he thought with a hard shake of his head as Larry, his vice president stationed in Japan, formally thanked everyone for attending the meeting. Ian needed to keep his mind on business, if for no other reason than to keep it out of the gutter.

He shut down the conferencing system and looked up to find Tatiana staring at him, her gaze unfocused. Her ponytail had come partway free and several thick tendrils of hair softly curled around her face. Her mouth was slick and pink as if she'd been licking it.

Sweet Lord, how he wanted her. He wanted to taste her wet lips, wanted to grasp her curves in his hands and drag her against him and just *take* and *take* and *take.*

The ringing of his private cell phone yanked him from his utterly inappropriate thoughts. He looked down and saw that it was his cousin Smith calling. Guilt hit him square in the chest again, as though Smith had caught him red-handed mentally stripping away her clothes. Figuring it must be another question about Serena for Tatiana, he picked up and said, “Do you need to talk to Tatiana again?”

“I do. Is she with you?”

“She is.” Ian got up and came around his desk to give her the phone. “It’s Smith.”

After saying hello, she frowned at whatever Smith said. “No, I didn’t get any of your messages. I left my cell phone at home again. At least,” she said with a small smile for Ian, “I hope that’s where it is. What’s up? Do you want to chat more about Serena?”

A moment later, she shot up from the couch, her eyes wide with shock. When she looked up at Ian, her breath was coming faster and her skin had flushed a deep rose. “Wait a second, Smith, I think I need you to say that again so I can be sure I heard you right.”

Both her voice and her hands were shaking by then, and Ian instantly grew worried. Had something happened to her sister or mother? Or was Smith delivering other bad news?

Just as he had yesterday when they were in her kitchen, Ian didn’t think twice about his urge to comfort her. He simply moved closer so that he could put his hands on her waist to steady her. And, for the moment at least, what he felt for her didn't have anything to do with sex...it was simply about taking care of someone who had come to matter a great deal to him.

He felt her react to his touch with an instant answer of heat through her silk dress at the exact same moment that she looked up at him with eyes that seemed to cut straight through to his soul, her beautiful mouth opening slightly in surprise.

"Ohmygod." She was vibrating beneath Ian's palms as she said to Smith, "Yes, that's a good idea, a really good idea. I'll call you back once I've had a little time to process the news."

Ian was trying to figure out her contradictory signals—she was shaking and yet her entire expression seemed to be lit with excitement—when she suddenly tossed the phone onto the couch and threw her arms around his neck.

As she hugged him so tightly that he finally felt every single one of her luscious curves against him, Ian knew in the space of a heartbeat that no other woman had ever fit this well in his arms.

And that he never wanted to let her go.

But then she was moving to take his hands in hers and twirling around in the middle of his office, laughing. Watching her was like watching sunlight stream through a multifaceted crystal, shooting off light and bright color and vibrant life everywhere it spun. He'd never known another woman who was this open with her emotions, who didn't seem to realize that she had to protect herself or else she'd get hurt.

Just the thought of anyone or anything hurting her had his chest clenching tight. He pulled her to a stop in mid-twirl.

He couldn't understand her, and Ian made it a point to understand *everything* that was a part of his world. It was the only way to make sure he knew exactly how to play all his cards correctly. But worse than not being able to understand Tatiana was the fact that he couldn't understand *himself* whenever she was around. She threw off his perfectly ordered schedule and made him feel vulnerable in ways that he'd vowed never to be again.

And, still, he wanted her with a desperation that stunned him.

"You were shaking when Smith first spoke to you and I thought something bad had happened. But now you're laughing. Tell me what he said, Tatiana."

"It wasn't bad news. It was *great* news. *Shocking* news."

She laughed again, and he wanted to shake her for not telling him what the news was already. But even more than that, he wished he could laugh with her, wished he were the kind of man who could pull her back into his arms and dance with her without knowing better than to give a woman such easy affection.

"I just can't believe it," she finally added.

"Believe *what?*" His question came out rougher, and louder, than he'd intended, but at least it seemed to startle her into realizing that she hadn't yet told him the news. "I still don't know what happened."

She gripped his hands even more tightly and he honestly didn't think she had a clue that she'd put them between her breasts as she finally told him, "Smith was nominated for an Oscar this morning. And so was I." She pressed in even closer to his hands, as if only he had the power to help slow the incredibly rapid beating of her heart. *"For Best Actress,"* she whispered.

Her happiness was such a living, breathing thing between them that all Ian knew in that moment was that he would do anything he could, give everything he had, to keep her looking like this. Which was why it was the most natural thing in the world to say, "I'm so proud of you," then pull her back into his arms and swing her around and around while she laughed again.

Her cheeks were flushed as she looked up at him, and he had to stroke her face, had to get closer to the brightest, warmest sunlight he'd felt in a very, very long time.

She was still laughing when she pressed her mouth to his. A kiss of pure happiness, pure joy. Stunned by the beauty, the sweetness of her unexpected kiss, he didn't even have a chance to kiss her back by the time she pulled away.

Her eyes were wide with surprise, and when she looked at him, and said, "Oh my God, I just kissed you," he knew for sure that nothing about the kiss had been planned. She had simply been so happy, so excited, so expressive in her joy, that hugging him, dancing with him, even kissing him, was the way she'd needed to express herself.

Just as he now needed—more than anything he'd ever needed in his life—to crush her mouth to his again. He could still taste her joy in their second kiss, but within the span of several heartbeats, desire and desperate need quickly edged their way in.

With Tatiana in his arms and her mouth pressed against his, Ian momentarily forgot all the rules, all the restrictions he'd put on his life and his heart. He couldn't do anything but feel, couldn't stop himself from taking another kiss, and then another and another, dragging her closer with each one, falling deeper under her spell with every breath he stole from her lungs, with every gasp of pleasure she made against his lips.

He'd known it would be like this with her, hadn't he? So powerfully sensual, and so addictive as she opened for him so that he could stroke his tongue against hers and she could taste him just as intimately.

On and on their kiss went, her response utterly unrestrained, but it wasn't until he heard her moaning softly against his mouth that he realized his hands had slid up from her waist to cup her breasts, her nipples pebbling against his thumbs as he stroked her.

What the hell was he doing?

And now that they'd kissed, now that he knew just how good they could be together, how could he possibly go back?

Ian tried to think straight. Tried to remember all the reasons why they shouldn't do this, even as she told him, "I've never wanted anyone, or anything, as much as I want you, Ian."

And in that moment, when it felt to Ian as though everything he'd ever wanted was right there in front of him, even though he knew better, he simply didn't have it in him to move away from her.

But despite the hungry way she'd kissed him, he also instinctively knew that for all the lovers she'd already had, none could have needed her as badly as he did...or would demand as much of her unfettered sensuality as he would. Grasping at straws now, he decided the only chance—and the very last one—that he had of getting them to stop this madness before it slid all the way out of their control, would be if he could scare her with the force, the depth, the wildness of his need.

He slid his hand around to the nape of her neck, then fisted his hands in her hair and roughly tilted back her head so that he could scrape his stubble across the sensitive skin of her neck. "If you don't leave right now," he warned her in a voice made harsh with the inner conflict that rode him, "there's no going back."

"I don't want to go back. Not now." She shivered against him. "Not ever."

"I won't be gentle." He had one last chance to try to do whatever he could to get her to run, because he sure as hell couldn't figure out a way to let her go. "If you stay, I'm going to take what I want from you, Tatiana. *Everything* I want. Everything you've been offering to me since the moment we met."

But instead of running, all she said was, "Yes." And then again, even more emphatically, *"Yes.* I don't want gentle. I just want *you."*

And then she lifted her mouth to his again...and he was lost.

CHAPTER FOURTEEN

As Ian kissed her, for the first time in her life Tatiana knew—really knew—what passion was.

This was the kind of passion that people wrote songs and books and movies about.

This was the kind of moment that people waited an entire lifetime for.

She'd acted out passion a dozen times on screen to the best of her professional ability, but she'd never truly *felt* it before. No one but Ian had ever kissed her like this, touched her like this. Touching not just her body, but her heart and soul, too.

She hadn't meant to leap into his arms to kiss him like that, but she'd been so excited about being an Oscar nominee that it had been pure instinct to share her joy with him any way she could. They'd hugged, they'd danced, and then, before she knew it, she was kissing him.

Just a few moments of her lips against his—and yet it had been unlike any kiss she'd ever had, with warmth and arousal instantly swamping her system.

Feeling as if she'd just been struck by lightning, she'd drawn back, but before she could do more than exclaim her surprise at what she'd done, Ian was crushing her against him, his mouth devouring hers. And as he kissed her breathless, she forgot all about the nomination, forgot about everything except how badly, how desperately, she wanted him.

She heard it first—the sound of fabric ripping—before she realized he'd torn open the bodice of her silk dress with one tug of his hand on the fabric at her neck, leaving her standing before him in her bra, also in blue silk.

"You're even more beautiful than I dreamed you'd be."

The raw timbre of his words, and the fierce need in his eyes, sent shivers through her, along with a ravenous hunger for more of his dangerous passion. She didn't want him in his clothes any more than he seemed to want her in hers, so in yet another impulsive move, she shoved his jacket open and onto to the floor, then reached for the buttons on his shirt and yanked them open.

His tie still held the top of his shirt in place, but she'd pulled it open enough to bare a patch of his chest. Oh, how she wanted to feel his heat, his strength! She was just putting her hands on his chest when he tugged her hair back, his mouth diving for the pulse point in her neck. With his free hand, he cupped one breast through the silk of her bra, and she both heard and felt his aroused groan against her neck.

Being with him without any walls anymore, without any rules about what was and wasn't allowed to happen, felt so good. So shockingly good that the only way she could keep herself steady on her shaking legs was to hold on to him, and to arch closer, to offer more of herself—*all of herself*—to him.

Sliding his hand from her hair so that he was cupping both of her breasts through silk, he stroked over her nipples with his thumbs. As a new flood of heat and arousal rushed over her, she couldn't stop herself from bucking her hips into him.

He gave one more hard rip and her dress was gone, nothing more than a small pile of shredded silk on the rug in his office. Her panties were blue like her bra and as he just stood there and stared at her, a hint of fear at knowing she was about to do something she'd never done, go to a place she'd never gone, nearly made its way in past her excitement, past her joy.

But then, he was sliding a hand between her legs, and all thoughts of fear fell away as he found her hot and aroused.

"I knew you'd be like this," he murmured against her mouth as he tugged her close with one hand between her thighs, the other on her breast, for another heated kiss. "So responsive." He kissed his way down her neck, over the swell of her breasts, before pulling one bra cup down and covering her nipple with his mouth. "So sweet." She couldn't keep up with all of the sensations, with the heat of his tongue on her, with the thrill of his hand over her shockingly aroused flesh, especially when his teeth scraped so deliciously over her nipple.

Against her breast, he whispered, "You're just so goddamned sweet," and then he was pulling down her other bra cup to suckle on the taut tip of her other breast.

Overwhelmed with heat and arousal and emotion, when he slid his fingers beneath the elastic of her silk underwear and found her bare skin, she couldn't stop from crying out from the shock of pleasure at having his hands and mouth on her like this. Absolutely everywhere she'd wanted him.

He moved his lips from her breasts back to her mouth to give her another searing kiss, and to drink in more of her cries, but his hand stayed right where it was, slipping, sliding against her slick, heated flesh. "All week I needed this. Needed to feel you, naked, hungry, ready for me to take you over the edge."

His words were broken up by the kisses he gave her, but even if she hadn't heard them, she would have known what he wanted.

Because she needed it just as badly.

"Now, baby." He lifted his mouth from hers to stare down at her with eyes that had gone nearly black with desire. "I need you to come for me. *Now*."

But she was already there as with one of his hands between her legs, the other on the nape of her neck to hold her steady, she shattered into a million beautiful pieces in his arms in a climax so much more powerful than any she'd ever experienced before.

He stroked her all the way through her release, murmuring how beautiful, how breathtaking she was. Still, when he lifted her up with his hands on her hips and wrapped her legs around his waist, she was still trying to catch her breath.

"Now. I need to get you into my bed right now."

"Anywhere," she said as she put her arms around his neck. "You can have me anywhere."

He stopped halfway to the door to kiss her again in an utterly unrestrained tangle of lips and tongues and teeth. For a moment, she thought he might just push her up against the wall and take her right there like that. And though she'd dreamed of making love with him in a bed, she now knew that wild sex against the wall would be perfect, too.

Anywhere would be perfect, as long as she was with Ian.

On a low curse, he finally moved them out of his office, taking long, impatient strides down the hallway with her in his arms. He turned into a dark room, moving one arm from around her just long enough to flip on the light switch.

"I need to see you." He kissed her as he lowered her back against the bed covers. "I'll go crazy if I can't see you, Tatiana. All of you." He looked down as he moved over her, his gaze moving from her face to her breasts, to her naked limbs. "A thousand times I've dreamed of what you'd look like, the sounds you'd make, the way you'd smell. But I had no idea just how amazing you would be." He leaned down to kiss her again. "Watching you completely let go like that, feeling your body moving against mine, your mouth so damned soft and sweet as you kissed me...it *destroyed* me."

She pulled him closer, tightened her legs around him so that his full weight was over her. "I've never let go like that before, never knew I could." But she didn't feel destroyed, she felt *reborn,* as though everything was brand new and so shiny and beautiful she could hardly wrap her head around the wonder of it all. "Take me even higher, Ian. *Please.*"

His hands tangling in her hair and his mouth on hers sent her climbing again, so quickly, so fast, that she was already desperate for him. Before she knew it, he had her bra off and her panties shredded as he tore them from her, so that she was completely naked before him.

"I've never seen anything, or anyone, as beautiful as you."

There was pure reverence in his voice as he stilled above her. Balancing his weight on one forearm, he stroked his free hand down between her breasts, over her stomach, then between her legs.

"You're beautiful, too," she whispered back, still hardly able to believe they were here in his bed, naked and kissing, and that he was about to make love to her. "But I need to see more of you. I need you naked, too."

Both of them started to strip away his clothes, although by the time his shirt was off, Tatiana was so stunned by his incredible male beauty that her fingers pretty much forgot how to work and he had to take care of everything else by himself. When he finally kicked off his shoes and socks and pants and turned back to her, gloriously naked and hugely aroused with a condom already on, her mouth went dry, her eyes wide.

"Wow." Maybe if she'd had enough brain cells left to realize the way she looked, sounded, she might have been able to stop herself from coming across like a virgin who'd never seen a naked man before. Even if that's exactly what she was. "You're...I..."

She couldn't form any words that made sense, but she could go to her knees and reach for him where he was standing at the foot of the bed. Putting her hands on his shoulders, she brought them down slowly over his back, his taut muscles rippling beneath her fingertips. His skin was so warm, his shoulders and back so broad, that a little sound of pleasure left her lips right before she leaned forward to press a kiss to the hollow of his throat.

He growled her name, and before she knew it, he had her lying back on the bed again. "I need you now, damn it."

"Yes," she panted as she instinctively arched beneath him and tried to pull even closer. "Take me now."

Everything had happened so fast from the moment he'd told her that one kiss would change everything...and that there would be no turning back from it. He'd been right, more right than she'd understood. Barely a heartbeat later, he shifted his hands beneath her hips and positioned her right where he needed her to be.

"You're mine, Tatiana."

She'd never seen his eyes look so dark or so full of desire, and knew that she was staring into a mirror of her own need for him. His jaw tightened as he brought their hips even closer together, so close that she could now feel the intense heat of his erection beginning to press against her.

Instinctively, she opened her legs for him as she echoed, *"I'm yours."*

His eyes closed for a moment, his lashes dark against his cheekbones as he stopped to take such a deep breath that she swore she could feel it in her own lungs.

"Mine," he said again.

And then, in the next breath, he was driving into her, taking everything she wanted him—and only him—to have, stretching her wider than she knew she could go, pushing deeper than she'd ever expected.

She reached for him even as her stunned gasp fell between them. The shock of taking all of him so suddenly, so fully, had her winding her arms tightly around him and burying her face against his chest.

Ian went completely still above—and inside of—her. "Tatiana?"

She tried to breathe through it, but he was just *so big* that even that small movement made her gasp again. And yet, it never occurred to her to let him go or to push him away. Not when giving her virginity to Ian was the best decision she'd ever made.

The soreness would pass—it already was, as her body settled into the perfection of nature—but this closeness, this intimacy, would be forever theirs.

She didn't have any words yet, so she pressed her lips to his chest, kissing him so he'd know she was okay. But instead of holding her tighter, he shifted slightly away to look down at her.

"You're a virgin." He grimaced. "Damn it, you *were* a virgin." She could read his confusion, and the obvious guilt on his face, as if he thought he'd done something wrong by taking what she wanted him to have. "Why didn't you tell me?"

"Because I didn't want you to stop. Please—" She wrapped her legs even tighter around his hips so that he couldn't move any further away from her, realizing just how quickly pain was turning to pleasure. "Please don't stop loving me, Ian."

"I can't stop, damn it." She'd worked with some of the best actors in the world, but she'd never seen so many divergent emotions cross anyone's face. "Not now. Not now that you're here beneath me and I'm finally inside of you."

With every word that he ground out, she felt the joy—and pleasure—begin to build inside of her again, until she was instinctively lifting her hips closer to his so that she could feel more of the heady slide, and the wonderful stretch, of his erection.

"Oh," she breathed as she relished every last sensation, "I love having you inside of me."

He crushed her mouth to his again, and then there was only pleasure as he slowly slid nearly out of her, then back in. She gasped again, and when he lifted his head to stare down at her to make sure he wasn't hurting her, she smiled—the happiest smile of her life.

"It feels good. *So good.*"

His groan came along with his next kiss, and he held them connected like that long enough that she could feel the rhythmic pulse of his erection against her sensitive flesh, the same beat as his heart against hers.

She didn't know how long he kissed her like that, with their tongues tangling, their bodies pressed fully together, totally connected in every way they could be. But by the time he finally began to move his hips again it felt as if it was a dance they had practiced a thousand times before.

One to which only the two of them knew the steps.

All her life she'd been a student of sensation, so in the midst of more sensory input than she'd ever experienced before, Tatiana tried to memorize her feelings and emotions, along with the heavy press of his muscular thighs over hers, the rasp of his chest hair against her breasts, and the delicious taste of his tongue on hers. But then, he moved one of his hands between their bodies, and the sweet slide of his fingertip over her clitoris promptly stole every last thought from her brain.

"Ian." His name was a plea on her lips as she lifted her hips to try to get closer to his hand and take him deeper all at the same time. "I need—"

"Shhh," he soothed. "I know what you need, sweetheart."

No one had ever looked at her the way he did then. She'd seen desire before. She'd seen affection. She'd seen admiration.

But she'd never seen such possession, as if Ian was claiming not only her body, not just her heart, but her very soul with every stroke of his fingers over her aroused flesh, with every thrust of his hard heat inside her. And no one had ever used an endearment that sounded so sweet to her ears.

She hadn't wanted to seduce, or to trick, Ian into being with her. She'd wanted it to happen because he was all in, just the way she was. But knowing how strong his self-control was, she was certain that he couldn't possibly have let one accidental kiss change his mind. Which meant that somewhere between yesterday morning in her kitchen and this afternoon in his office, he must have already made up his mind to have her.

And to love her the way she loved him.

"I always knew you would," she whispered against his lips.

"All you have to do," he said in a deep voice that warmed every inch of her, "is let me give you everything you need."

With each sweet yet sinful word he spoke, she grew wetter, hotter, needier. Every muscle in her body was tightening down inch by inch as he took her higher and higher with every caress, every stroke. And when he urged her—*Come for me again, Tatiana. Show me how good*

I'm making you feel. Let me feel it, too—that tightening gave way to such freedom, such flight, that his arms around her and his heavy weight above her, were the only ways she could possibly have remained connected to the physical plane.

She'd never known an orgasm could go on and on forever, starting with an explosion of bright red behind her closed eyelids, then orange and yellow, before swinging back around to another bolt of scarlet red like the finale of a fireworks show.

But just when she thought she'd already hit the highest possible peak—beyond bliss, *way* past ecstasy—he gripped her hips tightly and whispered her name as he grew impossibly bigger inside of her.

"Ian." She loved the way his name felt on her lips, loved the way his body felt inside hers.

But most of all, she loved the love that she felt for him.

As he came closer and closer to his own release, his thrusts grew harder, went deeper, but Tatiana still wanted more, more, *more.*

She moved with him, lifting her hips into his as he slammed into her again and again, their bodies slippery with sweat. She kissed, licked, bit at his chest, his neck, his jaw, until he captured her mouth with his. And it was his kiss that sent her, awed, tumbling over the sweet edge of ecstasy again.

She'd wanted everything from Ian. His body. His pleasure. His laughter. His teasing. His love. And when he finally let loose the final reins of control and climaxed inside of her, it was knowing that he'd finally given her all of himself, without holding anything back, that was the ultimate bliss.

CHAPTER FIFTEEN

A virgin? How could she have been a virgin?

Ian searched his brain to think of any virgin he might have been with, but even his first time as a teenager, the girl hadn't been inexperienced.

He had no idea how to treat a virgin, but even if he had, he and Tatiana were clearly long past that point now that he'd taken her the way he had.

Rough.

Fast.

And with no control whatsoever.

The truth was that even if she'd been as experienced as he'd wanted to believe she was, it still wouldn't have been right to take her like that. Just as it wasn't right for him to want to stay here like this forever, her curves pressed tightly to his as he lay over her where he'd all but collapsed from the force of his own orgasm.

Especially when she was small enough that he knew he must be crushing her.

He'd only just begun to shift his weight off her when her arms tightened around his neck.

"No. Don't go." He was still inside her and when she moved to pull him closer, blood rushed south again. "Not yet."

But guilt was already hitting him so hard that he forced himself to get up and walk into the en suite bathroom. Inside the luxuriously tiled room, he made himself look into the mirror.

The face looking back at him should have been full of remorse, and the strength of will to send temptation away. But what he saw, instead, was a man who looked stunned from having just unwrapped an unexpectedly beautiful gift.

From the moment Tatiana had appeared in his office on Friday night, her questions, her vitality, her laughter—hell, her sheer presence—had thrown him off again and again. Even now, he wasn't sure he could trust himself to go back out into the bedroom and not take her just as rough, just as fast, just as desperately, when what she had really deserved was flickering candles, soft lights, romance...and tenderness.

He scrubbed a hand over his face, silently cursing himself for the bastard he was. For so long, he'd painted women—especially beautiful ones—with one brush. But he'd been wrong about Tatiana, so damned wrong about her not being as innocent as she seemed, simply because she was a famous actress.

And she'd been the one to pay for it.

"Ian."

He lifted his head to find Tatiana standing in the bathroom doorway. He'd just had the intense thrill of putting his hands on her naked skin and knew how hot she ran, how soft every inch of her was. And yet as she stood before him now, with her gorgeous curves on display in the moonlight that came in through the window, he was stunned stupid by her beauty all over again.

"Are you all right?"

Shock that *she* was asking *him* that rather than the other way around made it impossible for him to find a quick answer. Before he could reply, she'd moved toward him and had put one hand on his cheek to soothe him.

"Because," she said with a little smile that quickly grew big, "I feel *great*."

Relief shot through him even as disbelief tried to push the selfish feeling away. "But you—"

"Really loved every moment of making love with you." She went to her tippy-toes, and with her hand still on his cheek, pressed a soft kiss to his lips. "I knew I'd like going to bed with you, but I didn't know it would be like *that*," she whispered against his earlobe as she wound her arms around his neck and pressed her naked curves against him. "So good. So overwhelming. So *perfect.*"

Previously, Ian would have assumed that this was all part of her calculated seductive act. He knew better now, knew her sensual words and manner were wholly natural, as much a part of who she was as her green eyes and her talent. And yet, somehow, for some reason, she'd held back her sensuality all these years.

But he knew the reason, didn't he?

Tatiana had obviously remained a virgin because she'd been waiting for her prince to appear on a white steed.

But she'd ended up with him, instead.

"I was too rough." And yet, even as he said it, he couldn't keep from wrapping his arms more tightly around her. "I took you too fast." As fast as his rock-hard erection pressing into her belly was now eager to take her again.

"I loved everything we did," she insisted.

"You deserved slower, sweeter your first time."

She tilted her head back to look up at him. "Then why don't you give that to me now? And after, I'll let you know which way I love more."

Holy hell, he knew he should never have touched her in the first place. But considering he'd yanked her virginity away, didn't he owe her some tenderness?

In the morning, there was no question that they would have to deal with what had happened tonight. But while the moon was up and she was naked and soft and warm in his arms, wouldn't it be worse not to show her all the ways a man could—and should—worship her? And knowing just how responsive she was to even the slightest touch, how could he not want to teach her everything he knew about pleasure? Just the thought of it had him wanting to tie her to his bed and never set her free...

And since tonight was the first and last night he'd ever make love to her, he'd make damned sure every single second counted.

Slowly sliding his hands up from her lower back, he felt her muscles jump slightly beneath his gentle caresses up her spine, then over her shoulders and neck until he was framing her face in his hands.

"I should have started with this."

He lowered his mouth to hers in a kiss that was barely more than breath and the faintest brush of lips against lips. He let himself taste her slowly this time, the delicious flavors of her lips, her tongue, her skin bursting into his system one by one. She was a potent combination of sweet sugar and exotic spice and he deepened the kiss until they were both straining to take air from each other's lungs.

He could feel in the pliancy of her muscles how ready she was for him again. It would be so easy, too easy, to drag her back to his bed and take her. She was so eager, so responsive, that he knew he could be inside of her again before either of them had time to take more than a handful of breaths.

But he'd promised her slow and soft and sweet. And though he couldn't give her his heart, he could, at the very least, give her the memory of a few hours of perfect pleasure.

Tearing his mouth from hers, he slid his hands over her shoulders and upper arms. Goosebumps rose over her flesh as he gently caressed her. "Are you cold?"

Her nipples were hard points against his bare chest as she said, "A little. But I'm sure that if you take me back to bed, I'll heat right back up again."

Knowing the odds were extremely low that he'd be able to trust himself to go slow and soft once he got her back into bed, he decided to stay right where they were for a while longer.

"A bath will warm you the quickest." He drew her across the large bathroom to the tub beneath the window, then quickly had the taps running hot and full. He lifted Tatiana over the porcelain edge and was about to kneel on the floor beside the tub when she tugged at his hand to stop his progress.

"Join me in the tub, Ian."

Lord, there was nothing he wanted more than to get into the tub with her. "If I take a bath with you...I'm afraid I'll hurt you again instead of cherishing you."

"You haven't hurt me," she said softly. "You won't." She laid her hand over his heart. "I know you won't."

How could she have that kind of faith in him after what he'd done? Especially when he knew exactly how this would end in the morning, regardless of how much pleasure they found in each other's arms tonight?

But before he could say as much to her, her hand curled into a ball on his chest. "I should have told you that I was a virgin. It was selfish of me not to, especially now that I can see how much you're beating yourself up over it. I can't go back and fix that mistake, but from here on out I promise to tell you when something is new for me." She bit her lip, letting the plump flesh slide erotically from beneath her front teeth. "I've never taken a bath with a man before."

He had to pull her against him, had to kiss her again. "I like it hot," he warned her.

"Me too."

He got into the tub and lowered her down with him so that she was sitting between his legs, her back pressed against his chest. Tatiana let out a happy sigh as the hot water rose and steamed over both of them. Taking his hands in hers, she pulled his arms tightly around her, then reached out with her right foot and deftly turned off the faucets with her pretty painted toes.

"Perfect." She leaned her head against the crook of his shoulder. "This is absolutely perfect."

Ian couldn't stop himself from pressing a kiss to the top of her head. And when she shifted so that he could see her face, the brightness of the smile she gave him almost fooled him into thinking the sun had already risen on their one and only night together.

"You're perfect," he told her, knowing with total certainty that he'd never be this close again to such sweet perfection if he lived to be a thousand.

"I've seen perfect lots of times. So have you. We both know I'm not even close to perfect."

He could still hear her telling his ex-wife that casting directors had called her fat in the past, and though he'd already told her that they were wrong, he knew words alone would never convince her to see things his way. Deciding it would be much better to show her just how perfect she was, he slid his hands up from her waist to cup the fullness of her breasts in his large palms beneath the water. Her skin was soft and slippery as he lifted them so that her nipples peeked out from beneath the surface of the water.

"You not only have the prettiest breasts I've ever seen, but look how responsive you are to my touch." He slid the pads of his thumbs across both peaks at the same time and her nipples grew even tighter against his touch. "Have you ever come just from this?"

"No."

The one short word was more of a gasp from her lips than anything else as he continued to toy with her gorgeously sensitive breasts. No other woman had made him want so much, or feel this reckless. He knew better than to make any promises, but as he rained kisses into the curve of her neck and shoulder, he had to say, "Maybe later tonight, if you're not too tired, we'll give it a try."

His sensual words had her shuddering against him. Still, he was stunned when she said, "I want to try now." She covered his hands with hers so that they were both cupping her breasts, her voice barely above a whisper as she added, "I think I'm already close."

He groaned into her hair. How the hell was he supposed to take things slow with her when she said things like that to him? Especially when she wasn't saying it to try to turn him on, she was just telling him honestly how she felt.

"Just keep relaxing back against me, sweetheart, and I'll make sure you end up feeling good one way or another."

She laid her head against his shoulder with a contented sigh and for the rest of his life he knew he'd keep a picture of this moment in his mind. No other woman would ever compete with this memory of how perfect Tatiana looked in his tub, her eyes closed as she trusted him to touch her in just the right ways...and to show her the ecstasy her body was capable of.

Gently, slowly, he stroked her full breasts, caressing every beautiful inch of her, from her ribs all the way out to her hard nipples. She moaned her pleasure into the room, arching her back to press harder against his hands.

He could so easily, too easily, imagine teasing her like this for hours, taking her to the edge, then drawing away just enough that she'd be begging, pleading, for more. And if they could have had more than just this one night together, they might have been able to find out if she could come from just his hands, or mouth, on her breasts alone.

But the week he'd kept his hands off her had seemed more like years, and tonight he couldn't wait another second to run his hands over the rest of her.

She didn't protest when he slid one hand down to the smooth skin between her thighs, and she was slick and hot, hotter even than the water in which they were lying. She let her legs fall open against his, then arched her hips up into his hand. Barely remembering in time that he'd just taken her virginity less than thirty minutes ago, he only just stopped himself from thrusting his fingers into her. And if she'd made any sound of pain, if she'd stiffened against him even the slightest bit, he would have forced himself to immediately pull away.

Thank God, she was liquid pleasure in his arms as she rocked against his hand, his fingers slipping and sliding against—then into—her in an intoxicatingly sensual rhythm.

Already, he recognized the signs that she was about to come, and he needed her mouth against his, needed to drink in her cries of pleasure. But even that wasn't enough, not when he also needed to feel her breasts against his chest, needed to feel her heart beating against his, needed to be able to kiss her, needed to watch her eyes dilate as she climaxed.

Temporarily moving his hands to her hips, he lifted her out of the water, spun her around, then brought her back down so that she was facing him. She laughed as water splashed over the side of the tub when their limbs got tangled and then her long, wet hair temporarily blinded them both.

When they'd brushed it away, her eyes were hazy with desire as she smiled down at him. "Hi there."

Even as caught up as he was in the grip of intense desire, he found himself smiling back at her. "Hi."

"This is fun, taking a bath with you." She nuzzled her cheek against his. "*Way* more fun than taking a bath by myself ever was."

"Fun?" He nipped her earlobe between his teeth. "You think being with me is fun?"

"Mmm-hmm." She rolled her hips over his erection, making him groan at just how good she felt over him. "More fun than I've ever had with anyone before."

Ian had played plenty of games with women in bed, but it had always been about gunning for pleasure, never about having *fun*.

His surprising realization fell away as she ran one hand between their bodies to wrap her fingers around his erection. "I need you again, Ian."

Her lips were already swollen from his rough kisses, but knowing that wasn't enough to stop him from devouring her mouth again. Without breaking their kiss, he teased her nipples between his thumb and forefinger until she made a wild little sound that nearly had him thrusting to completion in her hand.

"Put your hands on my shoulders. Both of them."

She licked her lips. "But I like touching you."

"I like it, too. Too damned much."

He moved her hands for her, putting them around his neck, and she immediately rolled her hips back against his, the slick heat of her body taking him even closer to the edge of sanity than her hand just had. The thought of thrusting into her was so damned tempting that he was nearly there...when somewhere in the back of his lust-fogged brain he remembered his promise to be gentle this time.

"I can't just take you like this, Tatiana. Not again, not so soon after your first time."

Tatiana rubbed her breasts against his chest. "I'm not a virgin anymore," she reminded him in a softly seductive voice, one that now held tremendous knowledge of pleasure. "And yes, you should *definitely* keep taking me like this. In fact, if I had known just how amazing making love with you would be, I would have jumped you the day we met in Napa."

He covered her mouth with his, kissing her breathless before he admitted, "The first time I set eyes on you, I wanted you so badly."

"You could have had me, Ian."

He shook his head, her honest words wreaking havoc with the little bit of control he still had in his grasp. "No. Jesus, no. Don't tell me that."

"Just think of all the time we wasted, thinking about each other, wanting each other, when all along we could have been doing *this*."

She shifted her hips in an obvious move to take him into her, and it took everything in him to grip her hips and stop her from impaling herself on him. "Not yet, sweetheart. Let me make you come again. Let me make sure you're ready—that I won't be hurting you."

He slid one hand over her stomach down to the slick flesh between her legs. "I love touching you," he murmured against her mouth. "I've never felt anything so hot, so soft, so perfect."

"I love it, too," she gasped as she moved herself back and forth over his hand, her breath coming faster with every push of her hips against him. She had her arms wound around his neck and was holding onto him so tightly that he could feel her heart pound faster and faster as she rose higher, then higher still.

When she pulled her mouth from his, and threw her head back so that she could arch her hips closer to his hand, he had to taste her breasts, had to draw her nipples in between his lips to taste first one, then the other. Her cries of pleasure echoed against the tiled walls of the bathroom.

Moving his free hand to the nape of her neck, he threaded his fingers into the wet tangle of her hair. "Open your eyes, sweetheart." She blinked once, twice, before she was able to focus. "I want to watch you come. Let me see you. *I need to see you.*"

As if his request, and his desperate need, had flipped a switch inside her, a heartbeat later she was climaxing...and what he saw in her eyes, and in her expression that held back nothing at all from him, touched Ian in a way nothing else ever had.

Not only pleasure, not just arousal, but a depth of emotion that had him wishing, harder than he'd ever wished for anything in his life, that he was capable of loving Tatiana the way she deserved to be loved.

But it was the sweet and trusting smile she gave him even before she'd come down from her orgasm that nearly broke him. He'd already made the mistake of stealing her innocence. He couldn't make it even worse by making her promises he'd never be able to keep.

Lifting her out of the tub, he carefully wrapped her in a towel, and as he picked her up to carry her back to his bed, she said, "I'm ready for you to show me slow and sweet now, Ian." She kissed him softly, just the barest brush of her lips against his, before whispering, "Although if you want to know the truth, I'm ready for fast and hard again, too."

His hands shook as he gently laid her on the bed, the towel falling open to reveal one perfect breast and a long length of leg. He'd been little better than an animal their first time. So no matter how hard it was to hold back a little longer, her pleasure mattered more than anything else.

She seemed to believe he'd given her enough orgasms already. But she was wrong. If he showed her nothing else before the night was over, he hoped she'd come away knowing just how much pleasure she deserved.

"Not yet," he murmured against her skin as he moved over her to press a kiss to the underside of her breast.

"Please," she begged when he slid her towel the rest of the way off so that he could run kisses over her rib cage and stomach.

"We're almost there," he promised, nipping lightly at her hipbone, then gently putting his hands on her thighs to push them open. "But not quite." Lord, she smelled good, and for a few moments he just enjoyed looking, just let himself breathe in her heady scent.

"Ian." There was a faint hum of panic in the way she said his name as she looked down at how open she was to him, and then at him, clearly poised to put his mouth on her. "I promised I'd tell you if I hadn't done something bef—"

Her confession of further innocence fell away as he licked a wet, heated path over her aroused flesh.

"Now," he told her, "you've done it."

Just as quickly as she'd taken to everything else they'd done, she was instantly lifting her hips back to his mouth for more. Wanting to oblige her every sensual wish, he cupped her hips in his hands and drew her closer. He loved her taste on his tongue, loved the way she gave herself over so completely to him every single time, loved the thrill of knowing he was driving her back up to the peak again.

He knew the instant her orgasm started to roll over and through her, when on a low moan of pleasure, she gripped his hair in her hands hard enough to make absolutely sure that he wouldn't take his lips and tongue away. Of course, there was nowhere he'd rather be than taking her up and over another crashing climax.

She was still trembling from the force of it when he moved on to his back and tugged her over him so that she was straddling him. "You'll control everything this way," he explained as he reached for another condom. He was just ripping the package open when she took it from him.

"This is another thing I haven't done." She shifted slightly so that she could look down at his erection. She reached for him with one hand, gripping the base of his shaft to hold him steady while she slowly unrolled the condom over his tip with the other. "How am I doing?"

He was gritting his teeth so hard in his attempts at control that he could barely tell her, "So good that I might not last until you've got it all the way on."

Clearly delighted with the effect she had on him, the sweet sound of her laughter filled his bedroom. He was so struck by the beauty of it that it took him a few too many seconds to realize she'd moved again so that she was levered right over him.

She moved her hips over his in just the right way to make his eyes roll back in his head, and when she laughed again, the sound was utterly sensual, and full of newfound female power...and pleasure, too.

"You know what? I think I like being in control."

And though it just might kill him the way she took him into her one slow, torturous inch at a time, Ian liked it, too. *Loved* it.

Her eyes closed as she lowered herself onto him, savoring the moment as though she wanted it to last forever, and though he did, too, in the end his primal need to have her couldn't be denied any longer.

Gripping her hips hard enough that she'd likely have marks on her skin the next day, Ian held Tatiana right where he wanted her, then thrust hard into her. She gasped as he drove deep, but he knew this time that it was pleasure rather than pain that had her pushing just as hard down over him.

"It's so good, Ian. So, so good."

She was practically sobbing the words as she braced her hands flat on his chest and rode him, the muscles in her thighs working hard to lift her body up, then back down, over him. Her breasts bounced, tempting him, teasing him, until he had to cup them in his hands and stroke both nipples together with his tongue.

She moved her hands from his chest to thread her fingers into his hair and tug his mouth even closer, and when the new position took him even deeper, her body eagerly opened for every last inch of him. *"More.* Please, Ian. I need *more."*

Again and again, with words and her body, she begged him to take every last part of her...and that was exactly what he did, until they both climaxed together in a wild combination of kisses and gasps and hands that couldn't get enough.

* * *

A short while later, Tatiana was wrapped up in his arms beneath the covers, her back to his front. He stroked her hair and breathed her in...and worked like hell not to give in to saying something in the aftermath of the moment that he wouldn't be able to stand by come morning.

Soon, thankfully, her heartbeat slowed, and she was nestling her hips back into his and pulling his arm more tightly across her chest, holding his hand over her heart.

Ian hadn't thought he'd be able to sleep, but Tatiana felt so right in his arms that he was nearly under himself when he thought he heard her say *I love you.*

But when he came, instantly, fully awake again, and waited for her to say more, she was fast asleep, breathing so soundly, so serenely, that he decided he must have been dreaming.

CHAPTER SIXTEEN

Tatiana woke to an empty bed, but Ian's scent still lingered so she closed her eyes and smiled as she breathed him in.

Last night had been incredible, surpassing any dreams she'd had of what lovemaking might be like by miles. No character she'd ever played or movie she'd ever watched could have prepared her for just how amazing it was to be intimate with the man she loved. The wonder of Ian's body. The tantalizing way he stroked and caressed her. His hardness to her softness. Every whisper, every sensual command, every look of pleasure and satisfaction in his eyes, had stolen more and more of her heart. Every time she thought she'd experienced the peak of pleasure, Ian had continually found a way to take her even higher, and then higher still.

While shadowing him, she'd thought more than once that he was superhuman, both with regards to his drive and the way he obviously thrived on his intense workload. Now, she thought with a naughty little grin, she knew that he had just as much stamina in bed, too. And, oh how she'd thrived on it...

She knew most people would think it was crazy for her to wait this long to give up her virginity. But she'd been perfectly right to wait for Ian. Not only because she was head over heels in love with him—but because, she thought with another smile that felt wonderfully wicked and wanton on her lips, there was no way any other man could possibly compare between the sheets.

Smelling coffee, she slowly pushed back the covers and slid over to the side of the bed. In the sunlight that streamed in through his bedroom windows, she was more than a little shocked to see faint red marks on her hips. She blushed as she realized Ian had marked her in his passion, with the firm grip of his hands on her hips as he drove her over the edge of bliss again and again.

"I know I should be gentle with you, but all I can think about is how badly I still want you." Tatiana shivered as she remembered his heated words, and her own heated response: *"Then take me again."*

And oh, how he'd taken her. Rough, then sweet. Fierce, then tender. Then hard, fast, and wild again. All the while, even when he'd already pushed her body far past the limits of pleasure that she'd believed she could handle, she'd begged him for *more, more, more* in a blur of need and desire.

And, most of all, love.

Wanting nothing more than to be near him again, to see the way his dark eyes became even more intense whenever he looked at her, she looked around for her clothes. And then she remembered: Ian had *shredded* not only her dress, but her panties as well when he'd torn them off her.

She had to laugh, then, at the beautiful madness that had come over both of them yesterday. And thank God it had, because she couldn't imagine feeling this way all by herself. Besides, she'd seen enough relationships on set to know that *crazy* only worked when it went in both directions.

She opened Ian's closet and took one of his long-sleeved, blue striped shirts off the hanger. Wrapping her naked body in it, she breathed in his familiar scent as she rolled up first one too-long sleeve and then the other. Seeing his collection of ties, she decided the one she'd yanked off him the night before would be the perfect way to cap off her impromptu outfit. She headed into his home office, found his tie near the door, then quickly wrapped it around her waist.

Barefoot, she walked into Ian's open living room and kitchen. She should have known better than to expect all wealthy businessmen to live the same way, but in the morning light she was surprised all over again at just how normal it was. All of the finishes and furnishings were of spectacular quality, of course, and the view from the penthouse had to be one of the best in all of the Pacific Northwest. But where most other men with his wealth would have owned ten thousand square feet or more just because they could have anything they wanted, she guessed his home was maybe a third that size. Probably, she figured, because he had the foundation of a great family to guide him.

Ian's back was to her as he poured a cup of coffee and she had to stop for a moment at what a gorgeous sight he was in his well-tailored suit pants and starched shirt. Knowing exactly how broad his shoulders were beneath his clothes, and the way the muscles in his arms and thighs flexed as he levered over her and thrust deep, then deeper still, simply stole her breath away.

That was how he found her, standing and staring at him as if she could hardly believe he was real. Looking at his beautiful face, Tatiana knew she'd never been happier than she was just then as she smiled at him from across the room.

"Hi."

As she moved closer, a dark cloud in the sky shifted precisely so that a sudden ray of light coming in through the kitchen windows behind him obscured his expression. "I hope you don't mind my going through your closet," she said in a playful voice. "We were in such a hurry to get my clothes off last night that they're pretty much goners."

Expecting him to tease her back, when he didn't say anything, and she still couldn't quite see his face clearly, those old nerves she always used to have around him started popping back to life.

But that was crazy. There was no way he could have touched her, kissed her, spoken to her the way he had if he didn't feel the same way she did.

Only, when she finally stepped in front of him, he didn't reach for her, didn't drag her against him the way she loved so much. And he still hadn't said a word. Instead, he was looking down at her with an expression of such clear regret that, for a moment, she almost started to worry that she'd made a mistake.

No. She couldn't have.

Last night, Ian had shown her a hundred times over just how much he cared about her, hadn't he? First with have-to-have-you sex and then with the care he'd taken in her pleasure until she hadn't known where one orgasm ended and the next began.

She wanted to say something that would ease the strangely tense air between them, but before she could, he spoke first. "Tatiana, last night—"

"—was incredible." She lifted her hand to his smooth, freshly shaved jaw. "It was the most beautiful, perfect night of my life."

"You're right, it was incredible." His eyes gleamed with the same fierce emotion he hadn't been able to hold back when they were making love. "*You* are incredible." That was when she realized that he looked positively tormented with every word he spoke...and guiltier by the second. "But you were also a virgin, Tatiana." A muscle jumped in his jaw. "Untouched."

She didn't know how everything could possibly be going from beautiful to weird so quickly, just that she needed to make it stop. Needed to make him see that things didn't have to be weird or strained between them. And that she didn't want him to spend one more second feeling guilty about being her first.

"I thought we already talked about this last night, about the fact that I *wanted* to do everything we did together. But maybe," she said when she could see that she still wasn't getting through to him, "it would help if you knew why I was still a virgin when I could have slept with dozens of guys by now?"

"Tatiana." Her name was more a growl than anything else, but she wasn't nearly done making her point—had barely begun, in fact.

"All the guys who wanted to take me to bed were nice men. Good-looking men. Heck, most of them were rich, famous men. But I always knew I would wait to have sex until it wasn't just sex, but something so much bigger than that. So that's exactly what I did, Ian. I waited until I fell in love. *With you."*

* * *

Just as his body had immediately stilled over hers when he'd realized she was a virgin, now Ian's heart stopped dead in his chest.

It was one thing to think Tatiana had whispered *I love you* while falling asleep against his chest. He could have written that off as heightened emotion from all the orgasms, or even pure exhaustion right before she dropped into sleep.

But hearing her say it to him in the clear light of day, her eyes bright and sure...

No, he couldn't let himself believe her, and he needed to stop the warmth, the longing that had shot through him when she'd said it.

"You don't love me."

"I do."

He didn't want to hurt her any more than he already had...and yet that didn't change his boundaries or his limits. If she were someone else, maybe they could have had a fling, just enjoyed each other casually the way he had with other women since his divorce. But Tatiana wasn't like anyone else. Partly because she was going to become part of his extended family by marriage soon, but mostly because she deserved so much more than a simple no-strings affair with a man who could never give her anything else.

"We've only spent a few days together," he reminded her, "and one night."

"So what? People fall in love at first sight all the time."

"Nobody can possibly fall in love that fast," he insisted, despite how jumbled up his insides had felt from the moment he'd met her in Napa Valley. "You're just trying to convince yourself that you love me because—"

"Don't you dare try to say you know how I feel or why I feel it." Her eyes flashed emerald fire as she moved closer. "*I* know what I feel, just like I know that *you* could never have touched me the way you did last night if you didn't care about me, too. Maybe it's not love yet for you like it is for me, but there's something there inside of you for me. Something big. Something *real.*"

All morning long, he'd gone over and over what had happened between them, trying to figure out what could have driven him to go against everything he'd known was right. In the end, he'd decided it had to have been pure hormones and primal attraction, rather than an emotion Tatiana wanted to call *love.* And what man on the planet wouldn't have been infatuated with her beauty, with the sounds she made when she came, with the thrill of being with someone so full of life and boundless dreams?

The last thing he wanted was to hurt her, but at the same time, he needed her to understand without even the barest doubt that he simply wasn't capable of loving a woman more than he loved his company, his work, the power and the rush of business.

It was one of the hardest things he'd ever have to force himself to do, hurting her now so that he wouldn't hurt her even worse in the future, as he made himself tell her, "Of course I touched you like that. You're the most beautiful woman I've ever seen and I couldn't resist you, not after you kissed me. No one could have, Tatiana."

She narrowed her eyes. "You've been with *way* prettier women than me. I've seen pictures of the women you've been with, not to mention your ex-wife."

"Those women all bought their faces, their bodies, with high-priced surgeons. But every curve on your body, every expression on your face is *you*."

"Okay then, why don't you tell me—how was sex with those women compared with me?"

Just when he thought she couldn't shock him more, she went right ahead and did it without so much as blinking. First, she'd stunned the crap out of him by actually being as innocent as she'd seemed, and then she'd blown his mind by unleashing such sweet yet wild sensuality that he could barely keep up with her. Only to find that one little four-letter word falling from her lips could send him reeling harder and farther than any orgasm had.

And now, *this.* Actually asking him point-blank to compare his time in the sheets with other women to being with her just hours before.

When he didn't answer her fast enough, she just kept pushing, "Was being with any of them as good as what you and I shared last night?"

"No." Damn it. "Not even close."

She smiled at him like she'd just made her point, and maybe it felt too much like she had, like she was getting too close, too deep again, because even though he'd already been cruel enough, he couldn't stop himself from saying more. "You're so tied to the fairy tales you've been acting out your whole life, and to the happily-ever-afters that screenwriters tie up into a neat and tidy bow, that you can't see that nearly all of those perfect endings are just fiction. They're nothing more than great stories meant to keep the audience coming back for more. So just because we burned up the sheets together doesn't mean I love you. What it means is that I love your body. I love your face. I love touching you. And I love making you come. But that's all it is, Tatiana. Just hot sex. Nothing more."

Her skin lost more and more color as he kept going, kept swinging harder, aiming lower. But even if he had deliberately just said all those things to make sure Tatiana stopped saying how much she loved him, God, how he hated to watch her smile fall.

Hated it more than he could ever remember hating anything before in his life.

"Fine," she snapped. "I get it. You don't love me. You'll never love me. And I'm a naïve idiot for ever thinking you did. Happy now?"

She spun around, ripping off his tie from around her waist and then his shirt from her shoulders. In seconds she was naked again and Ian realized, with no little fury at himself, that he was scum enough to respond to her astonishingly perfect body after he'd just done everything in his power to shove her out of his life.

"No, damn it," he ground out, "I'm not happy about any of this."

But she'd already hightailed it out of the kitchen toward his office. By the time he caught up to her, she was shoving her feet into her heels. She looked with obvious dismay at her shredded clothes on the floor, then stalked past him out of the office and toward his front door.

"Where the hell do you think you're going without your clothes on?"

"Home."

He knew how mad she was, and how hard she was trying to be tough, but he could also hear the slight break in her voice in the middle of that one syllable. Her pain twisted up everything inside of him...everything he didn't want to feel for her but couldn't seem to find a way to stop.

She grabbed her trench coat—one that barely grazed her kneecaps—from where she'd taken it off by the front door, and as she covered her naked body with it, then did up the buttons with trembling fingers, he nearly grabbed her to make her stop. But he already knew that making the mistake of ever touching her again could only lead them back to his bedroom.

It had been hard enough to push her away once—nearly impossible, in fact. He was dead certain he'd never manage it twice.

"You can't leave dressed like that, wearing only your coat and nothing else."

"Yes, I can. I can do anything I want. I can even make the mistake of sleeping with a man who's too haunted by his past and too scared of what the future might hold to let himself believe that I love him."

With that, she threw open the door, walked quickly to the elevator, and pressed the down arrow. The metal door slid open immediately, but right before it closed behind her, he moved into the small space with her.

"I'll drive you home."

"I'm going to walk."

"You're not wearing clothes. Hell, you're not wearing underwear!" And Lord knew that in nothing but a coat and heels, with sex-tangled hair and her lips still slightly swollen from his kisses the night before, she was his every erotic fantasy.

But he couldn't touch her. Should never have touched her, damn it.

"Well, then I guess I'd better hope there's not a breeze coming in off the water today, or I'll be giving people a show they haven't paid for. And not the *happily-ever-after* kind this time," she said, echoing his harsh words in a brittle tone.

Frustration with absolutely, positively everything had him growling, "You're going to get in my car, even if I have to throw you over my shoulder to get you there."

"That would mean touching me again...and we both know you're not about to risk making that *mistake* again. So I'm pretty sure your car is off the list."

"I'll hail you a taxi, then."

When she didn't argue, he tried to convince himself that she was finally listening to reason. Not only was she barely dressed, it was pouring outside. Hard enough that even rain-hardened Seattleites weren't hoofing it through town and the sidewalk was completely empty.

God, how could he have screwed things up with her so badly? It was why he'd been a master of control all these years, because he'd already learned from the way things had turned out with his marriage how little he had to give to anyone else. He'd been careful not to let any of the women he'd spent time with over the past few years feel too much for him. It had been so easy to keep his heart separate from sex that he'd been certain there wasn't even the slightest chance of being tempted to lose himself over a woman again.

But he hadn't bet on Tatiana, on how open she was with her emotions, or that she'd choose him to be the one she gave her love and her innocence to. He'd never been able to think straight when he was around her, and mere hours after he'd had her in his bed his brain was more muddled than ever. Later, when he was able to think rationally again, he prayed he'd somehow be able to figure out a way to make all this up to her.

Right before the elevator doors opened in the lobby, she pulled a hat he hadn't known she had with her out of her bag, jammed it onto her head, then scooted right out the front door of his building and headed up the storm-battered sidewalk at a fast clip.

Damn it, she was stubborn.

But so was he. And though he knew the very last thing she wanted was for him to accompany her home, he kept pace beside her every step of the way.

CHAPTER SEVENTEEN

Tatiana's two-block walk home was a blur of rain and emotion. She made sure to keep her head down to lower the odds of anyone recognizing her, and tried to stay a couple of feet ahead of Ian. She'd been right about him not risking throwing her over his shoulder to get her into his car, but he had stubbornly refused to let her walk home alone.

Her heart wrenched in her chest with every step, not only at how something so unbelievably beautiful could turn ugly so fast...but at the fact that she hadn't seen it coming. Hadn't for one single second guessed that the love she felt for Ian, the love she'd thought they'd expressed to each other every moment they'd been together last night, wasn't being returned in full.

When he'd told her he wanted to cherish her, she'd assumed he'd been speaking about more than just her body, that he'd meant he wanted to cherish her heart, too, the way she cherished his. She'd been so sure that the sweetness and the intense heat of their lovemaking had been the ultimate proof of all the things Ian felt for her but didn't know how to say out loud.

Less than an hour ago, she'd been so full of joy, so excited about their future together, so painfully naïve as she'd wrapped herself up in his shirt then walked into the kitchen to find him.

Now, all she could hear was his voice in her head. *"Just because we burn up the sheets together doesn't mean I love you."*

She had never been so thankful for the wet Seattle skies so that she could pretend it was just the rain she was wiping away from her eyes. Looking up, she saw that they were nearly at her building. Ten feet more, and she'd be safe inside, away from Ian.

"Tatiana." He surprised her by reaching for her hand, and holding firmly on to it until she had no choice but to turn to look at him. "I never wanted to hurt you."

But she already knew that, and somehow, it made everything worse.

She'd been loved and protected her whole life, but even with his mother's warning combined with how hard Ian had worked all week to keep his distance from her, she'd still thought love would be straightforward and effortless and easy.

Easy.

Now she knew just how wrong she'd been.

Tugging her hand free, she walked into her building and into the elevator, waiting until the doors closed so that she could be absolutely certain that she was alone before she let her tears fall.

And fall.

And fall.

* * *

Every other time in her life when she'd been knocked down, Tatiana had reached out for her sister, and Valentina had always been there. It was pure reflex to go find her phone, only before she had, she was shocked to realize that making that call for help just didn't feel right this time.

Valentina had been there for her her entire life, and though Tatiana knew she would be again, this time they wouldn't be dealing with a skinned knee, or a rude co-star, or Tatiana feeling temporarily overwhelmed by the pressures of fame.

Love was so much bigger than all of those little irritations. So freaking big and confusing, in fact, that she finally understood why Valentina had kept her budding romance with Smith to herself during those early weeks when the two of them had been starting to fall for each other.

Tatiana's stomach rumbled, but she knew she wouldn't be able to keep any breakfast down. Not when she was churning inside—mind, body, and soul. Hurt warred with love, and pleasure warred with the fear that she'd been foolish to see something in Ian—in both of them—that wasn't actually there.

He'd told her that life, that love, wasn't a fairy tale, and that no matter how good sleeping together was, they weren't going to get happily-ever-after with each other. Tatiana had always believed that she had a good grasp on fantasy versus reality, and that she'd been careful to keep a wide distance between playing a role in her work life and being true to herself when the cameras were turned off.

But was that true? Or had she just been fooling herself?

After waiting all these years to go to bed with a man, after waiting to make sure it was love and not just sex, had she simply told herself the lie she wanted to believe so that she could take what her body had craved so badly? Had she been so focused on the butterflies and the fireworks shooting through her every time Ian looked at her that she hadn't stopped to look carefully enough at what was really going on? Had she been wrong to believe that there was more than heat and attraction and sheet-melting sex between them?

Even now, as she stripped off her coat, she could still feel the imprint of his mouth, his hands, his hard, heavy weight over her.

And even after everything he'd said, her body—and her heart—still craved him.

It was so tempting to slide under the covers of her bed, pull them up high over her head, and let the darkness of sleep temporarily shut down her brain and the ache she felt in her heart every time it pulsed in her chest.

But Tatiana couldn't stand the thought of being that girl who hid, who cried under the covers. She might not have the answers yet to any of the questions she'd been asking herself. But how would she ever figure things out if she didn't keep facing the situation head on?

Hoping everything would seem clearer after a shower, she was heading for the bathroom when she saw the invitation sitting on the corner of the small desk in her bedroom.

The Seattle Family Foundation event was tonight. She'd promised to go, and though she felt like a truck had run over her, there was no way she was going back on her word.

Maybe, she thought, this was exactly what she and Ian needed—to be forced to see each other again before he could retreat even further into himself. She'd picked out a dress to wear earlier in the week—black and white silk, belted at the waist and fluttery at the knees.

But that had been *before.*

After, though she wasn't nearly as angry as she'd first been when he'd deliberately tried to push her away in his kitchen with his harsh words, she was still hurt...and just human enough that she wanted to push Ian back in some way, if only to show him that she wasn't the only one who cared.

Flipping on the light in her walk-in closet, she scanned the clothes hanging in front of her, running through them with her fingers. They were all pretty, elegant, sexy even. But none of the dresses were exactly right.

She wanted to dazzle Ian tonight, wanted his eyes to pop out of his head and his brain to turn to mush when he saw her.

The rational part of her knew that she shouldn't use her looks, or his attraction to her, to prove that she mattered to him. But the hurt voices that were shouting a heck of a lot louder than the rational ones told her in no uncertain terms that she should do whatever she could to prove that she did.

Any way she could.

She pulled out a dress that a new designer had sent to her agent, asking if she'd consider wearing it. Slinky and gold, it fit her as if it had been made specifically to her measurements, but when she'd tried it on three weeks ago, she'd felt as if she were playing dress-up in a much sexier woman's clothes.

Now, as she drew the thin, shimmering fabric over her naked curves and looked into the mirror, she finally realized why wearing the dress had never before felt right.

Three weeks ago, she hadn't understood her own sexuality, how deep it ran, or how sweet it could be.

Now she did.

Her eyes, the glow of her skin, even the way her body moved—all of it felt new now that she'd learned about pleasure.

And—whether Ian wanted to believe in it or not—love.

Regardless of how harshly he'd reacted this morning, Tatiana knew deep in her heart that the hours they'd spent in each other's arms had been special. Unbelievably precious and beautiful.

Carefully taking off the dress and hanging it up, she wrapped herself in a robe, then finally found her phone tucked halfway beneath a pillow on her bed. Hoping to find a hairstylist and manicurist somewhere in Seattle who would be able to squeeze her in at the last second, after typing in her password on the screen saver, she was shocked to find forty-six voice mails and text messages waiting for her. The top few that showed on her phone's screen all said one version or other of *CONGRATULATIONS* with a special text from Mia saying she and Ford were hoping Tatiana would be free the following Friday night to celebrate her and Smith's nominations with the Seattle Sullivan crew.

She couldn't believe she'd completely forgotten about her Best Actress nomination. She hadn't called Smith back, hadn't called her sister, hadn't even spoken to her agent. Instead, she'd jumped into Ian's arms, kissed him, and forgot that anything or anyone else existed but the two of them.

As she stood raw and hurting—and utterly, totally in love with Ian Sullivan—in her bedroom, Tatiana had never felt less equipped to deal with the Hollywood circus than she did right then. But at the same time, she'd also never needed the distraction of it more.

CHAPTER EIGHTEEN

"Tatiana!" Joyce, the head of the foundation, looked surprised—and thrilled—to see her that evening at the entrance to the swanky downtown hotel's grand ballroom. "Ian told us you weren't going to be able to make it. And after we heard about your Oscar nomination, we weren't surprised to hear you were too busy."

"I wouldn't have missed this for anything." Not even a broken heart.

"We're all so happy for you, and your nomination is so well deserved. I absolutely loved *Gravity.* My husband did, too, and he normally falls asleep in a movie unless there are a dozen car chases. I'm positive you're going to win."

"Thanks for saying that," she replied with a smile, "although just getting the nomination was such a shock that I'm thinking actually winning would be completely overwhelming.

Honestly, even thinking about what I'm going to wear that night is too overwhelming, at this point."

Tatiana hadn't been able to reach her sister or Smith, who were in Ireland scouting locations, and she'd guessed it was because Smith's Best Actor nomination had made them as busy as she was. But while it felt funny not immediately sharing everything with her sister the way she always had since she was a little girl, in a way it had been a blessing.

She still wasn't yet ready to talk to anyone about what had happened with Ian as she continued to work through her thoughts and emotions about all of it, reeling back and forth from hurt to angry to embarrassed...but always, throughout everything, still desperately in love. And utterly convinced that she was right to do whatever she could tonight to shake him up just a little more.

Still, during the ride here in the taxi she'd been more than a little nervous about the dress she was wearing. Even now, she had her trench coat wrapped tightly around her. But since her bold outfit wouldn't be worth a thing if she didn't project confidence along with it, she took a deep steadying breath as she undid the tie at her waist and slid it off her shoulders.

"Wow," Joyce said, "that's a gorgeous dress."

"I love yours, too." Noticing that the photographers were already pointing their cameras her way, Tatiana asked, "Where would you like me to go? Maybe I could stand over there, in front of the foundation's logo?"

"That would be amazing. Thank you so much for doing this."

"I'd like to do more, but hopefully this will be a good start."

Joyce took her coat and Tatiana smiled for the flashing cameras that immediately surrounded her. She'd never stood in front of the press in quite so revealing a dress, and she could still feel the flutter of nerves inside, but amazingly, instead of wishing she could hide or cover up, she realized with some surprise that she felt beautiful.

Truly beautiful.

She'd posed for photographers a hundred times at premieres and other industry events and fundraisers, but she'd never felt quite so radiant, as though she could look down and find her skin sparkling.

Because despite the words they'd thrown at each other that morning, nothing could erase the beauty of the night she and Ian had shared. Every moment they'd been together—kissing in his office, making love in his bed, seducing each other in his bathtub—Ian had made her feel radiantly beautiful.

As a little girl Tatiana had been cute. As a teenager, cute had shifted to pretty. But now that Ian had made her his, she finally felt like a woman, inside and out.

* * *

Ian looked up from his conversation at the sudden commotion. All the invited members of the press were leaving the main ballroom at the same time to head out to the entrance hall. Instantly, he knew why they were all so excited. So thrilled.

Because it was exactly the way he'd always felt whenever Tatiana was near.

She was standing in the entry in front of the foundation's banner, already surrounded by photographers. Between the circus her life had to have become the day after her Oscar nomination and the way things had been left between them that morning, he'd been absolutely certain she wouldn't show. Any other woman would have stayed away, would have nursed her fury at him, or at least celebrated her own success by letting the world fawn over her.

But not only had Tatiana kept her word by coming to the fundraiser...she looked positively incredible. Through the excited crowd he could catch only flashes of her beautiful face, her long, red-blond hair curling softly over one shoulder, but it was enough to see that she was glowing. Sensual. Sparkling.

No one would ever guess that just hours before, she'd cried as she walked home in the rain. She'd tried to hide her tears, but he'd seen them, and knowing he was the reason for them only made him more convinced that he needed to stay away from her.

He'd already hurt one woman by thinking he was capable of giving her the love she needed, only to neglect her when he just didn't have it in him to be a true husband or partner. Ian would never forgive himself if he did anything more to damage Tatiana's bright, positive outlook on life and love. She not only deserved love, but she also deserved to find it with a guy who would devote everything he was to her.

After a long while, when it was clear that the photographers would never feel that they had enough pictures of her, Joyce carefully escorted Tatiana away from the group.

That was when Ian finally saw what she was wearing.

Almost nothing.

Her dress was barely more than a shiny scrap of gold fabric. Thin straps hung from her shoulders as if by a thread above a bodice that dipped way too low and clung much too tightly to her luscious breasts. A slim belt wrapped around her waist, and the shimmering fabric highlighted her hourglass figure as it hugged her hips. And her legs...

Lord, how was he ever going to forget what it felt like to have her perfect legs wrapped around him as she urged him to take her harder, faster? As she'd begged for *more.*

He'd seen pictures of her in the past with his cousin at their film premiere and had been in Napa with her at the family wedding months earlier. But he'd never seen her wear something so revealing, so purely sensual.

Last night, especially once he'd realized the harsh way he'd taken her virginity, he'd wanted to make it up to her by showing her the kind of deep pleasure her body was capable of. Of course, he'd desperately wanted to know her pleasures for himself, too.

Tonight, she was embracing her sensuality in a way she never had before. And if he saw it, Ian knew everyone else must see it, too.

She was still elegant, still sweet...but overlying both was pure sex.

He'd believed—or hoped, at least—that as soon as they'd had a few hours to cool off away from each other, he'd be able to think things through in the same calculated manner he would an investment gone wrong. That way, he could make the necessary corrections to set everything straight again and minimize loss and suffering for everyone involved.

Only, despite the fact that he hadn't seen her since that morning, and that his day in the office had been one of the busiest he could remember, Tatiana hadn't been out of his thoughts for one single second.

All day long, he'd thought about the way she'd trusted him with both her heart and body. He'd replayed, again and again, the way she'd laughed in the bathtub with him. He'd remembered how perfectly she'd fit against him as she'd fallen asleep in his arms. And his gut had twisted every time he'd remembered the way her face had fallen when he'd hurt her in the morning.

He'd sworn up and down that he wouldn't do anything to hurt her more. He'd vowed to remain rational no matter what. And, he'd promised himself he wouldn't give in to the desperate urge to kiss her, to make love with her, ever again...even if it damn near killed him.

But that had been before she decided to show up at the fundraiser wearing the sexiest excuse for a dress he'd ever seen. All his vows to remain rational, to focus on what he could do to make things up to her, vanished as she stood in front of hundreds of people with every single one of her lush curves on mouthwatering display. Surely, Joyce could find Tatiana a sweater, or some sort of cashmere wrap, to at least throw around her shoulders. It wouldn't help with the length of leg she was currently showing, but it would be better than the current situation, where every man between the ages of twenty and eighty was drooling over her cleavage.

Ian had never been a jealous man. Even with his ex-wife, who was indisputably beautiful, he'd never felt the need to hide her away from everyone else. But yet again, where

Tatiana was concerned, one look at her was all it took to scramble his brain.

And right now, all Ian could think was that he wanted to keep her all to himself.

But the crush of bodies was tight enough in her wake, and so many important donors stopped him to say hello, that by the time he finally got back inside the ballroom, instead of being able to find her to convince her to cover up, it was time to announce the silent auction that would provide the bulk of this year's funding for the important programs the foundation ran. A job that was too important, that impacted too many people, for him to screw up because he couldn't stop thinking about Tatiana.

At the microphone, he took a moment to look out over the crowd of people who had gathered in support of the organization and thank them for coming before launching into his speech.

"Ten years ago, the Seattle Family Foundation asked me if I would come and speak at one of their first fundraising events. When I wasn't able to accept due to a scheduling conflict, they asked me if I would come down to one of their classes and help out there, instead. I was so impressed with both the skills being taught by the excellent instructors and the students' thirst for knowledge that I hired three of them on the spot. Over the years, I've worked with a lot of outreach organizations, and I can tell you from personal experience that the Seattle Family Foundation is one of the very best. Tonight, I hope each and every one of you will think about the people you care about most, the loved ones that you would do anything to support, and do whatever you can to help them continue to provide families with the financial, educational, and career support right when they need it most."

As soon as he stepped off the stage, Ian was surrounded by potential donors with questions, as well as checks and verbal IOUs. Finally, the crowd thinned and Joyce handed him a glass of champagne.

"Thank you so much, Ian, for everything you've done to help us. It looks like we're going to have our highest operating budget so far to work with next year." She gestured toward the dance floor. "And thanks to Tatiana and the fact that the press has been going absolutely wild for her, I'm certain far more people will be hearing about us than ever have before. In addition to all the photos, she did a few interviews on our behalf, and was positively eloquent."

On autopilot, Ian made all the right responses to Joyce before she walked away to deal with the auctioneer. At least, he hoped he did. Because from the moment he looked out onto the dance floor and saw Tatiana in Quinn Patrick's arms, Ian hadn't been able to focus on anything other than tearing her out of them.

Quinn was suave, rich, and between wives. Even a blind man could see that the two of them looked great together. *This* was exactly the kind of guy Ian had known that Tatiana and her slinky, barely-there dress would attract. Some mogul who wouldn't care about her intelligence, her talent, her kindness. All he'd want Tatiana for was to be a stunning trophy who was hot in the sack.

Blood rushed in Ian's ears as he made a beeline for the center of the dance floor where the two of them were now holding court, cameras continuing to flash as they captured every seductive move Tatiana made in the other man's arms.

He had been working on loosening Quinn's pockets for the foundation for months. When Ian stole Tatiana away in the middle of their dance, Quinn would likely be furious enough that he wouldn't give one red cent of his fortune to the charity, but Ian didn't care. Not when the dirtbag was holding Tatiana too tightly and his hands were too close to the swell of her hips.

Ian would make up the difference himself—would double it—if it meant getting her out of the guy's arms.

CHAPTER NINETEEN

"Ian," Quinn said when Ian walked up to interrupt their dance, "you should have told me Tatiana was going to be here tonight so I could brush up on my dance moves."

"It was more fun to surprise him," she said softly.

When Quinn smiled down at her, there was more genuine warmth in his gaze than Ian could remember seeing before. Quinn turned back to him with a raised eyebrow. "She was telling me you two are practically cousins." Ian knew exactly what he was doing—trying to remind him that he should stay away from the beautiful woman who was nearly family.

Tatiana's skin was flushed, her eyes bright, when she finally turned her gaze to his. In an instant, Ian's brain rewound to the way she'd been just as flushed beneath him, and then over him, in those breathless moments in his bed. Standing in the middle of the dance floor, every muscle in his body clenched tight as he remembered how intense, how shockingly *right,* it had been to make love with her.

Barely nodding at the other man, he told her, "Valentina needs to speak with you."

Tatiana frowned. "Is she here?" She scanned the room. "I didn't think she and Smith were coming back from Ireland until Monday."

"No, she's not back yet. She needs to speak with you on the phone." When she looked down at the small purse dangling from her wrist, obviously wondering why she hadn't noticed her phone buzzing, he clarified, "She called my phone asking for you. I've got a quiet place I can take you to talk to her."

"I'm sorry, Quinn," she said to the other man, "but I need to make sure everything's okay with my sister."

"Of course," he agreed, though it was clear he hated to let her go. "It was positively delightful dancing with you, and please don't hesitate to take me up on my offer to bring you up the coast to that private beach I mentioned."

With a final smile for Quinn, she let Ian direct her through the crowd and into a small, empty kitchen off to the side of the ballroom.

Ian hadn't thought this through, he'd simply taken the first available opportunity to get her alone. Now, as he stood close to her again, close enough to smell her perfume, close enough to see the pulse beating at the side of her neck, close enough to see the little flecks of blue in her green eyes, he lost the thread of everything but how much he wanted her.

More now, he was stunned to realize, than ever before.

One night hadn't quenched his thirst for her. One night hadn't gotten her out of his system. On the contrary, the passionate hours they'd spent together had only made him increasingly desperate for more of her.

"Ian? Don't you need to give me your phone so that I can talk to my sister?"

Shit. He never lied. But he hadn't been able to think straight when he'd seen her dancing in Quinn's arms, so he'd simply said the first thing that popped into his head. "There isn't a phone call."

"There isn't?" She frowned again, looking up at him in confusion. "They why did you drag me off the dance floor?"

"Because I needed to ask you what the hell you were thinking, wearing that dress tonight!"

The room was so small it almost sounded like he was yelling at her. But the control by which he'd always lived his life was currently in such shreds—precisely the way her clothes had been last night when he'd torn them off of her in his office—that he couldn't moderate it.

The last thing he expected Tatiana to do in response was to give a little twirl. As the thin, sparkling gold fabric swirled around her knees, she said, "I was thinking that it's a pretty dress. Don't you like it?"

"It should be illegal." The urge to touch her was so strong it nearly broke him. "All a man can think of when he sees you in that dress is tearing it off you."

"Thank you," she said as if he'd just given her a great compliment. "But why do you care if other men see me in this dress?"

"Because you're—"

The word *mine* hung in the air between them, as potent as it had been when he'd said it to her the night before in bed, right before he'd claimed her.

Damn it, he was getting everything wrong with her again and again and again...when all he really wanted to do was figure out a way to make things right.

"I'm sorry about this morning," Ian said. "I handled everything badly." He shook his head and admitted, "And now I'm handling everything badly again. What I'm trying to say, what I need you to know, is that I didn't push you away because of anything you did wrong. Every bit of blame for the situation lies in my court." Not only for losing control and taking her to bed, but also for not being the kind of man who could give her the true love she deserved.

He couldn't read her expression as he fumbled through the apology. What was she thinking? And why wasn't she just saying it to him the way she always had before?

Of course, that was when his phone actually rang.

"I know that's the ring tone that means something's wrong. You should go take care of it. There are probably millions of dollars on the line right now."

She was letting him off the hook, just like that, and perhaps he should have been grateful. But he'd spent enough time with her these past three days to *know* this wasn't her. She should be getting up in his face and asking him *why* he was being an asshole. Hell, she should even be grabbing him and blowing his mind apart with a kiss to prove without a shadow of a doubt that they were meant to be together.

Anything but this.

Anything but giving up on him. On them. Even if he'd done everything he could this morning to push her into doing just that.

"The call can wait. I brought you in here to talk."

She looked as frustrated as he felt. "What do you want me to say, Ian? That I was really hurt this morning? That I felt like a fool? That I hated going from feeling as happy as I'd ever been one moment to sobbing my eyes out the next?"

"I swear to you, Tatiana, the last thing I ever wanted was to make you cry."

"I know that. It's one of the reasons I fell in love with you. Because you care so deeply, with everything you are, even when you're trying so hard not to." She shook her head. "All day long I've been trying to figure out what I feel, knowing it would be so much easier if I could stay angry with you. But then I watched you get up on that stage and say all those beautiful, heartfelt things. How am I supposed to stay mad at you? How am I supposed to fall out of love with you? And even if I could do either of those things, how could I ever forget how good making love with you is...or stop wanting to be with you again? I know you must have had lots of fun and meaningless one-night stands." There was desperation in her voice as she said, "Tell me how to do it, too. You must know how."

Ian reached for a lock of her hair, couldn't stop himself from touching her even when he knew he shouldn't. "You're right, I've always known how. But with you?" He moved even closer. "I don't have a clue."

* * *

Tatiana reeled from Ian's nearness, from the need she could see so clearly on his face...and from the fact that the most honest man she'd ever met had actually faked a phone call to steal her away from Quinn and get her alone.

She'd come to the fundraiser tonight planning to make him see he couldn't resist her, but now that it seemed to have worked, she couldn't play any more games with him.

Love would never be a game to her.

"I wore this dress to get back at you," she admitted in a soft voice.

"I know you did, sweetheart." The endearment slipped from his tongue as easily, as sweetly, as it had when they were making love. And just as it had last night, it warmed her all over. "You're beautiful in it. So damned beautiful."

"I wanted you to see everything you could no longer have." She'd thrown caution completely to the wind when she'd decided to make love with him last night, and though she knew a wiser, safer, more rational woman wouldn't make that same choice again now, how could she do anything else but say, "But you can, Ian. You can still have me if you want me."

"Of course I want you. But you want the fairy tale. You want Prince Charming to carry you off on his noble steed. You want romance and flowers and poetry. And it's not too much to ask for, Tatiana, not when it's everything you deserve."

"Then why can't it be you?"

"It just can't."

"If it's because of what happened with your ex-wife, haven't you and I spent enough time together already this week for you to know I'm nothing like her? I'm honest to a fault. I don't want your money. I don't need status. I don't want you for everything that you have. It's who you *are* that interests me, Ian." Maybe it was crazy to lay it all out for him now, especially after everything he'd said to her that morning, but she couldn't see how keeping it inside would be any better. "I know everyone makes mistakes, but I'm certain that being with you wasn't a mistake. I was waiting to have sex until I was in love, and even if not everyone does that, it was right for me. I waited this long for you and now that I've found you, I'm not giving up. And even if I have to keep waiting, I will."

"No," he said, the one word full of such inner conflict it tore at her heart. "You shouldn't wait for me. There are a million guys out there who would be a better fit for you."

"I can't imagine anyone fitting with me better than you."

As emotion and heady sensuality swirled around them both, Ian told her, "I would take you to bed again tonight, tomorrow, and the night after that, if I thought sex was enough for you. But we both know it isn't. And I can't hurt you any more than I already have."

She could feel, could see, his frustration, and wanted so badly to soothe it, even though she knew she was the cause of it. But how could she when she still didn't understand why he was so adamant about pushing her away? "How do you think you're going to hurt me, Ian?"

"Being with me—it will change you."

"Of course it will. The first time I met you in Napa, everything already started changing. And now that I know you better, now that we've finally made love—"

"I'm not talking about good changes, Tatiana. You were with me all week. You know how many hours I work. You need, you deserve, someone who will be there for you. Someone who won't think twice about putting you first, now and always."

She could have reminded him that he'd left his staff meeting to track her down on Wednesday morning, but because she was certain he'd brush that piece of evidence away, she simply said, "When I'm filming, I work crazy hours, too. I understand what your life is like, that our schedules will take a lot of work to figure out. But I'm okay with that."

"You might think that now, but you'd end up hating me. This warmth you feel for me would grow colder and colder until all that's left is ice between us."

Pieces of everything she'd seen Ian do during the past week, everything she'd heard him say about love, all swirled together into the answer. "Is that what you think happened with your ex?"

Thankfully, this time, he didn't put her off, didn't keep her out. "Yes."

"She was warm once?" She shook her head. "I can't see it."

"Not like you. No one is as warm, as open, as you. But she wasn't what she is now, either. I made her that. I turned her into what she is now."

"You're a very powerful man, Ian. And you might be able to control companies and industries through your will and determination and brilliance. But even you can't *make* someone become a total bitch. You can't turn someone with true warmth inside of her into a glittering, self-absorbed block of ice. I get that maybe Chelsea was a softer version of herself when you first met and started dating, but I can guarantee that cold, hard part of her was already there, just waiting to spring out."

"I would have seen it."

"Or maybe you didn't want to see it. Maybe you were in a place in your life where you were ready to share it with someone and create a family the way your parents did with each other, so it was easier not to see it. Especially if she was trying her best to make sure you didn't."

Tatiana could see him turning her suggestions around in his head, and maybe if he were anyone else, she would have kept pushing, kept trying to make him see things her way.

But Ian Sullivan wasn't a man anyone would ever be able to push around. And because it was yet another one of the reasons she loved him so much, she simply said, "Having seen you in action all week long, I know not only how hard it is to change your mind, but also that I'm not going to do it tonight. So since I don't want to begin *and* end today fighting with you, I'm going to say good-night now." Before he could stop her, she went up on her toes and kissed him. One soft, sweet, gentle kiss into which she poured her entire heart. "I'll see you on Monday at your office."

And then she made herself walk away.

CHAPTER TWENTY

Ian was sitting in his home office staring blindly at his computer screen early Saturday morning when his phone rang. His first thought, before he could stop it, was *Tatiana.* But it was his brother Dylan's name that popped up on the screen.

"Hey, looks like a good day for a sail. I could use a crew."

Ian had lost countless productive hours this week. He needed time to focus on the eAirBox deal he'd put two years of work into. When Flynn accepted his offer on Tuesday, Ian needed to be ready to move forward immediately.

But he couldn't concentrate on anything but Tatiana. He'd known plenty of beautiful women, had even married one, but he'd never had such a hard time keeping his hands—and worse, his thoughts—off one.

Tatiana wanted love, wanted the happily-ever-after, wanted someone she could count on through thick and thin. And in his weakest moments, Ian wanted to be all those things for her. But even caught up in her spell, he knew better, knew he'd only hurt her worse if he were stupid enough to think love could change who he was at his core.

Work had always set him straight, and at this point, Ian could have worked for the next forty-eight hours and only barely caught up to where he needed to be. But there was no way he was going to get one damned thing done sitting here, rolling everything over and over in his head, like a teenager caught up in his first crush. What had happened between him and Tatiana was way past a crush, a million times bigger than a no-strings night of hot sex. She thought she loved him, believed it with a faith so fierce that, frankly, it awed him. And scared the shit out of him, too.

So instead of blowing off his brother's invitation, Ian slammed the screen shut on his laptop.

"I'll meet you at the harbor in fifteen."

* * *

The speed, the cold air, and the water spraying over him helped to clear his head. Ian and his brother didn't say much to each other during the sail, but they didn't need to. Not when they knew each other so well that they were, as always, a perfect team out on the Sound.

It had been way too long since he'd done this—not just the sail, but hanging out with one of his brothers. Sure, he'd seen them at the recent Sullivan weddings he'd flown in from London to attend, but there hadn't been time to really talk to any of them.

Suddenly, he couldn't lie to himself any longer by trying to claim it was because his schedule was out of his control. Sullivan Investments was his company, and as Tatiana had pointed out earlier that week, he'd built it up to the point where he had plenty of trusted people working for him to whom he could pass more responsibility.

So it wasn't that he didn't have time if he wanted it.

He simply hadn't made the time for his family. And now, for the first time, he forced himself to ask why.

At first, his single-minded focus on business had been all about saving his family so they wouldn't lose their house, and so that his brothers and sisters would have enough money to go to college and follow their dreams. But then, by the time his family had been taken care of, he'd been wholly caught up in the game, the thrill of winning, and of always reaching for more. Not because he'd been turned into someone else. It was more that he'd uncovered, or discovered who he really was. He'd never meant it to come at the expense of everything else.

Or had he? After all, wasn't it easier to keep them all out then it would have been to let them in? Especially when all of this emotional turmoil with Tatiana was the perfect example of what happened when he let anyone get too close?

A couple of hours later, they were back in the harbor taking down the mainsail, when Dylan said, "So, how was your week with Tatiana?"

The halyard slipped in Ian's hands. "Fine." He cursed as he barely kept the rope from getting away from him. "I don't know if I've been much help to her, though. She still seems frustrated by her role." And, definitely, by him.

Dylan gave him a look that Ian couldn't quite read. His youngest brother had always been so quick to grin, and to make a joke, that people often missed the depth that was just as much a part of him. Ian had always known it was there, though, even when Dylan was a little kid.

"I'm sure she's working on it, and that she'll figure it out," Dylan said. "She's never struck me as the kind of person who gives up easily."

Thinking that Dylan had no idea just how right he was, it was the affection in his brother's voice as he spoke of Tatiana that caught Ian's ear.

"Why haven't you asked her out?"

Dylan's eyebrows shot up. "Tatiana?"

"Yes, Tatiana. What are you waiting for?"

"Dating her would be like dating my sister. Don't get me wrong, she's gorgeous and fun, and it'd be great if things were different. But that's just not what's between us. Never has been. Besides—" Dylan paused, grinned. "—she only has eyes for you. So I think a better question is, why haven't *you* asked her out? Or," he said as his gaze sharpened, "have you?"

"I haven't." And it was true. Ian had made love to her all night long and then broken her heart the next morning...all without ever asking her out.

"Why not? And don't bother repeating my she's-like-a-sister line. Because there were some major sparks shooting off between you two at dinner on Friday night. So hot they practically melted the chocolates."

Ian worked to keep his hands steady on the boom as he said, "I'm not looking for anything serious. She is."

"Look," Dylan said, "I'm not looking for anything serious right now, either, so I get where you're coming from. But I've got to tell you that if a girl like Tatiana came along who I connected with, who I couldn't stop thinking about, who was clearly one in a million, I'm pretty sure I wouldn't stop at anything to make her mine. And I'd make sure I did whatever I needed to do to keep her happy."

"Of course I want her to be happy." Ian knew he was losing his cool now, but damn it, the last thing he needed was his little brother lecturing him about love. "I've never met anyone with her inner strength before. When she believes something is true, is real, she'll go down with the ship, never wavering for one second, no matter how dangerous the waters might be."

"Then why aren't you making a move?"

"Because more than anything else, Tatiana believes in true love. She wants it, deserves it, and I hope like hell that she gets it one day. But I can't give it to her. She thinks I can, but I can't."

"Wait a minute." His brother pinned him with a serious look. "Something happened, didn't it? Between the two of you this week."

"I screwed up. Big time."

Ian cursed as he ran his hands through his hair. He'd already shared more with Tatiana than he'd shared with anyone else—not just the inner workings of his company and day-to-day schedule, but particularly about his ex-wife. And he knew why he had.

Because he already felt a hundred times more for Tatiana than he ever had for anyone else.

But she had her whole life, and the whole world, in front of her. She could have and be anything she wanted, and he simply couldn't believe that a cynical, brooding workaholic like him was right for her.

"I can't screw up with her again. I can't hurt her again."

"Then don't," Dylan told him. "But don't lie to yourself, either, and think that you'll be able to stay away if you keep seeing her every day in your office."

Ian had always been decisive, had never wavered over the right path to take. Even when he'd left football behind to go into business, he'd never second guessed, never hesitated, never wondered "what if?" But while it was true that he didn't want to hurt her more than he already had, at the same time, Ian knew that he couldn't keep lying to himself and say he was only staying away for her benefit.

In college when his family had been hurting, he'd found out what it was like to be vulnerable, to come face-to-face with the cold fear of how quickly everything you'd ever taken for granted could be lost. He'd vowed never to let himself, or any of the people he loved, be vulnerable like that again. Work, money, success—those were the things that Ian could always count on to save his family. And himself. But somehow, Tatiana had begun to get behind his shields...

All week long he'd known that being close to her every day was a bad idea. But at the same time, he'd wanted to be close to her too much to put a stop to it. Now, thanks to this conversation with his brother, Ian knew exactly what he needed to do.

Even if it killed him.

CHAPTER TWENTY-ONE

"Thanks for meeting me on a Saturday, Tatiana." Ben Mitchell hugged her hello. "Now that they've decided to move up the first day of filming to Thursday, everyone is scrambling." He squeezed her extra hard before adding, "And *huge* congratulations on your nomination! You're going to win, I just know it."

Ben was one of the best costume designers in the business and Tatiana had been lucky enough to work with him twice before. When he'd called to ask if they could do a last-minute fitting, she'd been happy to pop by the Seattle set, which was already partly transformed for them to begin filming.

Laughing, she reminded her very fashionable friend, "You do realize four of the biggest and best actresses in the business were also nominated, don't you?"

But Ben didn't reply because his eyes had narrowed in on her. "You look different. Your skin has a different glow to it. And," he added with a little sound of disapproval, "you're thinner. You're not tanning and dieting because you're feeling pressure from the nomination, are you?"

Tatiana could already feel herself blushing as she shook her head.

"Ah, I see what's going on now," Ben said, his lips curving up into a slightly wicked smile. "Is the lucky guy anyone I know?"

"No. He's not in the business." Or, rather, only very peripherally, since Ian had invested in a couple of Smith's films.

Ben waited for her to say more, and she wished she could shout Ian's name from the rooftops and claim him as hers, but she couldn't. Not until he changed his mind about being with her.

The fact that he hadn't been able to resist her last night had to be good, didn't it? And the blue sky she'd awakened to this morning must also be an omen that things were going to change for the better, right?

All the overthinking she'd been doing since she'd left Ian at the fundraiser last night had a sigh escaping before she could hold it in. Thankfully, though Ben clearly noticed both her sigh and the fact that she was purposely not telling him who the guy was, he was kind enough to let it be.

He handed her a fitted blue suit and when she put it on, he frowned again. "Don't you dare lose any more weight. Tell that secret loverboy of yours he should be feeding you chocolate-covered strawberries round the clock."

She laughed, then, utterly unable to imagine Ian ever doing something like that. He'd told her last night that wooing and romantic gestures were what she deserved, but didn't he realize that she wouldn't want him to be like other men who went straight to ticking through the list of standard romance tropes?

A couple of hours later, she'd tried on nearly two dozen outfits so that Ben could perfect the fit and take pictures of her in each of them for the director. Instead of taking a cab home, she decided to walk back along the waterfront. Fortunately, everyone was too busy flying kites and playing tag with their kids and smooching on blankets laid out across the grass to pay any attention to the familiar-looking woman with the dark hat and glasses.

But even though it was really nice to be outside enjoying the sunshine for once, her stomach was clenched tight. Her role was still bothering her, especially now that production had been shifted up by a handful of days to Thursday of the coming week. But mostly, she was worried about Ian's reaction to what she'd said to him last night. Particularly since she hadn't been able to let the subject of his ex-wife go, and it wasn't exactly his favorite subject.

Just then, her phone buzzed in the pocket of her jeans. Hoping it wasn't Ben texting to ask her to come back to the set because he'd just found another rack of clothes she needed to try on, she nearly dropped it when she saw Ian's name on the screen.

Had he thought about everything she'd said last night and realized he wanted to be with her, after all?

Her heart was leaping in her chest as she stopped in the middle of the busy sidewalk to punch in her security code so that she could see his full message. Strangers bumped into her from all sides, but as she read his text once, twice, then a third time, she simply couldn't figure out how to make her legs move.

LAST MINUTE BUSINESS TRIP TO ALASKA MONDAY. WILL SEND YOU LIST OF OTHER CEOS TO SHADOW.

Her throat felt tight and her chest ached right beneath the breastbone. Less than forty-eight hours ago, he'd made her feel so wanted, so needed, so precious to him with every kiss and caress. And last night, she'd thought there was a chance that she might actually be getting through to him.

But now he'd made it perfectly clear that he didn't want her around at all anymore.

She was tempted to give in to the urge to throw her phone down on the pavement, purely for the satisfaction of hearing it hit and watching it shatter. But before she could do something so impulsive, her phone jumped in her hand, ringing with her sister's special ring tone.

Yesterday she'd felt too confused to talk, but though her thoughts about Ian were only *more* jumbled up now, Tatiana needed her sister more than ever. Finally moving off the sidewalk, she headed across the grass of the waterfront park to find a more private spot.

"Hey, Val." Tatiana's voice sounded really weird to her own ears, but she couldn't quite figure out how to modulate it back to normal. Not when she was still spinning from Ian's terse farewell text. "How's Ireland?"

"Amazing. Although Smith has been overrun with media requests since the nominations came in for *Gravity,* just like you must be. And when we dropped by a local pub to see if they'd have any interest in letting us film a few key scenes there, I swear the whole town must have turned up to dance and sing and celebrate with us. That's why I wasn't able to get ahold of you yesterday to congratulate you on your amazing achievement."

Sitting down on an empty bench and listening to her sister talk had, thankfully, helped Tatiana get a little bit of a grip by the time she had to speak again. "Honestly, it all feels kind of surreal."

"Promise me you'll let me know if you need anything, T. Anything at all." After Tatiana made a sound of assent, Valentina said, "I've been dying to know, how did your week with Ian go? Has it helped you with your new role? I kept hoping to catch you earlier in the week to ask, but the time difference as we've jumped through Ireland and Scotland always meant it was two in the morning whenever I got a chance to call you."

Oh, she wanted so badly to confide in her sister. But what would she say? *"Ian and I slept together. It was amazing. Magical. Because I love him. But even though he obviously wants me and can't keep his hands off me, he won't let himself love me back. And now I don't know what to do."*

Just hearing the words play out in her own head, Tatiana knew with perfect certainty that there were a good dozen ways Valentina would freak out from across the Atlantic if she actually said them aloud.

"Shadowing him has been great. And exhausting. I've never seen anyone work as hard as he does."

"I remember thinking that about Smith when you were filming *Gravity.*"

"Val, can I ask you a question?"

"Of course, T. You can ask me anything, you know that."

"When you and Smith were just starting to date, you felt unsure about things for a while, didn't you?"

"Only constantly." But she could already hear her sister's brain going into overdrive from her simple question, so she wasn't surprised when Valentina asked, "Are you dating someone? I know I've been really busy lately, but I'm always here for you, T. All you have to do is let me know you need me and I'll be there. Anywhere you need me."

The tears that had threatened when she read Ian's terse and emotionless text nearly came spilling out at the love in her sister's voice. Which made her doubly glad that saying, "No, I'm not dating anyone," didn't constitute lying to the one person who had always been there for her. "But, Val, if you were so unsure, then how did Smith convince you to be with him?"

Valentina was silent for a few moments, obviously thinking through her answer before she gave it. "There were lots of little, sweet things he did along the way. Remember when he gave me that framed picture of us?"

"It's still one of my favorites," Tatiana agreed. "So that's what did it? Knowing he was thinking of you and what would make you happy?"

"Honestly, while those little things he did were all lovely and sweet and made me realize he cared for me, they weren't enough to make me believe love could conquer all. I was still scared. Still worried about the past and the future and every moment in between."

Tatiana could understand why her sister had been so afraid to fall for Smith. The spotlight constantly shone on him because he was one of the biggest movie stars in the world, and her sister had always been much happier hidden in the shadows on the side of the stage. Plus, after their father had died and Valentina had pretty much taken over raising Tatiana, the way their mother had dated one wrong man after another had been really hard on her sister...and had made Valentina question everything about love. At the same time, she'd always protected Tatiana so that she never had to doubt that love was real.

"I still don't understand how he got you past those worries. What did he do to make them all go away?"

"He couldn't do that for me. I had to work through my fears myself in my own time, and if he had tried to push me to speed things up, I was stubborn enough that I would have only retreated further and put more walls up to block him out."

"So, you're saying he didn't push you to make a decision about the state of your relationship, but..." Tatiana paused to try to think of a subtle way to say the next part, but when she couldn't, she finally just blurted, "Weren't you guys having all kinds of wild and wicked sex the whole time you were working through things?"

"Given that you found us in the screening room that night on set," Valentina said with a slightly embarrassed laugh, "I think we both know the answer to that question is a big, fat yes."

"But why did you keep sleeping with Smith if you were unsure about sticking with him in the long run? Why didn't you make yourself stay away, or tell him to keep his distance, until you'd made up your mind one way or the other?" When her sister didn't answer right away, Tatiana belatedly realized she'd gone too far with her questions. Just like Ian always said she did. "I'm sorry. I know this is really personal stuff and I'm being way too nosy. You don't have to answer any more of my questions about your sex life with Smith, obviously."

"You can ask me anything, T. You know that. So don't apologize. It's just we've never really talked much about sex before, so I'm a little surprised." Her sister paused for a beat before saying, "The answer is that I couldn't stop myself from being with him. Smith is...well, you know how he is. Gorgeous. Sexy. Brilliant."

"And totally, completely in love with you."

"Yes, just as much as I finally admitted I loved him. And the truth is that part of that realization of how much I loved him came because I simply couldn't find a way to resist going to bed with him, even when I was certain that I needed to. At first, I tried to call what we were doing just sex, just a fling, a way to let off steam, but I think I always knew I was lying to myself. I never realized how closely connected the body and heart are until I met him."

Tatiana felt as though the light bulb went back on inside of her, then, burning more brightly now than it ever had before. That deep connection between her heart and her body was precisely why she'd never slept with anyone before Ian. Because she simply couldn't have given her body to a man who didn't also have her heart.

From the answers her sister had just given her, Tatiana now knew that while Smith had given Valentina space to accept her feelings for him, he'd also been smart enough to keep their physical connection burning hot and steady so that her sister couldn't shut herself off from him.

Tatiana had said it herself in the limo on the night of the gala—Ian wasn't a man who changed his mind easily. She hadn't planned to use sex to change his mind. But while she was giving him the space to come around to realizing he could risk loving her without hurting either of them, was it so wrong to hope that their intense attraction and sensual connection would help him see the light a little sooner?

"Tatiana?" Her name was mostly static. "My connection's just gotten bad. Are you still there?"

Before they were cut off, Tatiana quickly said, "Thank you, Val. For everything."

All her life, her big sister had protected her and guided her toward making good decisions.

Yet again, Valentina had helped her. More than she even knew.

Tatiana could now see that she'd been naïve to believe that she could heal Ian's past and show him that it was safe to love her in one short week. But while she wasn't naïve anymore...she wasn't giving up, either.

And now, thanks to this conversation with her sister, she knew exactly what she needed to do.

CHAPTER TWENTY-TWO

By Monday morning, the skies that had been so clear all weekend had turned a dark purple-gray. Just as dark as Ian's mood.

All weekend long, he had firmed his resolve to keep his distance from Tatiana. Again and again, when she crept into his mind, he pushed thoughts of her away. Discipline. Determination. Focus. Work. That was all he'd ever needed to get himself back on track, he reminded himself as his driver pulled up on the tarmac behind his private plane. Surely, if he just kept his eye on the ball, he'd eventually be able to forget her. Especially now that he wouldn't be seeing her every single day anymore. By the time they met again at a family dinner or party, he would have his head back on straight...and his life back on track with no emotional or romantic entanglements screwing with things.

And if he missed her, if the week already felt too empty, too dark, too *wrong* without her, well, that was just too damned bad, because—

What the hell?

He blinked hard to clear his vision, but when he looked again, Tatiana was still standing beside his plane chatting with his pilots, David and Linda. She had a medium-sized canvas bag slung over her shoulder and was wearing dark jeans, a blue and white striped sweater, and flat-heeled black boots that ended just below the knee.

Clearly, she was planning on making the trip to Alaska with him.

As soon as he stepped out of the town car, Tatiana turned to greet him. "Good morning, Ian."

She looked truly happy to see him, her expression as bright and sunny as ever. Just as happy as the sudden leap of his heart in his chest proved he was to see her.

He'd told her to go shadow someone else, but she hadn't listened. Talk about determination. He could learn something from her.

"Good morning, Tatiana."

Knowing he couldn't ask her what she was doing there in front of his pilots without embarrassing her, he turned to greet them, as well. They'd come with him to England years ago and then had followed him back to Seattle, but he hadn't seen them since their return to the States.

"Are you both settling back in to life in Seattle all right?"

"Everything's great," David said.

"Thanks again for the maternity hospital recommendation you got from your mother." Holding her husband's hand, Linda was radiant. "We just did the tour yesterday and it looks amazing."

"Oh, how lovely that you're pregnant!" Tatiana exclaimed. "When are you due?"

"In five months. We've been trying for a while, so we're very excited."

"Do you know yet if you're having a boy or a girl?"

David drew Linda closer as she said, "We want to be surprised."

"I would, too," Tatiana agreed. "I love surprises, and that would be one of the very best."

Knowing Linda had had some trouble with morning sickness in her first trimester, Ian asked, "Are you feeling back to your normal self yet?"

"Pretty much. Thanks for asking, Ian." With a look at her watch, she said, "David and I have a few final pre-flight preparations to take care of, and then we should be on our way to Alaska before the storm rolls in."

As soon as his pilots disappeared into the cockpit, Tatiana told him, "I know you sent me a list of other CEOs to shadow this week, but I'm not here to shadow you anymore." Before he could respond, she added, "And I'm not here to talk about Thursday or Friday night, either, I promise. You see, the character I'll be playing next week was born and bred in Alaska, and I was hoping you'd consider letting me catch a ride with you so that I can do my final bit of research for it. Getting a feel for where my character grew up will really help me."

In the week he'd spent with her, Tatiana had never shied away from confronting him. So then, why wasn't she bringing up their conversation from Friday night? And why wasn't she trying to pin him down, trying to get him to change his mind about being with her? She'd planned to give him some time to change his mind, but had *hers* been the feelings that ended up changing instead? Had she realized he was right when he'd told her that she was simply so overwhelmed by finally making love that she'd wrongly assumed that meant she was in love with him?

Or, was it simply that she knew him better than anyone else ever had...and understood that it was killing him to try to stay away when the very best moments of his life had been with her in his arms?

"I'm happy to give you a lift to Alaska if it will help you with your research." Hell, he was miles beyond happy about the chance to spend more time with her when he'd missed her more with every hour that had passed since she walked away from him Friday night.

When she was buckled into the seat across from him, he let David and Linda know that they were ready for takeoff. Just as the plane began to taxi down the runway, Tatiana pulled out her script and scowled at it.

Though he had planned to get some work done on the flight, instead of taking out his laptop, he asked her, "How's your work on your part going?"

Though her scowl deepened, it did nothing whatsoever to detract from her incredible beauty. "Not well. And I'm supposed to do a read-through of a couple of scenes with my male co-star on Thursday so that we can see where we are and feel each other out a bit." She shook her head as the plane lifted into the air. "I can already tell you how he's going to feel. He's going to beg the producer for a new leading lady."

She looked so upset that Ian didn't think twice before offering, "Would it help if I read through it with you now?"

Her eyes widened with surprise. "That would be amazing."

Ian had to move to the seat beside her so that they could share her script. Lord, he thought as he breathed in her scent, it was good to be close to her again. So damned good.

"I'm Rose, and you'll be reading the part of Aiden, the man who's..." She lifted her gaze to meet his. "He's in love with her."

Her eyes were so green and so beautiful that he nearly forgot that he couldn't kiss her.

"This is the scene where he finally tells her exactly how he feels, and she reacts badly." Tatiana's voice was a little breathless now as she told him, "Aiden leads off the scene when he barges into Rose's office."

"Rose."

"Aiden? What are you doing here? Didn't you get my message?"

"Did you think I'd just let you leave like that, with a note that said you were sorry, but you couldn't be with me anymore?"

"I'm already late to my next meeting. I can't do this now."

"What about after your meeting, Rose? Will you finally admit that what we have is rare and beautiful and that you love me? Or will I have to come back again tomorrow and the day after that for you to admit it?"

"I do love you! But that doesn't change anything. I can't be that girl I used to be, the one you fell in love with. Not now that I have to manage all this. Not when so many people are depending on me to make sure they don't lose everything if I screw this up. And not when, for the first time in my life I finally feel like I've found the place I'm supposed to be."

"Do you think I'd ever want any less for you? Do you think I can't see how well the suit, the office, even the pressure of it all, suits you? And do you think I'd ever ask you to give it all up for me? That I won't love you anymore because you're not the girl I first fell for?"

"You say that now, that you'll love me no matter what, but just because it's easy to say the words doesn't mean it will be anywhere near easy to actually pull it off. People make promises all the time, but they rarely keep them. And I can't risk everything here on a promise, on a hope that love will actually last. I just can't. So, please, I have a meeting now, and I need you to leave. And I won't change my mind after it. Not today or tomorrow."

After they read through a couple more pages, Tatiana laid the script down with a sigh on the table in front of them.

"It sounds good. Why are you so frustrated?"

"Good. Not great. I swear, I know the script backward and forward, but I can't get to the heart of Rose at all. If I can't root for her, then how is the audience going to be on her side?"

In the same way that Ian analyzed every angle of a potential investment for a business deal, he figured it couldn't hurt to try the same thing with this character she was so stuck on. "What's your biggest issue with Rose?"

"Who would choose money over love?"

"Someone who knows just how hard it is not to have money. Someone who knows just how unpredictable love is, that it isn't all roses and sunsets. Someone who can see the rhyme and reason to making money, but knows there isn't any whatsoever to love. Someone who's willing to believe in what she can count and add up, but who has only ever known chaos when it came to her heart."

"Okay, I can see that makes sense, but this hero, he's laying it all on the line. He wants to love her. And he's a good guy. A really good guy. I still don't see how I can play her so that it makes sense that she'd keep holding back."

"From the part we read, it sounds to me like she knows the damage love can do. And she also knows that the sacrifice and compromise needed to make it last are bigger than a quick flash of lust and the promises some guy is making to her."

"He's not promising her just a quick flash of lust, though. He's promising her all of him, everything, forever and ever. She's got to see that."

"No, I think all she can see is what she's learned from her own life, her own previous experience with people who made promises they never kept. And now it's going to take a hell of a lot more than some guy saying he loves her to make her take that risk again. Whereas if she keeps her focus on money and business and how hard and risky it is to take on such a big company with so little experience, she figures she can at least minimize that part of the risk in her life."

"She's already a billionaire, though, now that she's inherited the company. I get that she wants to prove herself, but I don't understand where the risk is."

"Even when you're at a point where money will never be an issue again, it's impossible to forget that helplessness. That's why I've set up trusts for my family that they don't know about, but that will kick in for each of them if they ever need it, just in case something goes wrong down the line. For any of them, for any reason, I need to know they'll be taken care of."

He didn't realize just how much he'd shared with her until he saw her expression, but just then, the plane dipped and pitched from side to side. Ian had never been a nervous flier, but though he wasn't too bothered by the turbulence, Tatiana had tightly crumpled the corner of the script in her hands.

Wanting to soothe her flight nerves, he told her, "I'm sure we've just hit a little rough patch and will be through it soon."

He watched as she deliberately loosened her grip on the pages. "After all the flying I've done the past few years, you'd think I'd be better at it." Turning away from the window as if by doing so she could forget that she was in a little tube shooting through the sky, she said, "Thank you for reading through this with me and talking it over. It helped a lot. More than anything else has so far, actually."

Just then, the plane did another couple of hard bounces, and her face went white before she plastered on a smile. "I had a really nice chat with my sister this weekend. It sounds like she and Smith are having fun scouting locations in Ireland. Evidently, they closed down the local pub."

Just hearing Valentina's and Smith's names had Ian's gut twisting with so much guilt that even though Tatiana had told him she wasn't going to bring anything that had happened on Thursday or Friday night up again—and he should have been glad for the reprieve—he had to know, "Have you told her about us?"

"I promised that what happens while I'm shadowing you stays between us."

Ian wasn't sure if it was the rough flight—or the difficult conversation they were having—that was the reason for the quick rise and fall of her chest as she answered his question. All he knew was that what she'd just said had pissed him off.

"Damn it, Tatiana, don't try to act like having sex with me is the same as sitting in on a business meeting. I might be an asshole, but even I wouldn't stoop so low that I'd ask you to sign an NDA before we slept together."

"You're not an asshole."

"I swore to you that I wasn't going to treat you badly. I promised myself I would stay away. I blew both of those promises, big time."

As if the tension between them was directly connected to the weather patterns, just then the plane banked sharply to one side, and then a few seconds later, to the other even more sharply. Tatiana screamed and every thought flew from his head but protecting her as he put his arms around her and pulled her close. She was ice-cold and trembling as he held her.

"Ian, Tatiana," David's voice came to them over the on-board speakers, "it looks like we're going to have to make an unexpected landing on Vancouver Island. Please make sure you're buckled in. We'll be safely on the ground soon."

When he looked down at Tatiana, her eyes had dilated with full-on panic.

"Tatiana, we're going to be fine." When it was clear that his words hadn't registered, he tucked his hand beneath her chin so that she had to focus on him. "David and Linda are the best in the business. I wouldn't trust anyone else more to get us down safely."

But when the plane hit more turbulence, Ian knew he needed to do something more to get her mind off the rough flight.

"When we were kids, our parents gave all of us really heavy-duty umbrellas. But we didn't really use them much, because it wasn't cool to be seen walking to school carrying one. Looking back, I don't know how we sat through class every day soaking wet, but I guess when you're a kid, stuff like that doesn't bother you much."

He could see that she was a little surprised by the way he'd just up and started talking about his childhood, and was glad that he'd managed to capture her attention, given the way the plane was wildly rocking back and forth.

"One day, I suppose my mother got sick of dealing with our soggy clothes and made us bring the umbrellas to school. The other kids snickered at us behind our backs, but Adam, Rafe, and I decided we'd make all of them wish they had brought their umbrellas to school, too."

"How'd you do that?"

He smiled at her, running the back of his hand down her cheek. "We holstered our umbrellas through our belts and climbed up the rain spouts to the roof of the school. Our mom was a big *Mary Poppins* fan, so we'd all seen the character fly through the air holding her umbrella plenty of times."

"You guys didn't actually jump off the roof, did you? Someone stopped you before you could, right?"

"Nope." He grinned at Tatiana's wide-eyed expression. "We were quicker than any of the adults. Besides, they already called us the Wild Sullivans, so I'm pretty sure they knew no threats or punishments were going to reform us. Odds are they were less surprised that we were planning to jump off the roof with our umbrella parachutes than they were that we hadn't thought of it sooner."

"So what happened?"

She had, it seemed, forgotten entirely about the lurching plane, and he'd never been so thankful for his childhood idiocy as he was now. If he'd played it straight when he was kid, he wouldn't have had this story to tell her now.

"Half the school was out on the blacktop waiting for us to make our move." He shook his head, laughing at the memory. "On the count of three, we opened our umbrellas, walked to the edge of the roof, and jumped."

She gasped. "Were you all okay?"

"Sure." He said the word easily, throwing in a shrug as he added, "Rafe knocked his arm up pretty good and Adam lost a tooth, but the real damage didn't come until the principal expelled us and Mom had to come pick us up."

"How mad was she?"

He grinned again. "Mad. But later, when I caught her holding the open umbrella on the driveway, looking up at the sky, I knew why we'd only been grounded for a month as opposed to forever." He could tell that they were getting close to making their landing, so he pressed a kiss to Tatiana's hands to make sure she didn't lose focus on him. "Part of the reason she loved watching *Mary Poppins* so much was because she always wished she could fly like that, too."

A moment later, they made as smooth a landing as he could have hoped for. Ian wrapped his arms around Tatiana and held her tightly against him, giving silent thanks that everything was okay. If anything had happened to her, he would have been destroyed. Completely destroyed.

And as the plane finally came to a shuddering—and safe—stop, she whispered, "Thank you for making me forget how scary this was."

CHAPTER TWENTY-THREE

Ian was still holding Tatiana when David and Linda came out of the cockpit. “Are you both okay?”

“We’re fine,” Ian told them as he continued to stroke Tatiana’s back. “And in one piece. Thanks to both of you.”

Despite how shaky Tatiana was, she immediately asked Linda, “Are you feeling all right?”

Linda looked confused for a moment before she realized what Tatiana was asking. Putting one hand over her stomach, Linda reassured her, “I’m perfect. Junior here is already quite the flier, just like his parents.”

“We can’t apologize enough for this,” David said. “We had an eye on the incoming storm, but never would have taken off if we’d thought it would blow in that fast. Or that hard.”

Ian had flown more than a million miles with his pilots, and he’d meant it when he told

Tatiana he trusted them. "You don't have anything to apologize for." But he needed to know something. "How long does it look like it will be until the storm clears?"

"Honestly, we're not completely sure at this point, but I'd plan on at least a day, maybe two. We'll do our best to stay on top of it and get you out as soon as it's safe. Fortunately, we were able to get a message out on the radio," David told them, "though we seem to be in a cell reception dead zone."

They were all surprised by the sound of someone yelling outside the plane. The door nearly blew off when David opened it to find a man in a dripping yellow slicker standing on the tarmac. David lowered the stairs, then wrestled the door closed once the man was inside.

"Thank God you all got down safely. Welcome to Port McHardy. I'm Tim. As soon as we got word on the radio that you were making the emergency landing, I headed here. You were on your way to Alaska?"

"We were," Ian confirmed, before introducing everyone and letting Tim know how much they appreciated his coming out to the plane so quickly. "Since we'll be here until the storm ends, if you could take us to a hotel, we'd greatly appreciate it."

"Be happy to. We don't have any hotels here, but my sister runs a B&B. It'll be a little tight in my car, especially with your bags and my pup, but I think we should all be able to cram in all right for the few miles through town."

David and Linda left to gather up their things, and Ian turned his attention back to Tatiana. "How about we get off this plane?"

The breath she inhaled shuddered in her chest, but she smiled at him. "Getting off this plane is one of the best ideas I've heard in a long time." He kept her hand in his as she stood up, making sure her legs were steady before he let her go to grab her canvas bag and his own.

"Pretty wet out there, eh?" Tim said, a massive understatement if ever there was one. "I'd offer you an umbrella if it would help, but it would just blow away in this wind."

By the time they'd all climbed into the car, they were soaked pretty much through. The front window fogged up on the inside and Tim wiped it away with his forearm as he headed away from the airport on a tiny country road.

A little black and white dog decided Tatiana's lap was the best place in the car to plop his wet rump down. Tim said, "That's Buster. He's still a puppy and learning his manners. I can take him up here if he's bothering you."

"No, he's perfect right where he is." And when Buster stood up on her lap, then put his paws on Ian's chest and began licking his face like he was a tasty dog treat, everyone laughed as Tatiana said, "Besides, it looks like he's found a new best friend."

The B&B was a small private home where Tim's sister and her husband rented out a couple of spare rooms in the summer to the few travelers who made it all the way up to the northernmost point of the island. Tim had barely brought them inside and explained their predicament, when his sister did a double take. "Oh my gosh, you're Tatiana Landon."

Tatiana smiled. "I'm really sorry that we're dripping all over your floors."

"My floors have seen worse than this when the steelhead are running. Oh, I so wish my girls were home from university to meet you. They'd be absolutely thrilled."

Her brother cut off her gushing to remind her why they were there. "This time of year, you've got both rooms open, don't you?"

"Didn't I tell you? Bryan and I decided to completely redo one of them." She was clearly distraught to have to tell them, "I'm so sorry, but I've only got one room open."

"David and Linda will stay here with you," Ian said. When they immediately protested, he shook his head. "You've both already been too flexible where I'm concerned, and after what you pulled off getting us down safely through that storm, I insist. Tatiana and I will figure out something else."

"I've got that space above my barn," Tim offered, obviously thinking they were a couple.

"My youngest uses it when he comes home from school."

"Oh no," his sister protested, "you couldn't put guests up there."

"A room above your barn sounds perfect," Tatiana said. She turned to look at Ian, and even with her wet hair plastered to her head, she was so beautiful she took his breath away. "Doesn't it?"

They all smelled like dog. His wool suit was destroyed. His entire schedule had just been thrown entirely out of whack. And they were going to be stranded on an island in a college kid's room above a barn for who knew how long?

But as Ian looked down at Tatiana's smiling face, he couldn't bring himself to worry about any of it. Not when he'd just been given the most unexpected and precious gift of his life—a few more hours with her.

"Yes," he agreed, unable to tear his eyes from hers. "It sounds absolutely perfect."

* * *

"It really is perfect!" Tatiana declared when Tim let them into the private space he had created for his college-age son.

Straight out of Tatiana's "one day I'll live in the country" dreams, the floors were pickled pine, and the pine bed frame on the far wall looked to be homemade, as did the kitchen cabinets in the small eating area. There was an old TV set and baskets of games and movies, along with a comfy-looking couch that evidently pulled out into another bed.

They'd stopped by Tim's home so that his super nice and pretty wife could load them up with some food to get them through to the next day. At Ian's urging—in the event that someone in town heard Tatiana was here after being on a plane that had made an emergency landing and posted the news on Twitter or Facebook—she'd used Tim's phone to leave a quick voice mail for her sister and agent, to let them both know she was fine. He'd also placed a couple of calls. One to Bethany so that she could make the necessary adjustments to his schedule and to let his executive staff know they should deal with anything urgent that came up—apart from Flynn, because he'd given the man his word that they would deal with each other directly. His second call was to the head of the company in Alaska he should have been meeting with right then to let him know what had happened.

Tatiana knew how important Ian's Tuesday afternoon meeting with Flynn was, and she hated the thought of anything going wrong with the acquisition when he had put so much time and energy into it. But when she'd told Ian she hoped the weather would clear up in time for him to get back for it, instead of agreeing with her, he'd given her a look she hadn't quite been able to read.

"If you need to use the phone in the house again," Tim said, "just drop by and go ahead. We always meant to put one in here, but never got around to it. The doors are always unlocked, so no need to wait for one of us to let you in."

"I can't think of the last time I haven't been near a phone or the Internet. What a gift that is," Tatiana said, smiling at the man who had been their knight in shining armor all afternoon. "Thank you so much for everything, including this chance to unplug for a little while."

"We really can't thank you enough for putting us up like this," Ian agreed. "If there's anything I can do for you in the future, just let me know."

"When I heard over the radio that your plane was having trouble, I was just praying you'd make it down in one piece. Had to have been pretty scary. We're all just happy to help."

But Ian was already handing him a damp business card. "This has all my contact information. I hope you'll let me do something really nice for you and your family one day soon."

"Well, thanks. And don't hesitate to come on in if you need anything. Two more for dinner would be no problem if you change your mind."

When he closed the door behind Tim, Tatiana told Ian, "It feels like we've landed in another world, another reality, doesn't it?" She looked out one of the barn windows. "Even outside we can't see more than a few feet in front of us. It's as if the storm has blocked out every—" The chatter of her teeth suddenly made it hard to finish the word. "Everything."

Ian lifted a hand to her cheek. "You're frozen solid."

Suddenly, she realized just how true that was, especially when he'd miraculously managed to stay so warm. "I'm sure I just need to get out of these clothes." But it was darn near impossible to get them off when she couldn't get her numb fingers to work right.

The next thing she knew, Ian had her in his strong arms and he was carrying her over to the bathroom. He turned the shower on, and when steam rose, he took them both under the spray, then put her back on her feet.

"I nearly got you killed in my plane. I won't let you get sick, too."

"You're the one who got me through the flight in one piece," she protested. "I would have lost it if you weren't there, telling me about all the fun you used to have with your brothers and Mia." The warmth of the shower was heaven sent, but Ian's warmth affected her even more. And though he was focused on taking care of her, the sensuality and attraction that had always sizzled between them was quickly rising up as he began to strip her icy clothes off. "It feels so good, being here with you."

His hands stilled as his inner conflict showed in both his expression.

Ian was constantly trying to take care of everyone. His family, with the trusts he'd set up for them. His pilots, both by asking after Linda's health and then by making sure they would be comfortable during their unexpected stay in town. Everyone involved with the Seattle Family Foundation.

And now her.

He thought he needed to pull away to "protect" her, and the truth was that she still didn't know how to convince him otherwise. All she knew was that being here with him now, in their own private world, wonderfully captive in a storm, felt like the best thing that had ever happened to her. Especially when she thought about the way he'd opened up to her on the plane when they were running through her script together.

He'd told her about the safety nets he'd put into place so that his family would never feel vulnerable or scared again, and she'd known with absolute certainty that Ian would do anything in his power to keep from feeling that way himself. That he'd push away anything—or anyone—that made him feel vulnerable.

Wishing that she could find a way to convince him that he was safe with her, she said, "For as long as we're here, for as long as the real world is beyond the storm, let's pretend this is all there is. Just you and me."

She was watching his face so carefully that she could see just how much her suggestion tempted him. Still, he tried to caution them both, a protector to his core. "The storm won't last forever."

"I know. But it's here now. And so are we."

She wanted desperately to kiss him. But she'd been the one who had made the first move on the night of her Oscar nomination, and had been the one to kiss him again on Friday night at the fundraiser.

This time, he had to be the one to decide.

His gaze was so dark, his expression so conflicted...before he uttered one low, heartfelt curse, then lowered his mouth to hers.

Ian's mouth was so warm, felt so good, tasted so delicious, that Tatiana could have kissed him like that forever if he hadn't needed to lift her sweater over her shoulders. She was yanking his shirt from his pants when he abruptly pulled back.

"Damn it, we can't do this."

"The real world doesn't count here, remember?" She couldn't keep the need, or the frustration, from her voice.

"I don't have any condoms. There's been no one but you since the wedding months ago, but—"

"I'm on the Pill." She had already finished stripping away his shirt as she told him, "I've been on it for years to deal with bad cramps."

He quickly ripped off the rest of her clothes and lifted her up so that her back was pressed flat against the tiles. His hands were everywhere at once—her breasts, her hips, then back up to thread through her hair so that he could take her mouth at exactly the right angle to drive them both to the brink of insanity.

"Every single second since Friday," he said as he found her wet and hot and ready for him, the words resounding raw and deep in the small tiled shower, "I've wanted you again. You're all I've been able to think about, Tatiana."

"It's been the same for me."

And, oh God, when he entered her skin-to-skin, even bigger, even harder than she remembered, it felt so good that she moaned and arched her back and neck, heedless of the hard tile behind her head until she knocked into it.

He cradled her head in his hands. "Sweetheart? Are you okay?"

"I'm perfect. Just please," she begged, barely noticing the slight throb in the back of her skull, "please don't stop. You feel so good inside me like this, with nothing between us."

The next thing she knew he was turning off the water and carrying her from the shower to the bed. She clung tightly to him, loving the way he moved inside of her as he took them across the room.

They dropped onto the covers in a wet tangle of limbs and their lovemaking was a perfect blur of desire and desperation as he stroked, aroused, *possessed* every last inch of her. She loved it, loved when he lost control, loved knowing she could do this to him when he was so utterly controlled in every other moment, even when it had looked like their plane might go down.

She knew she'd been all he'd thought of then, just as she knew she was all he thought of now. He was utterly focused on her pleasure, and her happiness, as he sent her tumbling heart-first into a climax that already felt so good she wasn't sure she'd survive it.

And when he stared into her eyes as he finally let himself go, too, she knew with perfect certainty that he'd truly never meant to hurt her. Because everything he'd ever done, even pushing her away, had been because he cared.

CHAPTER TWENTY-FOUR

"Can I ask you something?"

Ian's lungs still burned with the need for oxygen. The need to take Tatiana, to possess her and make her his, had become such an obsession that desire obliterated common sense every time he touched her. Hell, so much as looking at her or catching her scent in a room made him go a little crazier.

Now, in the aftermath of *crazy*, they were tangled in each other on the small bed, with the quilt bunched beneath their damp, naked bodies. He growled, "If you're going to ask me *why...*"

She laughed, her breasts bouncing against him as she said, "I'm pretty sure I already know *why* this time. Although—" She gave a little nip at his shoulder. "—I may ask you later, anyway, just to see you get all riled up. But only because I never quite know what you're going to do or how you're going to take me when you're like that." She made a little hum of pleasure. "A little rough. A little angry. A little fast. A little hard."

Even as a fresh hit of need nailed him, guilt rose. "Tatiana, I shouldn't—"

"I've told you again and again, you *should*. In fact, speaking of all the things the two of us should be doing together..." She purposely left him hanging there for a few seconds, not because she was an actress who knew how to play her audience, but because she was a beautiful woman with an innate sense of just how to make her lover crave her more with every second she spent in his arms. "I know I don't have the sexual experience you do—"

"Jesus, if you knew anything more we might never make it outside a bedroom ever again."

Did she have any idea how sensual her answering smile was? Clearly, she liked the idea of being locked in a bedroom with him forever. And because something told him her question would likely do more than just rile him up, he decided to do whatever he could to get her to forget all about it. But though she let him roll her beneath him for yet another heated kiss that he couldn't resist taking from her, when he made himself pull back for a moment to let her breathe, he could see that she hadn't forgotten what she wanted to say. His beautiful, brilliant girl never did.

His?

No, she wasn't really his, he reminded himself silently, and brutally. But even as he thought it, his hands tightened on her.

Only here, in this strange island world so completely separated from reality, could he let himself possess her.

Only for as long as the rain and wind drove the leaves from the trees outside, and the rough waves of salt water carved out chunks of the cliffs, could he reach for her and know that she was right there reaching for him, too.

Only for this rare moment in time when he was completely cut off from phones and computers could he devote himself entirely to the beautiful woman beside him.

The storm outside, he knew, would end too soon. But the storm inside of him would rage, crashing between desperate desire and the knowledge that what he had to offer could never be enough for Tatiana.

Ian came out of his swirling thoughts to find Tatiana's eyes, clear and sparkling, on his. How many of his thoughts had she read? Too many, he was sure. Enough that sometimes he might as well just speak every thought he had out loud.

"Go ahead, ask your question," he said, in a voice rough with desire—and affection for her that grew from moment to moment.

"Well, I was hoping while we're here and real life is on hold for a little while, maybe you could teach me..." This time she didn't draw out her words to tantalize. She did it because she was clearly embarrassed. Her skin was flushed as she finally said, "Things."

"Things?" The word came out strangled from his throat. "You want me to teach you *things?*"

"Yes." Such innocence, even as she made the sexiest request on the planet. "Sexy things." There was another pause, another moment of obvious bashfulness, before she lifted her bright eyes back to meet his. "Please."

It was the sweet and simple *please* that got him. That, and the fact that for all his legendary self-control, in this small room, on this island, in the throes of this storm, he was lost.

Completely, utterly lost in Tatiana. Even when he knew better than to drag either of them deeper...

She watched him, clearly confused as he got up off the bed and walked naked—and aroused—across the room to pick up one of the red-painted wooden chairs. Deliberately, he set the chair at the foot of the bed and sat down on it.

"Touch yourself."

He could see a thousand new questions pop up in her eyes, but she finally settled on only one. "Is this your way of saying yes?"

He didn't smile, though he wanted to. He didn't reassure her, either. She'd said just minutes earlier that it turned her on when he was a little rough. A little hard. Lord knew his erection was as hard as it had ever been from nothing more than looking at her sitting sweet and naked on the crumpled quilt.

"Touch. Yourself." Each word was spoken as a command, because for all her strength, for all her determination, it was obvious to him that she also loved giving herself up to his dominance in the bedroom. Not every time, perhaps, but definitely tonight.

While he taught her things.

Jesus, he thought as his erection pulsed hard between his thighs, he wanted to pounce on her, wanted to take her again and again until he'd figured out a way to burn through his fierce need for her. Instead, he forced himself to remain on the chair as she blushed and began to slowly slide her hand on top of her stomach.

She bit her lip, the flush now moving from her cheeks to spread over her breasts. "Do you want me to touch my breasts? Or...between my legs?"

He didn't stop his lips from curving into a smile this time. Of course, as an actress, she would ask him for direction. And he would give it to her. Only, it wouldn't be anywhere close to the kind of direction she was expecting.

"I want you touch yourself the way you have, alone in your bed, naked beneath the sheets, since the day you met me at the wedding." Her eyes grew even wider as he said, "I want you to show me if my own fantasies about you were right."

"You fantasized about me?"

"I thought you wanted me to teach you things," he replied in a deceptively gentle voice, "but from the way you keep stalling with more questions, maybe you aren't serious, after all."

That was all it took to persuade her to shift on the bed so that she was lying on her back with her legs falling open on the messy bed covers. From his perfect vantage point, he could see that she was still aroused from their earlier lovemaking, the smooth skin between her thighs plump and slick. Her hair was wet and tangling over her shoulders, where a few marks from his lips and teeth were starting to come into stark bruised relief against the pale skin. There was no order whatsoever to any part of the picture she painted before him...and yet, she was the most beautiful thing he'd ever set eyes on.

Order, he was beginning to believe whenever they were together, was vastly overrated.

She brought her hands up to her breasts and as she softly cupped them, her eyes fluttered closed. Looking as if she was going deeper into her imagination, into the fantasies she'd once created about the two of them, her hands squeezed, pinched, caressed her soft flesh and nipples that grew harder by the second. When a low moan fell from her lips, he decided it was time to push her a little farther.

"Very pretty," he said, wanting her to know how much he appreciated, and approved, of what she was doing before he shoved her all the way past comfort. "But I want more, Tatiana." Hell, he wanted so much from her that it was nearly ripping him to shreds.

"Tell me what you want, Ian. Tell me and I'll do it."

"I want you to tell me what I'm doing to you in your fantasies."

Her hands nearly slipped from her skin as a number of different emotions—surprise, lust, fear, along with determination to see this through—raced across her beautifully expressive face. But when only lust and determination remained, she held his gaze as she began to speak in an intoxicatingly sensual tone.

"After we met at the wedding and you shook my hand, I couldn't forget the way it felt. Your hand was so big, so warm, and rougher than I thought it would be for a businessman. I couldn't stop thinking, fantasizing, about what it would feel like if you were touching me somewhere else." She didn't so much as blink as she told him, "*Everywhere* else."

He swallowed hard as she moved her hands away from her breasts to slide over her neck, and then to her flushed face. "I wondered what it would feel like if you held me still so that you could kiss me exactly the way you wanted to. And how it would be if you fisted your hands in my hair—" She moved one hand from her cheek to her damp locks. "—so that I had to go wherever you decided to take me." Her hips shifted slowly up and down on the bed in a rhythm that told him just how ready she already was to take him again. "I wanted so badly for you to take me."

She was whispering now as she ran her hands back down over her neck, her collarbones, and then the upper slope of her breasts. And, oh, how he'd wanted it, too, wanted to take her every single second from that first handshake. Knowing that she'd been just as hungry, just as desperate for him, didn't just send him all the way to the edge, it nearly tipped him into the abyss. But if he moved, if he spoke, he knew she'd stop confessing her erotic fantasies to him, so he stayed exactly where he was, even as he watched her fingers move over her nipples, rougher on the second trip so that her flesh stood hard on the tips of her full breasts when she finally continued her journey down over her ribs.

"I knew that if—*when*—you took me, it would be good, better than anything I'd ever known." Her mouth curved up into a sexy smile as she brought one hand back up to her breasts and let the other move lower, then lower still, until her fingers hovered just above her sex. "I was right."

Her fingers had barely slicked over her clitoris when Ian could no longer hold back from touching her, too. On a deep groan of need, he got up from the chair, moved to the bed, and slid one finger, then two, into her. She lifted her hips into his hand, but when she began to slide her own fingers away, he said, "No, I want you to keep touching yourself."

"But you're—"

"Needing to be closer to you."

The words that should have come out simply as sexy, ended up being about so much more. Because as much as he wished he could hide from her just how deeply and strongly she affected him, in moments like this when she gave herself entirely up to him, he couldn't find a way not to give her at least part of himself, too.

"I need it, too," she said, and then just as he'd told her, she continued sliding her fingers over herself in a circular pattern that matched perfectly the deliberately slow pace he'd set between her thighs. She watched through heavy-lidded eyes the way their hands worked in unison over and into her, to bring her higher and higher with every stroke, with every swirl.

"Did you ever dream of this? Of both of us touching you this way?"

"No." The short word was little more than a gasp as he pushed just a little deeper, a little harder. "In my fantasies it was always just you touching me. Never both of us." She shook her head, admitted, "I didn't know we could do this together."

"So much," he said in a low voice, "there's so much we can do together. Like this." He took one of her nipples into his mouth. And as he suckled it, both of their hands naturally picked up the pace between her legs.

Now that he knew just how sweet, how soft, how hungry she was, every time he had her only made him wild with craving more of her. "I want all of your orgasms to be mine." He'd already taken too much from her, but he couldn't control the urge to want more.

"They are yours. Only yours, Ian."

He loved the way his name fell from her lips again and again, growing more and more ragged as they both took her closer to her climax. On a light scrape of his teeth over the tip of her breast, he growled, "Come for me. Only for me, sweetheart."

A sob tore from her throat as she went completely taut at his command, then broke apart, inch by gorgeous inch, beneath his mouth and hand and her own, as well. Nothing in the world but Tatiana would ever be this beautiful, this precious.

Between Thursday night and today, she'd come apart again and again for him. But his utter lack of control meant that he needed to see more, needed to feel more, needed to take her up even higher, needed to be right there as she experienced greater and greater pleasure, until he was absolutely certain that she had nothing left to give to him. And maybe then, he told himself, he would finally be able to sate his desperate need for her.

He wouldn't let her recover, not wanting to let her catch her breath or think or do anything but feel. She was still trembling as he moved to kneel on the rug beside the bed. Putting her legs over his shoulders, he found her core to be deliciously hot and wet against his lips and tongue. With his fingers still moving hard, fast, and deep into her, he nudged her own hand away from her sex.

This time, there was no slow buildup to her climax, no need to coax—or demand—that she come apart for him. And as one orgasm spiraled into another, though she'd already given him so much more than he deserved, when he moved again to his feet and gripped her hips in his hands to pull her to the edge of the mattress, he couldn't catch his own breath.

All he could do was feel.

A heartbeat later he was completely inside her and he couldn't look away from her beautiful eyes, so green and so full of love for him.

She'd done exactly what he told her to do from the moment he'd pulled the chair up to the foot of the bed, but now she surprised him by reaching up to wind her hands around his neck and kiss him so sweetly that before he knew what had happened, she'd rolled them over so that he was flat on his back and she was on top.

They'd moved straight from lesson one to lesson two, but this time he wasn't the teacher.

She was.

And, Lord, the things she taught him as she kissed him hungrily while rubbing her breasts over his chest and grinding her hips into his.

He'd never known desire could be this sharp, this sweet, this overwhelming.

He'd never known a woman could be this soft and this strong, this innocent and yet so beautifully sensual all at the same time.

And he'd never known, until they drove each other higher before reaching the pinnacle of the storm together, just how high it was possible for a man to reach...or how far it was possible for a man to fall.

CHAPTER TWENTY-FIVE

Ian couldn't remember the last time he'd awakened with a woman in his arms and wanted to keep her there. Even when he'd been married, he'd gotten out of bed as soon as his eyes were open to work. And with the women he'd had casual flings with, both before and after his marriage, he'd never been tempted to stay overnight or to have them at his place.

But with Tatiana breathing softly and steadily in his arms, her chest rising and falling against his, with her hair tickling his chin and her warm curves pressing against him as he lay with her spooned against him, he now knew exactly what he'd miss if he got up to go use Tim's house phone to check in at the office.

So damned much.

Loving the feeling of waking up with Tatiana in his arms was just one more thing that set her apart from every other woman he'd been with. Lord knew making love with her was on a whole different plane, as well. It would, he thought, be easiest to chalk it all up to their break from real life, but even back in Seattle when they'd been going from meeting to meeting, he'd been attuned to her in a way he'd never been with anyone else.

Ian had never known a woman's body so well. Before they'd landed on the island, before they'd been caught in this storm, he would have tried to tell himself that it was because they were discovering her pleasure together, kiss by kiss, caress by caress, climax by climax. But by now, there was no point trying to convince himself to believe such a blatant lie...not when he knew that what had grown between them was so much more than just pleasure.

Ian had never *wanted* to understand a woman's reactions this much. He'd never been so compelled to give a woman pleasure. He'd never worked so hard for a gasp, for a moan, for a smile. And yet, what stood out most for him wasn't their phenomenal lovemaking, but the way she reacted when she'd walked into their room above the barn: Like it was heaven.

The other women he'd been with, and especially his ex, had not only expected five-star luxury, they'd demanded it. Since he was rich enough to give it to them, he always had.

Tatiana, on the other hand, was totally undemanding when it came to anything materialistic. It would be so much easier if she were, if she would ask him for something, anything, other than the one thing it would be impossible for him to give her.

The night before, after making a simple spaghetti dinner, when Tatiana hadn't been able to stop yawning, he'd tucked her into bed. By the time he was done pulling their damp clothes out of the shower and laying them over various pieces of furniture to dry out, she was asleep.

This morning, with the rain still battering the barn, and the sky outside the window still a dark gray, he didn't need to check with his pilots to know that they weren't going anywhere today.

Ian knew he should have been worrying about missing his meeting with Flynn. But when every stolen hour he spent with Tatiana was more precious than the last, all he could think was, *What the hell am I going to do when the storm finally ends?*

How was he ever going to let her go?

He was holding her so close that he felt her come awake from moment to moment, her heart rate just starting to pick up its pace, her breath coming a little faster, her limbs stretching out one at a time, her toes curling against the top of his foot.

"It wasn't a dream, was it?" She slowly turned in his arms, putting hers around his neck. "Good morning."

He had to kiss her once, soft and sweet, to tell her without words that it was the best morning of his entire life. "Good morning."

"Mmm, you've never had a beard when you were kissing me before." She rubbed her cheek against his. "It's so rough, so rugged." She nuzzled against him. "I like it. Kiss me some more, Ian."

Lord, how he loved the way she talked to him—she never weighed her words or spent so much as one second calculating her gain or his response the way other women did.

He kissed her good and long to please both of them, then showed her how good it felt when his morning beard scratched over the sensitive skin on her neck, her breasts, her stomach, and the patch of slick, heated flesh between her legs. He took her up once with his mouth, and then again with both his fingers and tongue when he couldn't get enough of her taste.

She was drowsy liquid heat beneath him by the time he kissed his way back up her luscious curves, and he couldn't wait to feel her surrounding him, couldn't think about anything but being inside her again, when she whispered, "I want to touch you, too."

When she reached down to cup him in her hand, he nearly lost it right then and there as she stroked him.

"You're so hot, and so hard." There was wonder in her voice, along with infinite curiosity as she said, "I was dreaming last night of holding you like this. And tasting you." When he pulsed again in her hand, she made a hungry little sound. "I want so badly to make you feel as good as you just made me."

When she slid down his body to kiss her way down his torso, it was as close to an out-of-body experience as he'd ever had, the first tentative swipe of her tongue over his erection nearly enough to hurtle him over the edge. So when she went all the way from base to tip the second time, he knew that if he didn't yank her up inside of the next five seconds, it was all going to be over.

But before he could pull her back up his body, her mouth came fully over him. *Oh Lord, it was good.* So good that he couldn't do anything but thread his hands into her hair to pull her closer and push even deeper between her lips.

Once, twice, three times he gave himself over to her before he made himself break free from her incredible mouth and rolled her onto her back on the bed. He reached up to lock her hands around the bed posts, then gripped her hips hard and drove into her, as they came together in a dance of desire that was at once hotter and wilder and yet more tender than ever before.

* * *

An hour later, when they were finally out of bed and finished with their shower, they opened the door to find raincoats, umbrellas, and gumboots outside. Tatiana was impossibly cute in the pink raincoat and matching boots that Tim's wife had lent her, her hair extra curly in the rain as they stood under the eave of the barn and watched the wind whip through the branches of the Douglas fir and arbutus trees.

"I'm thinking we might as well leave our umbrellas here. The wind will just tear through them otherwise." She slipped her hand into his and smiled up at him. "Plus, it'll be easier to hold hands."

If they'd been anywhere else, in a city crammed with people rather than on a farm in the middle of the wilderness, they couldn't have held hands without making the covers of the gossip rags. But here, in the middle of a storm so severe that everyone else was staying inside, with the thick fog and rain making it too hard for anyone to get a clear line of sight on them from out of a window, they were free to be together.

Neither of them spoke as they walked down the deserted farm road, but the silence was an easy one. A little more than one week ago, when he'd found her waiting in his office, he could never have imagined any of this. Not only more pleasure than he'd ever known before, but learning that holding Tatiana's hand could be just as good as making her come.

Or that being with Tatiana, both in bed and out, would feel so right. So easy.

A light through the fog about a half mile away in the direction of town caught their eye and they headed toward it.

"What a gorgeous lighthouse!" Tatiana's eyes were wide with wonder as they came close enough to see it clearly, the red-roofed lantern room rising from the trees that surrounded it.

"Dylan used to make us visit every lighthouse he could find when we were kids. I've always been amazed that they were able to create a light that was bright enough and strong enough to cut through even the darkest, fiercest storms. The light, the strength, the hope," he found himself saying, "reminds me of you."

Rain spiked her eyelashes as she turned to face him and her cheeks were flushed from the cold. "I know I promised you I wouldn't talk about certain things while we're here." She moved closer and turned to face him. "But I have to do this."

She lifted her mouth to his and in her kiss he heard and felt the words of love she'd promised not to say aloud.

What, he wondered when she pulled back, had she heard, and felt, in his kiss?

And was it more, even, than he was ready to admit to himself?

* * *

The island's shoreline was green and rugged, and so was Ian in the raincoat and gumboots that Tim had left outside their door. Every time she'd seen Ian before today, he'd always been perfectly clean-shaven and polished. Both looks suited him, she realized. The master of the universe in the tailored suit *and* the rugged outdoorsman with dark scruff on his face, and muddy boots.

They walked past the lighthouse and toward the tiny little strip of stores, and as they came closer, she could see lights on inside the post office and grocery store. Though she and Ian remained the only ones out on the street, would he pull away when they got close enough to be seen together? He'd clearly been on edge when he'd asked if she'd told her sister about them, so how would he feel if the rest of the world found out that he'd made her his?

A little sigh escaped her, one that puffed white in the air around her mouth and had him turning to give her a questioning look. But they'd agreed not to talk about their relationship—what it was, what it wasn't, what it could be—and just be with each other in this storm. So she simply said, "While we're here, why don't we pick up a few things to eat?"

He stared at her for a few seconds longer, continuing to hold her hand as they stood in the middle of the empty, rain-filled street. She wanted to kiss him, wanted to declare her love for him not only in front of the shop owners, but the rest of the world that would surely be alerted within seconds once they saw who she was.

But since she suspected it would break her heart if he let go of her hand, she made herself do it first before heading inside the store.

"How do you feel about meatloaf?"

"Sounds good."

For the first time all day, things between them felt strained. In their room above the barn, they'd been entirely in their own world. But this little grocery store felt more like the real world than anything else had since they'd landed. There was a rack of magazines, a couple of which had her face on the cover, and a flat-screen TV on in the corner.

She'd already loaded up her hand basket with ground beef, ketchup, a bell pepper, garlic, and onions when she rounded the aisle and saw the cutest display of jewelry. "Look, they're perfect little replicas of the lighthouse."

Ian took one off the display and, without a word, walked up to the front counter to pay for it. She stood right where she was, unable to move, barely able to breathe, until he came back to where she was standing. They were hidden from the man at the checkout by a tall shelf, so no one could see Ian undo the clasp and lay it against her collarbone, then lift her hair and move it to the opposite shoulder so that he could close the clasp. It was such an intimate gesture that for one brief, perfect moment, she felt as though they were a real couple.

"I never got you a gift to celebrate your nomination. Nothing was right. Not until now. Not until this."

"I didn't need a gift," she replied in a soft voice, "but I'll cherish this one forever." The lighthouse charm necklace was better than jewels for her. Sweet and fun and a memory she'd have forever of the most wonderful days of her life. No matter what happened between them in the future, she'd always treasure these precious, stolen hours with him.

She recognized the look in his eyes—he wanted to kiss her—along with the frustration that he felt because he couldn't.

"Do we need anything else to eat?" he asked.

She'd temporarily forgotten all about why they were in the store and when she looked down at the basket in her hands it took her brain a few seconds to click back into gear. "Maybe some fruit. Cheese and crackers might be good, too." Her stomach grumbled. "And bacon."

Quickly, they gathered up the rest of the groceries. It had been good to get outside, to walk in the rain together, to see the pretty lighthouse. But now, they both wanted to get back to their own private world. One where they didn't have to worry about what the man at the checkout would think seeing them together, or whom he might tell.

"Wicked storm, eh? Hoping it will blow out just as fast as it blew in, the way it usually does." The grizzled man didn't wait for them to pipe in, just kept talking. "Thought I saw a piece of blue sky earlier." He peered out the window. "Thought maybe the rain slacked off for a bit there."

Tatiana was so attuned to Ian's moods that she felt his tension beside her without needing to look at his face. She knew he couldn't afford too many hours or days away from the office, yet it didn't seem as though he wanted the storm to end any more than she did.

The man shook his head as he dropped their groceries into a canvas bag. "Probably just wishful thinking, though. Not too many people out today, apart from you two. Not too many tourists this time of year, either. You see the lighthouse?"

"We did," Tatiana said with a smile. "It's beautiful."

The man's hand stilled on the package of ground beef he was scanning to take a closer look at her. "You remind me of someone."

"I get that a lot." Normally, she would have been happy to sign an autograph, but today she simply paid and took her groceries so that she wouldn't lose one more second with Ian.

Especially if the storm was going to break soon.

* * *

After checking in with Linda and David at the B&B and confirming that they would be grounded until the following day at least, when they got back to the barn, Ian surprised her by offering to make the meatloaf. While he cooked, she sat cross-legged on the floor in front of the wicker basket of CDs and combed through the huge number of old movies. There were some great ones, some bad ones, and some she'd never seen.

She picked one of each for Ian to choose from. "*Back to the Future. Total Recall.* Or *Wayne's World*?"

He didn't hesitate. "*Wayne's World*."

"I've never seen it." But she'd always meant to see what Mike Myers had done before *Austin Powers* and *Shrek*. "Is it good?"

"It's a classic," he said with a grin, and her heart flopped over in her chest at seeing him look so carefree and so happy. "It doesn't have to be good."

How many other people had seen Ian like this? Scruffy, cooking, grinning, wearing jeans and a T-shirt while choosing bad movies for them to watch.

She reached up to touch the lighthouse on her necklace. They were all such simple things. And yet, each one of them meant so much to her.

She put out the cheese and crackers and sliced apples onto a plate while he finished getting the meatloaf ready to go into the oven. After washing his hands, Ian came over to the couch, where she was already curled up under a blanket and the opening credits of the movie had begun.

It felt so good, so easy, so right, when he wrapped his arms around her and she tucked her head against his chest while they watched. The story was simple, about a small-town rock band, the funny guy getting the pretty girl, and good triumphing over evil. And, much to her delight, it turned out that Ian knew all the words from when he was a teenager, especially the part where they went into a long string of "she's a babe" jokes.

Her stomach growled just as the timer on the oven dinged. Putting the movie on pause, they headed back into the kitchen to eat their simple meal. She'd found a candle and matches on a shelf and placed it, lit, in the center of the small pine table.

"Have you ever thought about being in a movie like that?"

"Casting directors have always seen me more as the dramatic type."

"You're great in the dramas," he said, "but you'd be great in a comedy, too."

"You really think I could be the slinky guitar-playing heroine?" She vamped a line from the movie, putting on her best sexy attitude.

He blinked, clearly stunned for a minute. "Wow, that was good. So, yeah, you could totally play that part. Though I was thinking more about you killing it as the goofy lead singer with the cable show in the basement."

She laughed, barely covering her mouthful of meatloaf in time. "You know," she said a few moments later, "now that you mention it, it would be fun to do a comedy. Although I have a feeling that if I'm going to get one, I'll have to show those casting directors a thing or two they don't expect."

"If anyone can do it, it's you, Tatiana. You're extraordinarily good at what you do."

"Thank you." She suddenly felt shy. "So are you. Actually, I wanted to ask you something."

"Of course you do," he teased her.

For a moment, she hesitated. Neither of them wanted to let the real world intrude on their day any more than it already had in the grocery store, but now that they'd spoken about her career, she had another question for him about his. And since it hadn't felt weird to bring up her job in the midst of having fun, she hoped it wouldn't be strange to talk about his, either.

"When Flynn was walking you through his new idea, he talked to you like you were a tech guy, rather than just some guy in a suit."

"I drive my tech guys crazy," he admitted with a cute smile. "They're always telling me to stop breaking their toys."

"Actually," she said in a teasing voice as they took their empty plates over to the sink, "I could see you as the geeky guy down in the basement downing Red Bull and pulling a pen out of his pocket protector."

Laughing, he tugged her back under the blanket on the couch to finish watching the movie. But Tatiana was listening so carefully to every beat of his heart as she lay against his chest that she barely heard another word of dialogue in the film.

She didn't know who started kissing whom first, but it didn't matter this time. All that mattered was that it was so good, so sweet. Being with Ian was everything she'd ever wanted, everything she'd ever dreamed of. Soon, they had each other's clothes off, and she was lying naked on the couch with his wonderfully heavy weight pressing her deeper into the cushions.

She loved the sweetness, the softness, he was giving her, at the same time that wild hunger vibrated between them the way it had from the very first moment she'd kissed him. He'd been slow, gentle, this morning when he'd put his mouth on her and taken her over the edge again and again. She was unabashedly greedy for all of it, for everything she could experience with Ian, for every new sensation.

"More."

Just one word spoken so softly against his lips, but he immediately stilled, his lips against hers.

"Show me more, Ian." It was what she'd asked for their first night together, and she remembered what it had done to him...and then what he'd done with her. "I love all the different sides of you. Gentle and sweet. Rough and wild. I don't want you to hold anything back when you're with me."

Since she was the one doing the asking, she should have been prepared for what Ian did next, but he had his hands on her hips to spin her around so fast that she was momentarily disoriented when she realized she was on her knees.

The couch cushions, warm from the heat of their bodies, crumpled in her fisting hands as she tried to ground herself. But how could she do anything but fly wild and free when Ian was running his hands over her, shoulders to hips, breasts to the vee between her legs, with hungry abandon? He wasn't gentle anymore, was simply taking everything she had offered to him by asking, by begging, for *more.* She loved it, loved every second of his hands, his mouth, the heat of his naked skin against hers.

Again, he moved fast, giving her no warning as he gripped her hips to plunge into her.

"Oh." She heard the wonder in her voice, couldn't have held it in even if she'd wanted to. "Do that again. Please, just like that."

His answering groan sounded as raw and as desperate as she felt, her name at the center of it. And when he went impossibly deep into her again, his hips slamming into hers, she gasped with pleasure.

So much pleasure that she could hardly believe she'd lived this long without knowing it was there.

"I like it when you do that. I like it so much. *So, so much."*

"I do too, sweetheart." To her ears, his words spoke not just to sex, but to trust, and to a depth of emotion between them she'd never shared with anyone else. *"I do, too."*

She trembled, shook, knew she was going to shatter any second. And in the end that was all it took, one more slip, one more slide of his fingers over her breasts, between her legs, for her to completely break apart, with Ian only moments behind her.

With no breath, or brain cells, left for words, all that existed in their little room above the barn was pleasure, and a connection that was twining deeper and deeper with every laugh they shared, every orgasm that exploded between their bodies...and later, when passion had temporarily run its course and he tucked them both into bed, every quiet moment in each other's arms.

CHAPTER TWENTY-SIX

The sound of giggling outside woke Ian up. "Sounds like we have a couple of little visitors outside."

Tatiana made a sleepy sound of agreement, then pressed a kiss to the arm he had slung over her body and pushed off the covers so that they could both get out of bed to put on jeans and T-shirts. Her hair was a tangle of curls and her eyes were still heavy-lidded with sleep as she walked over to the door and opened it with a smile.

The little black and white dog bounded in first. Two young twins, a boy and girl that Ian figured were probably around four years old, were staring up at her with big eyes. "You're pretty," the little girl said.

"So are you," Tatiana said as she squatted down to come face to face with the children.

"I'm Sadie. This is Jamie. He's my brother."

"I'm Tatiana." She gestured behind her. "That's Ian."

The boy held out a basket of eggs. "We are supposed to bring you these."

"Our chickens made them," Sadie informed them both.

"Wow." Tatiana smiled over her shoulder at Ian. "Look at the marvelous gift our new friends just brought us." She turned back to the kids. "Does your mommy or daddy know you're here?"

"Mummy is the one who sent us," Jamie said as if it should have been obvious. "She said not to bother you, though."

"Oh, that's the last thing you could ever do. I'm just happy Ian and I will have someone to share all these eggs with. Do you like to eat them raw or do you think I should cook them?"

They both made a face at the first suggestion, then hollered, "You have to cook them!" in unison, though Sadie had to tell her, "Once I saw my uncle put a raw egg in a drink."

"Did you ever do that, Ian, to pump up those muscles of yours?"

"Rafe dared me to drink a full glass of raw eggs once." He shook his head, laughing at himself. "It was disgusting, but he did end up doing my chores for a week when I won the bet, so it was worth it."

While Tatiana went into the kitchen to start cooking up eggs and bacon for all of them, the kids immediately ran over to the cabinet in the corner and pulled out a box filled with Lego pieces.

"I know how to build a car," Jamie told Ian.

"I can make an airplane," Sadie one-upped her brother as she sat crossed-legged on the hooked rug on the pine floor and dug her little hands into the Legos to dump a bunch all around her. "Want me to show you how?"

"You bet." Ian found a spot on the rug between the kids, both of them talking over each other as they tried to show him the best way to put together a moving vehicle out of the scratched-up, worn Legos in the plastic box. Between Ian and his brothers, they'd probably had nearly every set of Legos as kids, and soon he was reaching over the dog on his lap into the box to make a spaceship of his own.

"I can't get these two pieces apart!" Sadie whined, so he put down his own creation and focused on helping her with hers.

The way the little girl went from zero to sixty, from happy to frustrated in the blink of an eye, reminded him of his sister Mia when she'd been little. They hadn't played much with Legos, but she'd been a whiz at Chutes and Ladders and, when she was a little older, Battleship. Oh yes, he thought with a grin, she'd *loved* to sink his ships.

He looked up, then, to find Tatiana smiling as she watched the three of them and the puppy play together on the floor. "I should have known making Lego spaceships would be yet another talent of yours," she teased him.

Her skin was flushed from the steam rising off the pans on the little stove top, the small hairs around her forehead curling even more wildly than the others. A little Lego truck driving up his arm made him turn away, but not before he read with perfect clarity the emotion in her green eyes.

More than once she'd told him she loved him. More than once he'd told her it was impossible, that love couldn't come that fast. But when she called out to them that bacon and eggs were ready and the kids dashed over to squeeze around the small table, moving behind her to stroke her hair and press a kiss to the top of her head was the most natural thing in the world.

Being here with Tatiana was so simple—board games and splashing in puddles and laughing at old movies. Life hadn't been this normal or this fun for him since he was a kid. Being with other women had always meant fancy dinners, grand gestures, glittering jewels. And as he watched her help the kids settle with food and orange juice, he was struck by a sudden vision of having a life like this with Tatiana that stretched out past the storm—a life full of fun, laughter, games. She'd make every second joyful.

But just as quickly as that picture formed, he saw another one—a vision where he was too busy with work to enjoy being with her, with their kids. She'd be busy too, with her films, and tensions would surely rise when they both tried—and failed—to carve out anything extra for each other.

A knock sounded on the door and when he got up to answer it, he found a very apologetic brunette on the other side. "Sadie, Jamie, you were supposed to bring the eggs and then turn right around and come home."

Around a mouthful of eggs and bacon, Jamie said, "They asked us to stay."

Sadie pointed at the pile of Legos on the floor. "Ian needed us to show him how to build a spaceship."

"I did. They're great kids. I'm Ian, by the way, and this is Tatiana."

The twins' mother's eyes went wide as she finally caught sight of Tatiana. "I'm Kelly. It's so nice to meet you both. And I'm sorry again for the intrusion. Tim thought it would be nice if we dropped off some eggs for you. I thought the kids were back down with the horses, otherwise I would have come looking for them earlier."

"We really enjoyed them," Tatiana said with the gentle smile she gave people when she knew they were nervous around her. She gestured to the food. "I'd love it if you could join us."

"Oh, I really wish I could, but we've got to get going to preschool." The woman flushed even deeper. "I can't believe I'm asking this, but is there any way I could maybe get a picture with you?"

"Absolutely. In fact, why don't we do a big family shot together?"

Ian took Kelly's phone and snapped several pictures with it, then just as he had at the warehouse visit, did the same with Tatiana's at her request.

The power flickered a couple of times during their impromptu photo shoot and before she and the kids and the puppy left, Kelly said, "Looks like the power might finally go. There are some lanterns just down the stairs if you end up needing them."

* * *

They'd only just finished washing the dishes when the lights did indeed go out. Ian had already brought the lanterns up and when he turned them on, the room was bathed in a soft glow that made everything seem even more unreal that it already was.

"You were so great with those kids." Tatiana moved into his arms as though it was the place she was meant to be. "You were concentrating just as hard on those Legos as you do in your meetings dealing with millions of dollars."

"Building a spaceship is serious business."

She laughed as she laid her cheek against his chest. There was no music playing in the room, but the sound of the rain hitting the roof had enough of a beat for them to dance to in the kitchen.

"I've had a really good time here with you, Ian."

"So have I."

And as they danced by the lantern's light on the old wood floor with the rain falling outside, Ian knew he'd never been this happy in all his life. No amount of money, no amount of power or wealth had ever given him what this beautiful woman always gave so effortlessly, so endlessly.

But even as they danced, he could hear the rain starting to slow.

He pulled her closer, held her tighter, wishing that the rain could just keep falling, that the fog would continue to shroud them forever, that the wind would always blow hard enough to keep airplanes out of the sky.

Here in the storm, on the island everything had been so simple. He'd been a man falling head over heels for a beautiful woman with a heart so pure, so sweet, that it humbled him...and made him see everything with new eyes.

Even—as their dance transformed from sweet to sinful in the span of one kiss and he drew her across the room past the Legos and old movies to the bed—love.

CHAPTER TWENTY-SEVEN

Tatiana woke from their late-morning, post-sex nap to the shine of bright sun pouring in the windows. But when she reached out for Ian, his side of the bed was empty. Rolling over, she found him sitting in the chair at the foot of the bed by the window, staring out into the beautiful day and looking utterly grim.

Her chest clenched even as her heart felt fuller than it ever had. She hadn't known it was possible to love someone so much, so deeply, that she could almost swear she could feel his emotions roll through her.

Pushing the covers off, she moved naked onto his lap. He'd pulled on his jeans, but his chest was bare. When he automatically put his arms around her to draw her closer, she leaned into his warmth, his strength.

She didn't say anything, just listened to the steady beat of his heart and breathed him in. He already knew what was in her heart. Today, she guessed, he would finally tell her what was in his.

"When we leave this room today," he finally said, "when we walk into the sunshine, when we get back on the plane, everything is going to be different."

She couldn't deny that everything was about to change. She'd heard the rain ease off when they'd been dancing together earlier. And the way he'd just made love to her, so sweetly, so reverently...hadn't she known that he'd been touching her as if he was afraid that it was the last time?

So many times since they'd landed on the island and she'd promised not to speak about what had happened on Thursday or Friday, she'd barely been able to keep from blurting out everything she was feeling. But now, with their entire future hanging in the balance, she couldn't find a single word. All she could do was bury her face in his neck and press her hand flat over Ian's chest to count the beats of his heart.

"I don't want this to be the end for us, Tatiana. I can't imagine going through a day without seeing your smile, without touching you and having you in my bed, without laughing with you."

Tatiana knew she should have been over the moon, should have been jumping for joy. But Ian didn't look happy about what he was saying to her. On the contrary, he looked as grim now as he had when she'd woken up.

And she could see how conflicted he was still, as he brushed a hand over her hair, looked into her eyes, and said, "I love you."

Tatiana was certain her heart stopped beating and her lungs stopped pumping as the three words she'd been dreaming of hearing Ian say echoed in the room. It should have been because everything was perfect. She'd assumed that if he ever confessed his love to her, it would be a perfect moment she'd want to capture so that she could replay it over and over forever.

But no matter how much she wished she could fool herself into believing everything was perfect, she couldn't. Especially not when he lifted his hands to her face and held her gently, as if he was worried she might break under the pressure.

"I love you," he said again, "and I can't make any promises right now, but—" He paused, a muscle jumping in his cheek. "I want to try."

His *I love you,* she realized, had come so much easier than this, than the *I want to try* that he'd nearly had to yank out of his own throat.

"I want to try, Tatiana," he said again. "I want to try to love you the way you should be loved."

She already knew just how he'd do it. How he'd *try* to work fewer hours for her. How he'd *try* to put up with her Hollywood events. How he'd *try* to be the man he thought she wanted and needed him to be.

And she also knew that no matter how many times she told him she didn't need him to do any of those things, he would never believe she meant it when she said that all she needed was for him to be himself.

All that would ultimately happen was that he'd end up being completely, totally miserable. And so would she. Only this time she would be the guilty one, because she would know that she could have stopped him from making all those mistakes.

By leaving.

Now. Today. Before they walked out of this room, before they stood in the sunshine, before they got back on his plane heading for the real world.

Untangling her limbs from his and moving off his lap was one of the hardest things she'd ever done, but she couldn't keep touching him and say what she knew she had to say. Couldn't be that close to him and do what she knew she needed to do.

"I know it should be enough," she said softly, speaking as much to herself as to him. "I know all my dreams should be coming true. But—" She reached blindly behind her for the bedcover to draw over her bare shoulders. "—I love you too much to ever want loving me to be that difficult, or for you to think you have to *try* to become something you're not."

She could see how surprised he was by her response, and worse, how hurt. Especially when he stood to reach for her and she instinctively shrank back.

"I wasn't looking for you, Tatiana. I didn't see you coming. I didn't expect you to burst into my life and turn it upside down. But I'm not sorry that you did, that you have. These past few days with you have been the best of my life, but everything has happened so fast between us that I still can't see yet how things are going to work in the real world. I want to try to see if they can."

So much of her wanted that, too. But she knew better. "Can't you see? It's exactly what you did with your ex-wife. You *tried* to make a relationship work around your job and what she wanted from you. It didn't work, and I love you too much to let you make those mistakes again."

"You were the one who first said you're nothing like my ex," he argued. "And neither are the two of us when we're together. Not even close."

"All along, you've been worried that you would hurt me, that I'd end up crushed and you'd end up guilty. Are you telling me that all of those worries are gone now?" When he didn't immediately reply, her heart sank even lower than it had already fallen. She asked in a soft voice, "Or was I right to feel that those worries, those fears, were still lying in wait beneath everything we've shared here on this island, in this room? They are the real reasons why you don't want to make me any promises, aren't they? Not because it's all happened so fast."

She'd thought the hardest thing she'd ever done was to leave his arms a few minutes ago, but when his continued silence and bleak expression gave her his answer, Tatiana now knew it was much, much harder not to move back into his arms to give him comfort.

But love, Tatiana had always known, would be all or nothing for her. It was why she'd waited so long to sleep with a man—until she was certain that he was *the one.* She would never be happy, truly happy, with halfway. And neither would Ian. After more than a week in close quarters with him, she knew that he never moved forward with a business deal unless he was absolutely, positively sure that it was the right move to make. At which point he never looked back. He would never *try* to win a client or take over an industry. He would simply *do* it without ever second-guessing himself.

Love—and forever—would be no different for him.

"I love you, Tatiana. Why can't knowing that be enough for now?"

His words tore at her resolve, but it didn't change the fact that *enough* couldn't ever be. Not for either of them.

"During the storm," she said in as steady a voice as she could manage, "there were moments when you forgot to be on guard, when you forgot about your fear of hurting me or letting me down, and we were close. So close. Those moments showed me what it's like to have all of you. Or nearly all, at least. I can't go backward when what I really want, what I really need, is for those moments to grow and build into minutes, hours, weeks, years. And I know now that I was unfair to you when I told you I would wait, that I would just keep holding on until you came around. I thought I could, I swear I did, and maybe I could have if we hadn't been caught in the storm." Her eyeballs ached from the pressure of all the tears threatening to fall. "But now that I know just how much there could be, how much *love* can be, I also know that anything less would break me apart."

"The last thing I'd ever want is to break you, sweetheart."

"I know." His endearment hit her straight in the center of her heart, just as it had every time he'd said it to her before. And, oh, how she longed to be back in his arms, even as she said, "So that's why I'm leaving before you do."

"Tatiana—"

The guilt etched into the beautiful lines of his face made her forget to keep her distance for a moment as she took his hand in hers. "You never asked me to fall in love with you. You never promised me anything. You warned me that you weren't ready to love anyone, that you didn't think you'd ever be ready. But I was, so I chose not to listen, and to love you with everything I am. I don't regret it, not any of it. And you shouldn't feel guilty for anything that happened between us." Every single part of her ached as she looked into his dark eyes. "Being here with you on the island has been the perfect fairy tale. But you were right when you told me fairy tales aren't real. We both have real lives, great ones full of family and work and friends that we love. I don't want you to give all of that up. Not for me, or anyone else. I want you to have it all, Ian, and I want to have it all, too. Amazing, fulfilling careers along with love that's big enough and strong enough not just to deal with, but to celebrate, in all of the messiness of real life."

That was when she made herself draw back from him, made herself force a smile and say, "Speaking of messy, I'm going to go hop in the shower so that we can get out of here before the weather changes again."

And before her tears began to fall again...

CHAPTER TWENTY-EIGHT

By now, they both needed to get back to Seattle—Ian to close the deal with Flynn and Tatiana to begin production on her new movie—so the trip to Alaska was shelved for another day. During the flight, she made notes on her script while he worked on his laptop. He offered her something to drink and she politely declined it. He asked if she needed to do another read-through and she said she thought she finally had it under control thanks to his earlier help.

The flight back was as smooth as the trip there had been rough, which should have been great news...and yet...Ian found himself wishing that they'd hit rough air again so that he could have another chance to hold Tatiana's hands and be close to her.

With every mile they covered, as the distance between them grew bigger and bigger, Ian knew that all he would need to do to make her change her mind about leaving him was to pull her back into his arms and kiss her. One kiss and she'd feel, she'd remember, what was between them—how extraordinary it was. And then she'd come back to him and give him the chance he'd all but begged for, and he wouldn't have to face the thought of a night without her in his arms.

But how could he do that when he knew she'd done exactly the right thing by getting out before he eventually destroyed the light inside her?

Finally, the plane landed, but once they'd both unbuckled and stood, Tatiana stayed standing before him. "Ian—" Her mouth trembled and she pressed her lips together for a moment before continuing. "Before we get off the plane and the real world swallows us up, can I ask you a few last questions?" She laughed a little then, but he could hear how shaken she was beneath it. "Really, I mean it this time. These will be my last ones."

"Anything, Tatiana."

"If I call you tonight. Tomorrow. Next week. Next month. Will you promise not to pick up? And if—" Tears welled up in her beautiful eyes. "—if I come by your office, if I tell you I need to do more research, will you promise not to let me in?" She lowered her head to brush tears away. "And if you find me standing on the tarmac again waiting to spin you a tale about needing to get on your plane with you for a role, will you promise not to fall for it?" She pulled her canvas bag up and held it in front of her chest like a shield. "One day I hope I'll be my old self again and the memories will have faded enough that I'll be strong enough to resist you on my own. But until then...I'm going to need your help, and your promises, not to fall for any other ideas I might come up with in the middle of the night when I'm missing you like crazy."

He'd told her he'd do anything for her. But he hadn't known—hadn't *truly* known what it was like to love until now. Not until the most beautiful woman in the world stood so close and just out of reach, at the same time as she asked him to help her stay away from him.

It nearly killed him to say the words, "I promise."

He watched as she forced the corners of her lips up. "Thank you." But she still didn't walk away. "I also wanted to wish you good luck with your meeting with Flynn today, although I know you won't need it. He's going to sign the deal." Her smile was genuine now. "And I'm going to be so, so happy for you when he does. Let him know I said hello."

When she finally turned to go, Ian felt as though his insides were tearing in two. "I don't need to do the deal, Tatiana." She turned back to him in shock as he said, "If I walk away from it, I'll have more time to spend with you."

Tatiana had surprised him right from the very first time he'd met her, but even though he now knew her better than he'd ever known anyone else, the very last thing he expected to see on her face was anger.

"Would you ever ask me to give up acting?"

"Of course not."

"Then why do you think I would ever in a million years want you to give up on your own dreams?" She shook her head. "I saw firsthand how excited you are about Flynn's company, and about working personally with him. I know how much you thrive on your work, and I love that you do. Can't you see that you've never let me, or anyone else, down before by being true to yourself? But if you blow this deal on purpose, if you walk away from working directly with Flynn after you gave him your word, all because you can't get it through your thick skull that you're already perfect just the way you are...well, then, you won't just be letting me down. You'll be letting yourself down, too."

As she turned for the door and he followed her, he felt like he was watching them both on screen, like all of this was happening in a movie, rather than his real life. Because how could he have finally found something so beautiful, so incredible, and then lost it so quickly?

"T!"

Tatiana had called Valentina to let her know they were finally coming back to Seattle, and now Valentina and Smith were standing at the bottom of the steps waiting to fold Tatiana into a hug.

"I'm so glad you're back safe and sound." Ian watched Valentina brush the hair back from Tatiana's forehead so that she could look into her sister's face to make sure she really, truly was okay. "But you're crying. Why are you crying?"

"I'm just so happy to see you."

Valentina pulled her sister closer and lifted her questioning gaze to Ian's face. He'd barely been able to hide what he felt for Tatiana a week ago.

Now he simply didn't have a prayer.

Valentina paled even as Smith, who had clearly already put two and two together, came forward with hands curled into fists.

"What the hell, Ian?"

His cousin was clearly spoiling for a fight, but when Tatiana said something in a voice that was too soft for Ian to make out, Valentina cut Smith off with a hand on his arm. "Tatiana's ready to head home now."

* * *

Tatiana sat in Smith and Valentina's living room on a soft chair under a blanket with a cup of tea in her hand. They'd both been kind enough to give her some space on the drive over and to let her settle in for a few minutes while they spoke softly to one other in the kitchen.

About her and Ian, of course.

When they both finally moved hand in hand to sit on the couch kitty corner to her, Tatiana suddenly realized that everything really had changed. It wasn't just she and her sister anymore. Valentina and Smith were a team in all things now, even loving and protecting her.

"Are you ready to talk about it yet?" Valentina asked gently.

No she wasn't. Not even close, but seeing how worried her sister and Smith were, she knew she had to at least say something. "I'm in love with Ian. But I'm pretty sure both of you already got that."

"Why didn't you tell me, when we were on the phone last week?"

"I wanted to tell you, Val. I almost did, but I knew what you'd say." She looked at Smith. "What you'd both say. That you'd tell me to keep my distance. And—" She held up a hand to beat them to it. "That you'd only be saying it because you love me."

"We do," Smith said, "so much that we hate to see you looking this way now."

"I know I'm a mess," she agreed, "so you're probably not going to believe me when I say that loving Ian was the best thing I've ever done in my entire life."

Valentina moved from Smith's side to put her arms around her, and by the time Tatiana finally looked up from her sister's comforting arms, Smith was gone.

* * *

Ian wasn't at all surprised when Smith walked into his office and slammed the door behind him, snarling, "You should have stayed away from her."

He stood, figuring he'd make it easier for his cousin to do what needed to be done. "I know."

"What the hell is wrong with you, leading her on like that, making her fall so in love with you that I'm pretty sure she's going to be pissed at me for coming here to beat the crap out of you?"

"I'm in love with her, too. And you *should* beat the crap out of me."

"You'd better believe I'm planning on—" Smith broke off. "Wait, what did you just say?"

"You should beat the crap out of me." Ian had the most important meeting of his career in a couple of minutes, but he'd just have to do his best to clean up the mess Smith was going to make of his face before he headed into it.

"No, before that."

"I love her."

"Jesus." Smith ran a hand over his face in obvious confusion. "I don't get it. She loves you. You love her. So what's the problem?"

Bethany knocked once before letting herself in. "Ian, Smith, I'm so sorry to interrupt, but Flynn is here." She shot Ian the same concerned look she'd given him when he'd returned to the office thirty minutes ago. Clearly, he looked as bad as he felt. "I thought you might like to know that he's already looking at his watch."

Having missed their previously scheduled meeting this morning when Ian couldn't get off the island in time, Flynn had shifted his own tight schedule to come again this afternoon. If Ian stood him up a second time, it was likely he'd feel he'd just been jerked around by another investment company. If that happened, it was unlikely Flynn would come back to Sullivan Investments.

Ian couldn't stand the thought of Tatiana crying over him, couldn't stand not being there to take her into his arms and soothe her. If he left now, he could be with her in fifteen minutes. But though seeing her again, touching her again, would make him feel better, he knew with perfect certainty that she would be absolutely infuriated.

"If you blow this deal on purpose, if you walk away from working directly with Flynn after you gave him your word, all because you can't get it through your thick skull that you're already perfect just the way you are...well, then, you won't just be letting me down. You'll be letting yourself down, too."

Turning to Bethany, Ian said, "Let Flynn know I'll be there as soon as I can."

His assistant nodded and closed the door behind her with a soft click.

Smith stared at him like he couldn't believe what he was seeing. "I just want to make sure I've got this straight. You're in love with an amazing woman who's currently crying in her sister's arms over you, but instead of doing anything and everything you can *right this very second* to convince her you're sorry for screwing everything up and won't make the same mistakes again, you're in here getting ready for a meeting." Smith shook his head. "I've figured out the problem. You're an idiot. You were a good man once. What the hell happened to you that makes you think this—" He gestured to Ian's office. "—is what really matters?" With that, his cousin left the same way he came in, with a good, hard slam of Ian's office door.

Ian knew that Tatiana had risked everything for him. Getting in his face with her questions when no one else would. Loving him when he'd repeatedly tried to push her away. And then walking away for both their sakes when he didn't have the strength to do it.

The very least he could do for her was not let her down now.

* * *

"Where's Tatiana? Isn't she still supposed to be shadowing you?"

Of course that would be the first thing Flynn wanted to know. The other man had clearly been smitten with her during last week's meeting and he'd only gotten to speak with her for a few minutes. Lord, if he only knew how sweet it was to hear her laugh over a bad movie, or how good it felt to dance with her to the beat of the rain in the middle of the kitchen, or the way she held absolutely nothing back while making love....

"Tatiana couldn't be here today, but she says hello, and—" He paused before deciding to tell the other man, "she also hoped we'd be agreeing to a deal today. So do I."

Flynn took his measure. "You look really tired, and with you missing our meeting yesterday because you had other meetings out of town that couldn't wait, I've got to ask: Are you sure you've got the time to give to my company?"

Ian laughed, then, all pretense of holding it together gone. "You want to know the honest to God truth? No, I don't have the time. I haven't had the time in over a decade. Longer than that. But I'm going to make the time for your company. Not only because I gave you my word that I would, but also because I haven't been this excited about working with someone else in a very long time."

"Honesty." Flynn looked surprised. "I haven't seen much of that in boardrooms these past couple of years. Until right this second, frankly, I wasn't sure that I could trust you. Look, I'm not asking you to give up having a wife and kids for me. Hell, I hope to have those myself one day. And I get that you might not always be the best person to work with in every area, that you've got a staff full of intelligent, enthusiastic people who know how to kick ass in their specific arenas. I just want to know that your interest in growing my company is serious."

"It is."

"In that case," Flynn said with a wide grin and an outstretched hand, "we have a deal."

CHAPTER TWENTY-NINE

It was a good thing, Tatiana thought the following afternoon, that filming had begun today. Even better that the director had wanted to start with the scene where Rose left Aiden. They hadn't needed much extra makeup to create the shadows under her eyes or the powder to make her skin look pale.

And when they were done with their first day on set, both the director and her co-star had told her that they'd never seen her be better. Having just channeled all of her pain and the brittleness she was feeling into her character, she was struck by the irony that just when she'd managed to keep her career from going off the rails, her personal life had completely crashed and burned.

After leaving the set, she headed out on foot through town for home. And it was true, Seattle really did feel like home already.

She was starting to know the city fairly well after the past couple of weeks, but not so well that she wasn't surprised when her route took her right past the restaurant where she and Ian had eaten on the first day she'd shadowed him. Her chest clenched as she stood outside and remembered how naïve she'd been, how easy she'd thought falling in love—and being loved back—would be.

All the previous night without Ian, she'd longed for him, had been so tempted to go knock on his door and beg him to forget everything she'd said about not *trying.* But Ian, she knew, had always protected everyone else.

Now, she needed to protect him from giving up everything he loved for her.

"Tatiana!"

She was surprised to see Mia stepping out onto the sidewalk. Looking up, she saw that the restaurant where she and Ian and his professor had eaten was just a couple of doors down from Sullivan Realty, Mia's office.

"I was just going to call you about Friday night and here you are walking past."

Oh God, Tatiana had forgotten all about the party at Mia and Ford's house to celebrate her and Smith's Oscar nominations. When Tatiana had first suggested it, the family celebration had seemed like a great way to make sure Ian wouldn't be able to avoid her. But now, after she'd made him promise on the plane to keep his distance...

She sighed. Hadn't she known there would be family parties? In fact, it was one of the reasons he'd been so hesitant to start anything with her in the first place, because of how awkward—and horrible—it would be to constantly see each other if things didn't work out.

Somehow, she told herself, she'd have to figure out a way to deal with seeing him at Mia's house tomorrow night.

Mia had been all smiles when she came out of her office, but her grin quickly fell away when Tatiana lifted her sunglasses and she got close enough to see Tatiana's face.

"You know what," Mia said, "let's go into my office so that we don't cause any more pandemonium out here on the sidewalk than Ford already did this morning when he decided to go out and pick up coffees for us." Mia put an arm around Tatiana to direct her inside. "I know falling in love with a rock star is every woman's fantasy, but let me tell you, the reality can be a little nuts sometimes. One woman actually stripped off her underwear in the middle of the sidewalk to give to him." Mia made a face. "Can we say *yuck*?"

"Serious yuck."

"People probably do weird stuff like that to you all the time, don't they?"

"Not *that* weird, thankfully," Tatiana said with a laugh. One that sounded so rusty she realized she hadn't laughed since she'd been in

Ian's arms on the island and they'd been dancing around Legos on the floor of their perfect little barn room.

As soon as they stepped into Mia's office, Ian's sister closed the door and then the blinds to make the glass-walled space private. "What's wrong?"

Yesterday, though Valentina had clearly been extremely worried about her, Tatiana's sister had accepted that she wasn't yet ready to say more. Since then, of course, Valentina had sent a half-dozen text messages checking in, and they were meeting in a little while at her place so that she could finally tell her sister everything.

But now that she was sitting with Ian's sister, who loved him as much as she did, Tatiana knew she wouldn't be able to keep it all from spilling out another second. And if she was going to tell it, she figured she might as well start from the beginning.

"When we were at your parents' house for dinner and I was helping your mom in the kitchen, I told her I had fallen for Ian."

"Wow." Mia's eyes were wide with surprise. "I'm going to go out on a limb here and guess that my mom *loved* hearing that."

"I think she did," Tatiana said with a small smile. "She gave me a big hug...and then told me to stay determined and not to give up on him."

Emotion swamped Mia's face. "We all love him so much."

"I know you do. How could you not when I fell in love with him the first time I met him in Napa at Marcus and Nicola's wedding? Partly," she admitted, "because he's gorgeous, but mostly because of how much he obviously loves you and wanted to make sure you were safe and happy."

"Love at first sight," Mia said with a sigh. "That's so romantic. Only you don't look happy, and I'm guessing that if I went to see my brother right now, he wouldn't look happy, either."

Knowing her voice would break on any words she tried to say, Tatiana simply shook her head.

"I was so sure things would turn out differently with you," Mia said. "Hoping, praying that he'd finally open up with you, even though he's isolated himself more and more from all of us over the years."

"Me too," Tatiana confessed in a hollow voice. "I kept thinking that if I didn't back down or give up or go away, if I was just *there* for him, if I could just smash through all of his boundaries, he'd let me in. And when we were on the island, for a while..."

"Island?"

Realizing no one but her sister and Smith knew about their aborted trip to Alaska, she explained, "We were headed to Alaska for one of his meetings, but when that bad storm hit, we had to land way on the north end of

Vancouver Island. While we were grounded there for three days without cell phones or Internet connections, I got to see another side of your brother when he actually let down his walls for a little while." Tatiana didn't realize she'd put one hand over her heart until it was already there. "Far enough that he started talking about wanting to try with me. He even said he'd give up the big deal he's been working on for the past two years so that we could have more time together."

Mia looked shocked. "He's been obsessed with investing in that company."

"He should be. I met the founder and the guy's a genius. And that's just the problem. If I let Ian give that up for me because he thinks there's some sort of rule about how much time and focus you can give to someone you love versus your company—"

"He'd be miserable."

Tatiana nodded.

"But if he didn't walk away from it all," Mia said, "if he still worked crazy hours, would that ever be enough for you?"

"After spending the past week and a half with him, and seeing how well he juggles it all—better than anyone I've ever seen—I know it would be. I don't want him to change. I don't need him to change. He's perfect just the way he is. But—"

"He doesn't see that, does he?"

"No, he doesn't. And if we were together, he would live in constant fear of hurting me, and feel guilty every time he thought he was letting me down."

"Ugh."

Tatiana nodded. "Double ugh."

Mia reached into her desk drawer and pulled out a box of Brooke's chocolates. "This definitely calls for my emergency stash." Once both of them had popped truffles into their mouths, Mia asked, "So, are you going to be okay with seeing him on Friday night?"

Tatiana figured there was no point in lying. "It's going to be really hard to see your brother." She sighed before admitting, "But—and I know this probably doesn't make any sense—it would be worse *not* to see him."

Mia's lips had moved up into a little smile as she held out the box of chocolates. "Want another?"

Tatiana shook her head. "No, thanks. And I'd better get going or else I'm going to be late to meet up with Valentina. She's already worried enough about me."

Mia gave her a warm hug. "See you tomorrow night. And if you need to talk again before then, you know you can call or come by the house anytime, don't you?"

"I do."

"I wish my brother knew it."

"He does, Mia."

"Then why has he been shutting me out for so many years?"

"I don't know. But maybe," Tatiana said with a small smile that she knew wouldn't make any sense to anyone but Ian, "it's finally time for you to ask him."

* * *

It had taken years of work, of focus, of dedication for Ian and his executive team to close the eAirBox deal. They'd celebrated last night, all of them, including Flynn and his team. But, for the very first time ever, Ian's professional triumph wasn't enough to make up for his personal loss.

There wasn't a moment when he had stopped thinking of her during the past twenty-four hours. Hell, during the past several months since the wedding, if he was being honest with himself. Again and again he replayed every one of her beautiful smiles, the sweet sound of her laughter, the softness of her mouth on his, the bliss of feeling her skin heat and dampen as she came apart in his arms...and the honest emotion that he'd seen in her eyes every time she looked at him.

He'd gone around and around in his head trying to figure out a way that they could make things work, what he could do to convince her to give him another chance, but every time he was stopped by Tatiana's voice in his head: *It's exactly what you did with your ex-wife. You tried to make a relationship work around your job and what she wanted from you. But it didn't work. And I love you too much to let you make those mistakes again.*

Ian was so lost in his thoughts that he didn't realize his sister had walked into his office until she threw her arms around him and said, "I love you, big brother. You were gone so long that I didn't get to tell you nearly enough. Now that you're finally back home, I've got lots of lost time to make up for." After a long while, she finally drew back to sit on the edge of his desk. "But before we get to the heavier stuff, I need to remind you about the party at our house tomorrow night. You're in charge of the bubbly, so you'd better not be late or we won't be able to toast Smith and Tatiana."

Damn it, he'd forgotten about Mia and Ford's party on Friday night. How could he go when he'd promised Tatiana that he'd—

Wait a minute, Ian thought, as he rewound back to the exact promise he'd made: not to answer her calls, or let her shadow him at work anymore, or take her away for a business trip on his plane. But he'd never made even the slightest promise about staying away from her at a Sullivan family event.

Thank God.

"Have you seen her?"

His sister nodded, looking far more serious than usual. "She just dropped by my office, actually, on the way back from her set."

"How is she?"

He was surprised by his sister's faint smile. "Head over heels in love with you. And I just found out that she talked to Mom about her feelings for you, too."

"She did?"

Mia's smile grew even bigger. "She did."

"Wait a minute," he said, his brain feeling even more muddled now than it had since he'd watched Tatiana walk away from him the previous afternoon. "If you just saw her, and you obviously know what happened, and she's talked to Mom, then why aren't both of you yelling at me for screwing everything up?"

"Seems to me," she said softly as she studied his face, "that you're doing a good enough job of that yourself."

But he knew his sister, knew there was plenty she wanted to say to him, and that there had been for a long time. "I didn't hold back with you when you were getting together with Ford in Napa. You promised me that it would go both ways."

She looked like she could hardly believe what he was saying. "Wow. I can't believe you actually just asked me to butt into your private life when you've held back so much from all of us for so long. Not just since your divorce, but before that. Before you met and married Chelsea, even. I actually think it happened once you left college and started working to support us all. Tatiana was the one who suggested I come here to ask you why."

"Of course she was," he said, easily able to see Tatiana encouraging his sister to push past the walls he'd put up around himself. "I'm sorry, Mia. I'm sorry I shut you out."

"No, it wasn't your fault, Ian. At least, not *all* your fault. Because we let you do it. We let you pull away. And now I can see just how wrong we were—one of us should have gotten in your face a long time ago and just stayed there until you had no choice but to lower your walls." She put a hand over his. "Tatiana did exactly that, didn't she—what we were all afraid to do? She stood up to you and every time you pushed her away, she didn't give up on you. Instead, she came back again and again."

His chest clenched tight as he told his sister, "She did."

"She's braver than every last one of us."

"She is brave. And brilliant. And beautiful." He ran his hands over his face and admitted, "It's only been one day, but I already miss her so damned much, Mia."

"I know things with you two are a big mess right now," his sister said as she squeezed his hands, "but I still have to tell you how completely amazing it is to know that you're as head over heels in love with her as she is with you."

Easily able to see every one of his sister's hopes and dreams for him on her face, Ian had to tell her, "If I were the right man for her, if I could give her everything she needs, if I could do it all—I would."

"When we were kids," his sister said softly, "you proved again and again that you could do, could achieve, could have anything you set your mind to. I know you're convinced that you can't possibly find a way to balance work and a relationship, because you never could before now. But I think there's a simple reason for that: You never *wanted* a relationship with a woman enough to give it your all." She paused for a moment to let her words sink in, before adding, "You've never truly loved a woman before Tatiana, have you? Not the way you love her—with everything you are."

* * *

"How sweet. A little family reunion. And how perfect that you're having it in your office, Ian, since I know how much you hate to leave it."

Mia spun around. "Chelsea." His sister sounded like she'd tasted something rotten. "It's been too long, and yet, I have to admit I wish it had been longer."

Ian didn't normally feel like laughing when his ex was in the room, but he was surprised to find himself swallowing a laugh after Mia's retort.

"Thanks for coming by, Mia," he said. "And for the update."

Knowing this was his way of kicking her out, Mia asked in a low-pitched tone, "Are you sure I can't stay and throw things at her?"

His laughter bubbled all the way up and out this time. "Thanks, but I can handle her on my own."

With obvious reluctance, Mia slid off his desk. But instead of leaving him to deal with Chelsea alone, she headed straight toward his ex. "Why are you here?"

Chelsea raised an eyebrow. "That's none of your business."

"Oh yes, it is." Mia advanced toward Chelsea in such a way that his ex-wife actually took a step back. "Mess with my brother and you're messing with all of us." Mia's gaze swept down, then back up Chelsea's body. "You know, that color makes you look *much* less pale than usual. You should thank your stylist for helping you out." Turning back to Ian, Mia smiled and blew him a kiss. "See you Friday, big brother."

Ian couldn't fault his sister for wanting to protect him. Not when he'd spent his whole life doing the same for her. As soon as the door closed behind her, he stood up to greet his ex-wife. "I'm glad you're here, Chelsea."

"You are?"

He nodded. "I was going to call you today."

"You were?"

"I'm assuming you read about the eAirBox deal?"

She pulled the front page of the *Seattle Post-Intelligencer* out of her purse as confirmation. "Remember how my phone kept running out of space for taking pictures and I said, they need to make more space on these things? Well, that's just what this company does, which means I can make a case that I gave you the idea." He was pretty sure she wasn't joking, not even when she said, "You made a mistake by not holding on to me, Ian. I was your lucky charm."

His ex was certainly creative, he had to give her that. And once upon a time, he'd found her beautiful, too. But now he saw just how false every part of her was, from her colored contact lenses to her artificially plumped-up lips and breasts to her fake tan.

And yet, none of that changed the fact that he *had* hurt her.

"You're right," he finally said, "I did make a mistake with you. Lots of mistakes. I screwed up in our marriage and I just kept screwing up afterward, too."

This time, she wasn't able to hide her surprise. "I can't believe you're saying these things."

"I've been beating myself up for years over our marriage, over not being there enough for you. I'm truly sorry that I wasn't, Chelsea. You didn't deserve to be ignored. Nobody does."

"Well—" For the first time, it looked as if his ex didn't know what to say. "Thank you for the apology. Even if it's long overdue."

It *was* long overdue, he realized. This whole conversation was, in large part because after the divorce he'd shut himself away from everyone by moving to London. Were it not for Tatiana being brave enough to confront him—and to keep on doing it, even when he'd repeatedly tried to push her away—he wouldn't be having any of these long-overdue conversations today.

From the first, he'd been struck by the way Tatiana always wanted to understand why people did what they did. But even more amazing was the fact that she wasn't afraid to go deeper than other people usually did. She wasn't afraid to push harder, or farther, either.

Now, it was time to channel her fearlessness to get some answers from his ex-wife.

"Can I ask you a question, Chelsea?"

His ex-wife was frowning now, at least as much as she could with a dermatologically frozen forehead. "I guess so."

"Why did you marry me?"

Her frown deepened until there were actual lines on her face. "Is this a trick question?"

"No, I promise you it isn't."

"You weren't like any other man I'd dated. You were more confident. More focused. More determined. It was exciting to be with you, especially since you were traveling for business so much that when I was with you, it never felt like we'd settled into a boring pattern like other couples."

"But eventually didn't you want that? Didn't you want to settle down? Didn't you want our life together to have more of a pattern?"

"No, I didn't. I just wanted you to turn your focus to me. I wanted to be more important than your company, your deals. I thought that once we got married, you'd change."

And it was true, he suddenly realized. All Chelsea had really ever wanted while they were together was for him to change who he was. Whereas, again and again, Tatiana had said the exact opposite, that she loved him just the way he was.

He hadn't been planning to give his ex any more checks, but since he had a feeling she hadn't been saving much of what he'd given her over the past several years, he decided it would be his last act of penance. At the same time, however, it wouldn't be fair just to hand it to her and let her think there were more checks coming in the future.

"I'm not giving this check to you because of my new deal. In fact, I never wrote any of these checks because I actually thought I owed you anything for any of my deals, or because I was afraid of your lawyers. I did it because I felt guilty that I didn't treat you the way a good husband should have. But now I think it's finally time for both of us to move on, past the mistakes we made with each other."

Chelsea stared at him for a long moment, before awareness lit her gaze. "This is because of Tatiana Landon, isn't it? I saw the way you looked at her. You're in love with her, aren't you? That's why you want me out of the way. You're hoping I'll accept your apology so that you can go to her and tell her you're not a big, fat jerk."

He could see the calculations already going on behind her eyes, was nearly certain that she would try to dig up something about him and Tatiana so that she could leak it to the press, and he was glad for it. Happy that it helped dissolve the final remnants of his guilt.

Misplaced guilt that he'd let drive Tatiana out of his life.

"You're right again," he said as he moved to the door and held it open for their final good-bye. "I am in love with Tatiana, and I hope that one day, you'll find what you're looking for, too."

CHAPTER THIRTY

Laughter was spilling out of Mia and Ford's house on Friday night when Ian headed up their front walk carrying a case of Sullivan Winery's finest sparkling wine. The house was lit up against the night sky, and though rain had been threatening all day, for the time being it was holding off.

And he was extremely glad for it, because clear skies were essential for the plan he'd spent all last night and today putting together.

What Mia had said to him about not ever truly *wanting* any woman enough to give her his all had really hit home. Speaking with Chelsea minutes later had only confirmed the truth of it.

He *wanted* to give Tatiana things he'd never given another woman. His time, his attention, and most of all, his heart. Only, he'd screwed things up with her so badly, and in such a big way, that he knew he needed to get them right in just as big a way. Tonight, he was counting down the seconds until he could see her again, until he could hear her voice, see her beautiful smile. And he was praying that when the helicopter landed on the grass behind Mia and Ford's house, she'd agree to get into it with him so that he could whisk her off for the most romantic evening of her life.

Everyone was busy chatting when he stepped inside, but Mia spotted him right away. "Thank God, you're finally here. I was afraid you were going to do something crazy, like change your mind about coming tonight. Although if you had, I would have dragged you here myself." She stopped and tugged at the case of sparkling wine in his hands. "Earth to Ian. I need you to let go of the bubbly."

But Ian could barely process what his sister was saying with Tatiana standing so close. She was beyond beautiful in a black and white patterned dress that skimmed over her curves and fluttered around her knees. Her elegant outfit wasn't extra-sexy tonight like it had been at the fundraiser, nor was it as pared down as the jeans and sweaters she'd worn on the island. But it didn't matter how she dressed, or what side of herself she chose to showcase. Ian loved them all equally. Because he, too, loved her just the way she was. Full of constant questions, boundless bravery...and endless passion.

Knowing he'd never be able to stay away from her until the helicopter came—and that she deserved so much more than an impromptu apology and declaration of his love for her in the middle of her party—he gave Mia the case of bubbly, then turned and walked out the door again, heading for the tower.

A short while later, he heard his father say, "Mind if I join you for a little air?"

"Sure."

"Congratulations, again, on closing your new deal. We're all very proud of you, and I know how thrilled you must be."

They'd spoken on the phone the previous day, so Ian already knew how proud his parents were, but it was nice to hear it again. "Thanks. It's a really good move for the company." And yet, he wasn't as over-the-top thrilled as he thought he'd be.

Because nothing felt right without Tatiana in his life.

"I'm in love with Tatiana, Dad." It was the first time he'd told anyone of his feelings, but it didn't feel right to keep it inside anymore. Especially not with the father he loved so much, whom he knew loved him just as much.

"She's a beautiful woman. Sweet and talented, too."

"Closing that deal should be the best thing that has ever happened to me, but nothing feels right without her."

"I know what it's like when things don't feel right." Max ran a hand through his hair. "Damn it, I've waited too long to sit down and talk with you about this." His father turned to face him. "All these years have passed since I lost my job, and yet the sense of failure still gnaws at me sometimes when I think back to how I couldn't figure out a way to provide for all of you."

"It wasn't your fault."

"No, but it sure as hell felt like it when you had to leave college to start working for a paycheck. But for as low as my own pride in myself sank, I couldn't have been prouder of you, watching the way you took the business world by storm. Even if my failures were the reason you'd had to get started with it in the first place."

"Any one of us would have pitched in to help. I was just the right age to be the one who was able to do it. And I was happy to."

"I know you were, but though you were so successful, and obviously thrived on the work you were doing, it wasn't easy to watch you turn so serious, and to give up your dreams of playing football."

"What I do now is a better fit than playing pro ball would ever have been."

"Maybe, but I only wish you could have figured that out without the pressure of needing to earn as much money as fast as you could to save our house. You were pushed headlong into starting your own business while other college kids your age were busy figuring out how to get their papers written by only reading CliffsNotes."

"For so long," Ian told his father, "work felt like enough. Even when I was married, it was enough, and that's why Chelsea and I didn't last. I couldn't run my business the way I wanted to, the way I knew I needed to, and also be there for her the way she wanted me to be. And the truth is that I never cared enough, never loved her enough to put her first."

"But Tatiana is different, isn't she?"

"I've never loved anyone the way I love her. The thing is—" He paused to look back toward the windows, through which he could see Tatiana standing in the middle of the living room looking so beautiful he could hardly believe she'd been his for a little while. "—I've screwed things up with her, Dad. Really, really badly."

"For so many years," his father said in a gentle voice, "your mother and I have hoped that you'd find someone who doesn't want or need anything from you but love. And from what I can see, you don't need to protect Tatiana like you protect your brothers and sister. You don't need to save her like you saved me and your mother. You don't need to prop her higher like you did your ex-wife, or prove that you can be a bigger and bigger success every year the way you do for your shareholders. All Tatiana wants is you. Nothing else." Max gave Ian's shoulder a squeeze before standing up. "Something tells me that regardless of how badly you think you've screwed things up, if you're willing to give her yourself—every part of you, heart and soul, without holding anything back—the two of you are going to be just fine."

And as his father's words played again in his head, Ian realized he'd been about to blow it again. He'd been sitting out here waiting for the perfect time to literally sweep Tatiana off her feet in the romantic gesture he'd been so certain she wanted.

When all along, *all she wanted was him.*

One question at a time, one kiss at a time, Tatiana had taught him about love. The kind of real, powerful, forever love that his parents had...and that he'd been so sure would never be for him. Everything about the way he and Tatiana had come together had been unexpected and impromptu and *messy.*

And meant to be.

At long last, with a hell of a lot of help from his father, Ian realized that tonight shouldn't be any different.

Nearly twenty years ago, he had done everything he could to save his dad and his family. Now, Max had just returned the favor a billion times over by saving Ian from himself.

* * *

Mia began handing out the champagne glasses to everyone, and Tatiana nearly dropped to her knees in gratitude that they were almost at the toasts, because she wouldn't be able to fake her smile for much longer.

It had been hard enough coming here tonight knowing that Ian would be close enough to touch and yet completely out of reach. She'd tried to brace herself for the moment she saw him, tried to remind herself that she'd need to stay strong enough not to throw herself back into his arms, even if the two days she'd spent apart from him had felt more like two horribly long, miserably dark years.

Of course, when he'd finally walked into the house, her heart had leapt so hard and so high that she was half surprised it wasn't dancing around on the floor from the sheer thrill of seeing Ian face to face again. But after one quick look at her, he'd immediately turned and left.

For a moment, she'd thought she would shatter right there, in the middle of Ford and Mia's living room with Ian's family surrounding her. Her hands and feet had gone numb, and she'd forgotten how to breathe.

Somehow, though, she'd gotten through it, partly with the help of Valentina's warm hand over her ice-cold one...but mostly by drawing from the love she felt for Ian to regain her cool.

She didn't want him to think he'd destroyed her, didn't want to add more guilt to the load he already carried.

For the past half hour, Tatiana was hopeful that she'd pulled off another Oscar-worthy performance with his family and friends, acting as if she were whole when she was certain she'd never feel whole again.

Once everyone had a champagne glass in hand, Mia tapped a spoon on the side of hers. "It's time to toast our guests of honor." The room quieted down as everyone turned with smiles for Tatiana and Smith. "And since it's our house," Mia said with a grin as Ford wrapped an arm around her waist from behind, "Ford and I have decided we get to go first. Smith, you wrote, directed, and starred in an amazing film that blew both of us away. I've always been proud to share the Sullivan name with you, and I always will be. And Tatiana, we want you to know how blown away we are by you, and how much we love you, too."

"Especially me."

Two dozen heads swiveled toward the deep male voice that had just sounded from the doorway.

Ian.

He only had eyes for her as he headed across the room, and the silence was so complete they truly could have heard a pin drop.

"The first time I saw you in the middle of the vines in Napa Valley, I knew you were special, but I couldn't let myself believe it. I wasn't prepared to let someone as unexpectedly bright and beautiful as you into the life I'd arranged so carefully. Or behind the walls that I'd worked for so long to build so high." Their families parted for him as he spoke in his strong, mesmerizing voice, until he was standing right in front of her. "But from the moment I met you, all of my carefully ordered plans, all the boundaries I'd built, started to come crashing down one after another until they were an even bigger mess than your living room."

She could barely take it all in, that right when she thought she'd never recover from her heart ripping in two, Ian was suddenly standing before her, staring down at her with pure love in his eyes. And yet, even as stunned as she was by the unexpected and beautiful words he was saying, how could she not smile at his equally unexpected joke?

He moved closer, then, reaching out to stroke the small dimple in her right cheek. "I never thought I'd find something, someone, I'd love more than my company, or would be able to count on the way I can count on it. But now I know just how wrong I was. You've proved to me again and again that I'll forever be able to count on you. And even if I tried my whole life to stop loving you, I would never be able to do it. Because *you* are the love of my life, Tatiana. Can you ever forgive me for not recognizing true love when you were right there in front of me?"

Just then, someone coughed and Tatiana remembered, with no little shock, that they weren't alone. The minute he'd walked back in the front door and started speaking, the world had shrunk down to just the two of them. But Ian hadn't just told her that he loved her—he'd declared himself in front of everyone.

Of all the words he could have spoken to her tonight, it was *how* he said them that said the most about his true feelings for her. He wasn't just opening himself up to let her into his heart tonight, he was breaking down the walls he'd put up around himself to let *all* of them back in.

"How could I not forgive a son who would do anything for his mother and father?" She reached for him and could have sworn sparks jumped when their hands touched. "How could I not fall for a brother who would protect his siblings with his dying breath?" He tugged her closer at the same time that she moved toward him. "And how could I not love a brilliant CEO who is excited by the work he does every single day...and who happens to wear a suit better than anyone else ever will?"

His mouth came down over hers, then, so warm and so full of love that the tears she'd barely been holding back all night long finally spilled down her cheeks from the sheer joy of being back where she was meant to be.

In Ian's arms.

Too soon, he was drawing back, but before she could protest, he said, "When I told you life isn't a fairy tale, it was because I'd never met anyone like you, and I honestly didn't think you could exist. You're everything I've ever wanted, needed, dreamed of."

"So are you. I love you so much, Ian."

"You said you needed to learn something from me, but I'm the one who's learned everything from you. *Everything,* Tatiana. Especially," he said with a heart-stopping grin that made her fall in love with him all over again, "the power of a well-timed question."

He brought both her hands up to his lips and pressed a kiss to them before dropping to one knee. Thunder rumbled outside and rain poured down onto the roof above them as he spun every question she'd ever asked him into the most beautiful one possible.

"Tatiana, will you be my happily ever after?"

And as her *yes* was drowned out by the cheers from both of their families, Tatiana knew there had only been one answer all along.

Love.

* * *

Everyone surely thought they were crazy for heading hand in hand out into the rain, but she knew storms would always be special for them, taking them back to the days and nights on an island where everything but love had been stripped away.

Together, they'd danced on the grass to the beat of the rain, and soon everyone was out there with them, getting thoroughly soaked and laughing their heads off. Or—as she noticed when she looked over at Ian's parents—kissing.

While they danced, he admitted he'd had plans to sweep her away in a helicopter to a romantic restaurant filled with roses and a band playing all her favorite songs, but that he hadn't been able to wait another second to be with her again. And Tatiana knew that even if they never made it on a fantasy date like that, or if he had to miss some of her movie premieres because of his job, or if her filming schedule meant she couldn't be there to celebrate every one of his new deals, that none of that was what really mattered.

"All I ever need is you, Ian. Just to be with you."

And this time, when she looked up into his beautiful eyes and saw that pure love had replaced the shadows and ghosts, she knew for certain that he felt exactly the same way...and that love at first glance really had turned into forever.

EPILOGUE

A month later...

Dylan Sullivan made it off his sailboat and into his parents' house just in time to hear Tatiana's name announced as the winner for Best Actress. Everyone in the Sullivans' living room cheered, clinked glasses and hugged, but Dylan knew there wasn't a person on the planet who was happier for her than his oldest brother.

Ian had accompanied Tatiana to the awards ceremony and now the two of them embraced and kissed in the audience as if they were all alone, instead of surrounded by thousands of audience members, with millions more looking on from all over the world. Finally, after he whispered something to her that made her smile, with one more kiss, she headed up the stairs to the stage to accept the gold statuette.

For a moment, she simply stood at the microphone and looked down, stunned, at the award in her hands. But while she was obviously overwhelmed with emotion, when she spoke her voice was steady. "Thank you so much for this incredible honor. My parents always told me I could be and do anything I wanted to. I can never thank you enough for that, Mom. And Dad—" She looked up toward the ceiling. "—thank you for continuing to watch over me every day." She stopped to compose herself again before continuing. "But the person who truly deserves to be standing up here tonight is my sister, Valentina." Tatiana looked out into the audience where Valentina was sitting beside Smith wiping away happy tears. "Thank you for everything you've done, and keep doing, to help make my dreams come true. You're the best sister anyone could ever have." A moment later, her gaze moved back to Ian. "Ian, you're the happily-ever-after I always dreamed of, and I love you more and more every single day."

When the camera panned to Ian in time to show him saying *I love you* back to Tatiana in front of the entire world, Dylan had to admit that he hadn't quite gotten over watching his brother be so open about his feelings.

Finally, Tatiana smiled into the camera, clearly speaking to the millions of people watching at home as she said, "Thank you to each and every one of you for letting me have the best job in the world!"

The crowd applauded and when the ceremony went to commercial, Mia asked Dylan, "Have you ever seen anything so wonderful or romantic? Tatiana and Ian are so *amazing* together."

He handed his sister a tissue to wipe away her happy tears. "They were definitely meant to be together. And we'll always owe her for giving us back our brother."

"We will," she said with another sniffly hug.

When Smith won for Best Actor a few minutes later, and they all saw and heard just how much his fiancée's love meant to him, Dylan couldn't have been happier for his cousin. For all of the Sullivans who had gotten engaged or married in the past few years.

Unlike Ian, love had never left Dylan fighting ghosts or guilt. He'd never loved and lost the way Mia and Ford had, either. And there wasn't a close friend who was waiting in the wings with her heart in her hands like Brooke had with Rafe. Dylan wasn't looking for love, but just as he'd told Ian, if he ever managed to find a woman who made his palms sweat and his heart race, he'd do whatever he needed to do to make her his.

And while he was happy with his boats, with the ocean, with the time he got to spend with his family, the sixth sense that he trusted to guide him safely across the ocean during a nasty storm was telling him that everything was about to change.

Really, really soon…

~ THE END ~

ABOUT THE AUTHOR

Having sold more than 4 million books, *New York Times* and *USA Today* bestselling author Bella Andre's novels have been #1 bestsellers around the world. Known for "sensual, empowered stories enveloped in heady romance" (Publishers Weekly), her books have been Cosmopolitan Magazine "Red Hot Reads" twice, have been translated into ten languages. Winner of the Award of Excellence, The Washington Post has called her "One of the top digital writers in America" and she has been featured by Entertainment Weekly, NPR, USA Today, Forbes, The Wall Street Journal, and most recently in TIME Magazine. She has given keynote speeches at publishing conferences from Copenhagen to Berlin to San Francisco, including a standing-room-only keynote at Book Expo America on her publishing success.

If not behind her computer, you can find her reading her favorite authors, hiking, swimming or laughing. Married with two children, Bella splits her time between the Northern California wine country and a 100 year old log cabin in the Adirondacks.

For a complete listing of books, as well as excerpts and contests, and to connect with Bella:

Visit Bella's website at:
www.BellaAndre.com

Follow Bella on twitter at:
http://www.twitter.com/bellaandre

Join Bella on Facebook at:
http://www.facebook.com/bellaandrefans

Sign up for Bella's newsletter at:
http://eepurl.com/eXj22

70965949R00229

Made in the USA
Middletown, DE
18 April 2018